"A smart, touching, time-bending romance. Funny and affecting."
—David Nicholls, bestselling author of *One Day* and *Sweet Sorrow*

"Hayes has created a moving, memorable, layered story where each new revelation brings the reader to a greater understanding of both the narrator and Theo, the complexity of their relationship, and, indeed, who they are as people. This story deals unflinchingly with tough topics: Love, sexuality, heartbreak, and hope are a given considering the storyline. But Hayes also deals with trauma and abuse and how those experiences affect a person's mental health, life, and relationships. It's rare to finish a book and immediately begin reading it again. For many readers, this will be just that book. A gorgeously told story of heartbreak and recovery that still leaves the reader feeling hopeful about love." —*Kirkus Reviews* (starred review)

"If you loved *Normal People* and *One Day*, this moving, messy, and magical debut is for you." —*E! News*

"Fierce and often funny . . . It's counterintuitive to be hopeful for a relationship you know is doomed from the start, but the sheer emotional intelligence of the unpicking, from horrible breakup to magical first kiss, kept me hooked. Wise, compelling, and beautifully written." —*Daily Mail* (UK)

"Hayes references Nora Ephron throughout the book and she's a pretty good successor judging from this debut." —*Stylist*

"[A] bittersweet love story without heroes or villains. Hayes strips away the layers to reveal the heart of a relationship between two flawed but appealing characters with their whole futures ahead of them. Recommended for fans of *One Day* by David Nicholls and *Normal People* by Sally Rooney." —*Booklist*

ALSO BY HAZEL HAYES

Out of Love

BETTER BY FAR

A NOVEL

HAZEL HAYES

DUTTON

DUTTON

An imprint of Penguin Random House LLC
penguinrandomhouse.com

The poem on page 301 is an excerpt from "Remember" by Christina Rossetti (1830–1894),
first published in 1862 in her book *Goblin Market and Other Poems*.

DUTTON and the D colophon are registered trademarks of Penguin Random House LLC.

LIBRARY OF CONGRESS CATALOGING-IN-PUBLICATION DATA
Names: Hayes, Hazel, 1985– author.
Title: Better by far: a novel / Hazel Hayes.
Description: New York: Dutton, an imprint of Penguin Random House LLC, 2024.
Identifiers: LCCN 2023053838 (print) | LCCN 2023053839 (ebook) |
ISBN 9780593472958 (trade paperback) |
ISBN 9780593472965 (ebook) Subjects: LCGFT: Novels.
Classification: LCC PR6108.A9665 B48 2024 (print) |
LCC PR6108.A9665 (ebook) | DDC 823/.92—dc23/eng/20231120
LC record available at https://lccn.loc.gov/2023053838
LC ebook record available at https://lccn.loc.gov/2023053839

Printed in the United States of America

1st Printing

BOOK DESIGN BY DANIEL BROUNT

Do mo mháthair

AUTHOR'S NOTE

You may not be aware of this, but most non-US novels are translated into American English for release in the United States. Words get Americanised, which is in itself a perfect example because, for starters, this word would be spelled "Americanized" instead. In a US edit, *s*'s become *z*'s, *r*'s and *e*'s are swapped in words like "centres" and "metres," and *u*'s are dropped from words like "colours" and "flavours." Don't even get me started on "lifts," "chips," "crisps," and "petrol." Thankfully, I've never mentioned "aluminium" in my work.

I agreed to the US edit on *Out of Love* thinking it didn't make much difference how words were spelled. That is until I was in a studio narrating the audiobook and, in order to be consistent with the text, I had to keep reminding myself (as did the director) to say "toward" and "forward" instead of "towards" and "forwards." I realised then that I missed my little Irishisms and I didn't want to lose them again.

Better by Far was never meant to be set in Ireland. Nor was

Irish culture meant to play such a prominent role in Kate's story. But sometimes, we writers don't get a say in what finds its way into our hearts or onto the page. Much like Kate, I've come to understand that I'm inherently, invisibly, and sometimes mystically connected to my homeland. Together, she and I have found a new appreciation for Irish customs, folklore, and, of course, an Teanga—our tongue, our language. Gaelic is as wild, beautiful, and hardy as the dandelions that dig their roots deep into our soil, sprouting up between whatever cracks they can and dispersing their seeds far and wide.

Many thanks to Dutton for allowing me to be one of those seeds. It was important that I keep this book just as it was written, and keep these letters from Kate to her ghosts exactly as she spoke them.

Le grá agus buíochas—with love and gratitude,
Hazel

BETTER
BY FAR

TILL FEBRUARY

I'm supposed to be writing a book, but instead I find myself writing to you. I prepare the blank page, ready to pour myself onto it, but all that comes out is your absence, which feels so much more like a presence. How odd that the language of grief is one of loss—people describe feeling empty, hollow, carved out—when for me, grief is heavy. There's a weight to it. A density.

In Irish we don't say I am sad; we say tá brón orm—there is sadness on me. And we don't say someone is grieving, we say they are faoi mhéala—under grief. The phrase "going into mourning" literally translates as "putting on a robe of sorrow." We wear our feelings, wrapping them around ourselves like cloaks that separate us from the world, and grief is the heaviest one of all.

Today, unsatisfied with simply weighing me down, grief finds a way to slip inside me, filling me up like some tar-like creature that clogs my throat and lungs and crams itself into the cavities between my organs. You've only been gone a few hours and already I am turgid with the lack of you.

￫

I say you're gone, but you're not really. Not yet. Your clothes are still hanging in the wardrobe. Your CDs are stacked, alphabetically, on the shelf above the stereo. Your squash racket is over there by the door—you said you wouldn't need it this week. You even left your passport here, in the top drawer of your bedside table; it occurred to me just moments ago to check if it was there, and I must admit my relief in finding it. Not that it matters where you are, I suppose, if we won't be seeing each other anyway; it's just easier knowing you're stuck here too—in drizzly, dark Dublin, where places carry with them reminders of me—and not sitting at a table by some quaint town square in Paris perhaps, or maybe Croatia. Yeah, that feels right—Croatia. With its mild evenings, cobbled streets, and local beer on tap. Local women too—all of them perfect, in your eyes, because you don't know them yet, haven't fought with them yet, haven't seen them sick or sad or suicidal.

Perched on the edge of our bed, with your passport in my hands, I picture one of these women approaching you with an easy smile, all-over tan, and oodles of sympathy for the brokenhearted boy reading a book outside her favourite café. I let myself linger on the scene for far too long, right up to the point where you wake up face down, ass out, legs tangled in her ridiculously white sheets. The whole scene, in fact, is impossibly white, bright to the point of overexposure. She opens her eyes, stretches her long limbs. One corner of her mouth curls up. "Good morning," she purrs.

Stop it, I tell myself, flinging your passport back in the drawer. *He isn't in Croatia. He's in his brother's filthy flat in Lucan.*

But even though I know that you and Scott are most likely on his sofa playing video games, and you're already exasperated by his plenty-more-fish-type platitudes, knowing a story isn't real doesn't make the feelings it evokes any less real. And so I'm left with all the jealousy and rage churned up by my own pathetic work of fiction.

Why can't I write an actual work of fiction?

A real writer would spin this breakup into gold. A real writer would chew it up and spit out a novel so magnificent it would make all the heartbreak worthwhile. Cure it, even. A real writer would sell a million copies and buy herself a mansion paid for with pain.

I mentally fast-forward to this imaginary point in my future, when I stand at the summit of my dreams and look back down at the jagged path I climbed to get there. I can almost taste how thin the air is. But then I remember I'm still at the bottom of the mountain, just a sad little Sisyphus with a book to write and a heart to mend, and today, both tasks seem equally insurmountable.

My shoulders slump forward, like my skeleton has suddenly vanished, leaving the vague shape of a human behind. I slide, sluglike, onto your side of the bed and instantly begin to cry. It's not a particularly loud or deliberate cry—my face doesn't contort or change—I just stare at the wall as tears flow involuntarily down my face, like blood pouring from a wound. I hate these walls. These bare, eggshell walls. I hate the potential I saw in them.

⫣

Your mother calls at two o'clock. I peel my face off the soggy pillow and pick up, half expecting an onslaught of concern over our breakup, maybe even a plea for me to call you, to make up, to make it work. Instead, she asks if we've made plans for Christmas yet.

She doesn't know.

And I'm certainly not going to tell her.

I say we'll get back to her and I hang up as fast as I can. Then I think about Christmas without you, and I resume crying. Hours pass. But when I check the clock again it's only eight minutes past two.

⫣

I am all too familiar with this feeling of time distended; when my mother died, time ceased to behave as it had before. It was a Wednesday afternoon. I was nine years old and idling in a geography class when it happened. She drowned in a freak current just off Colligeen Beach, not far from our home. At her wake I heard someone say one of her lungs had ruptured. Though I didn't know what "ruptured" meant then, I looked it up later in my father's dusty blue thesaurus, scraping one glittery pink fingernail down the list of increasingly upsetting words.

Crack. Fracture. Split. Breach. Burst.

Strangely, there was no word in that book, nor have I found one since, that conveyed how I felt that day, the day her body lay shrouded in our dining room. "Grief" doesn't even come close—its paltry five letters no less crude a symbol of the thing they are supposed to represent than a stick-figure drawing of a person; they lack all the nuance, magnitude, and magic of the real thing.

As a sign of respect, all four clocks in the house were stopped for her. Even the staunch grandfather clock in the hallway stood idle, its pendulum hanging limp as a broken limb. But time didn't stop with them. It didn't even have the courtesy to slow down, though I was positive it had. Time, unticking, ticked on. The clocks caught up. And so, too, did the calendar in the kitchen, which was dutifully flipped at the dawn of each new month. Counting ever further away from her.

My mother's death was like a puncture in the fabric of my existence, beginning as a pinprick and expanding outwards to become a gaping black hole around which every other moment seemed to catch and drag. Minutes, hours, days, all spiralled inexorably inwards, endlessly elongated by the brutal pull of that tiny, terrifying iris, that ineluctable instant, from which no light or life could possibly escape. My mother was in there, I was sure of it, beyond the event horizon, alive, preserved, pristine, just as she had been, but neither one of us could cross it; she couldn't exist after that point, and I could never return to a time before it. Nor could I move forward, it seemed, to the day it didn't hurt anymore, when time resumed moving at a regular pace. I was trapped in the space between grief and healing, no longer the person I was, not yet the person I would be, with no choice but to endure it.

Now here I am again. Trapped. Waiting. Enduring.

Scientists call it spaghettification, the stretching out of matter towards a singularity. That's how life felt. Spaghettified. Each new feeling was eternal while it lasted. Each new experience unnaturally prolonged. Even memories grew misshapen in that place, malformed by the gravity of my loss. Sometimes, still, the days and dates surrounding her death are indistinguishable. My father shows me photographs from that year and I feign recognition as he smiles down at some grainy six-by-four scene. All I see are spectres of myself: roller-skating down my street, blowing out ten candles, holding up a small glass trophy—I'm told I won a local spelling competition.

Maybe I should have been honest with your mam. But what would I have said? I imagine now, aloud, how that conversation would have gone . . . "Hi, Ruth. No, I won't be joining you for Christmas . . . Finn and I broke up . . . We're still living together . . . Well, we live in the same place, just not at the same time . . . Yes, Ruth, I know that's insane. Oh, and while I have you, can I get the recipe for your vegan lasagne, please?"

I decided to give up milk last week after seeing a video of a calf being taken from its mother. They drove him away in the back of a truck and the mama cow chased him for as long as she could before finally giving up. She just stood in the middle of the road, wailing.

"That's it," I announced, pouring my tea away. "I'm never

drinking milk again." And to your credit you didn't say or do anything derisive. The next day, you went out and bought me a carton of oat milk, and that was that.

I digress. Our plan is absolutely ludicrous. What were we thinking? I'm sure it made sense at the time, but now I'm struggling to remember. I wish you were here to explain it again.

We made the decision last night following a ridiculous argument that was entirely unnecessary—I couldn't even tell you now how it started—and almost comical in its ugliness. We said things I know we didn't mean. Things designed with the sole intent of causing pain. At one point, you looked me dead in the eyes and said, "I don't like you."

Fuck.

I mean, I know you love me. Despite it all, I know you love me. And I love you too. But loving someone and liking someone are two very different things. Loving someone is almost an impulse, a physiological response to your shared experiences. Loving someone means that their absence would make you sad, but their presence doesn't necessarily make you happy. That's reserved for liking someone—liking who they are, liking who you are around them, and therefore wanting to spend time with them. So basically what you said is that if I died tomorrow you'd be sad, but while I'm still living, you'd rather not be near me, if it's all the same.

As soon as the words left your mouth you stopped, and I stopped too. Like a pair of windup toys who'd been noisily oscillating on the carpet, we both ran out of steam and froze. Then you held your arms out and I fell into them, burying my face in your chest.

"This has to stop," I cried. You didn't disagree.

I can't remember when the world last slowed around us like it did then. We didn't stir. Or even sway. We just held each other and our breath as the moment ballooned outwards, holding us in a grasp as gentle as a daydream, and just as delicate.

The spell was broken when the doorbell rang, and we both started breathing again.

"I'll get it," I said, gathering myself.

There were three small ghosts on the doorstep, each one around hip height. They stood stock-still, silently staring up at me through circular black eyes. I waited a while for them to speak, but they said nothing. Eventually, one of them produced a plastic bucket from underneath his sheet and the others followed suit.

"Aren't you supposed to say 'trick or treat'?" I asked. Still nothing. One ghost shuffled slightly on the step.

"Fair enough," I said, grabbing a handful of Mars bars from the stash I'd left by the door and dropping them into the buckets. The ghosts nodded their satisfaction and went on their way, but as the last one turned to leave, he paused.

"Ghosts can't talk," he confided in an almost whisper, before tottering off after his friends and leaving me in the doorway, avoiding the conversation I knew we were about to have. The air was laced with smoke from nearby bonfires, and across the street another group of kids were calling door-to-door, tripping over skirts and capes as they went.

Give me autumn any day. Give me precious days made more precious by encroaching night, and halos of lamplight through fine rain. Give me crisp orange leaves that crunch underfoot, hands warmed by hot chocolate in thick ceramic mugs, and people planted firmly next to log fires, their bodies blocking the heat for the rest of us. Give me pumpkins and candles and kids heaving stolen shopping trolleys up muddy hills, full of wood for the bonfire.

I'm not one for sticky summer nights or sleeping before it's dark outside. And I could do without the eruption of freckles on my face after a solitary day of sun. But autumn, and the buildup to Halloween especially, was always my favourite time of year. Probably because it was hers.

When I was little, my mother would tell me stories about Samhain, the pagan festival that marked the end of the harvest season and the onset of winter. She said that on Oíche Shamhna— the eve of Samhain, which later became Halloween—the boundary between this world and the otherworld was thin, so people would disguise themselves to hide from the Aos Sí: spirits who crossed the thinning threshold into our world for the night. Most ghosts weren't dangerous, she assured me; they only wanted to visit. That was why she set a place at the table each year for her parents, who had passed, "just in case they wanted to stop by." But then there were the Unseelie, evil faeries who played horrible tricks on mortals for fun. Whenever my mam mentioned them she'd pretend to look around warily, as though she were afraid they might be listening. They were the ones to watch out for, she told me; they were the reason we hid behind masks and filled the house with friends and games and laughter till the sun rose and the veil thickened once again.

She and I would spend months planning matching costumes, then present our creations to my dad, who gladly wore whatever he was told to. Even my first Halloween, before I was in on the joke, they hosted a party as Gomez and Morticia Addams, with me as baby Pubert. My mam's sleek black hair was perfect for that one, but she had to don a blonde wig the year we dressed up as Aragorn, Legolas, and Gimli. She looked radiant in a forest-green cape she'd sewn herself, complete with an Elven leaf brooch. Meanwhile, my clothes were stuffed full of newspapers, and my ginger hair was backcombed and wild. I spent most of the night sucking Fanta through a hole in my beard and brandishing a plastic axe above my head. That was my last Halloween with her.

Which reminds me, our fight was about Halloween. Well, not Halloween itself but Jenna's Halloween party. You went to play squash with a friend after work and said you'd pick up dinner on the way home so we could eat before we left. Then you arrived back an hour late and empty-handed.

"Why didn't you remind me?" you asked, anxiously checking the time.

"Because I'm not your fucking secretary," I said, though

the weight of the comment was somewhat diminished by the fact that I was wearing a Tinker Bell costume, wings and all. You were supposed to go as Peter Pan. I'd laid the costume out on our bed for you.

"Well, you were home all day," you said. "Why didn't *you* pick up dinner?"

"Because you said *you* would!" I replied. "Also please don't say it like that."

"Like what?" By now you were fruitlessly opening and closing kitchen cupboards, staring at shelves full of condiments.

"Like I was 'home all day' sitting on my ass. I was unpacking boxes. Trying to make this place liveable. And there's no food in there, so you can stop looking."

"There might be something down the back," you said, shoulders-deep in a cupboard now. "Ugh. Gross."

You produced an unlabelled jar full of mould and held it towards me, your face twisted in disgust, then raised an eyebrow as if to ask what it once was. I shrugged and backed away. It's possible the jar had been left there by the previous tenants.

"I know you were unpacking."

"Well, don't say it like that, then; it's derogatory."

"Oh please," you said as you dropped the unidentified ex-food into the bin and began rummaging through the contents of the fridge. "Don't pull the sexist card."

"I didn't."

"That's what you meant, though."

"No, I meant derogatory," I said. "Which is, funnily enough, why I said 'derogatory' and not 'sexist,' or 'misogynistic,' or 'bigoted,' or 'chauvinistic,' or—"

"I'm not doing this. It's impossible to argue with you."

Another knock at the door. This time a horde of tiny witches and wizards. I practically threw the chocolate at them and stomped back to the kitchen.

"What the hell does that mean?" I asked. By this point you were searching for the best-before date on a probiotic yoghurt.

"It means I can't do it," you said. "You're too good."

"That's ridiculous. Arguing is hardly an art form, Finn."

"Arguing," you said, realising the yoghurt had gone off and chucking it at the bin, "is just expressing yourself really good with words. Which is what you do for a living."

"Really *well*," I corrected, and instantly braced myself.

"Fuck's sake," you roared, slamming the fridge door so hard that all your beer bottles rattled inside it.

And this is how it started. But by the time the fight ended, almost two hours later, we were way off topic; like a pilot trying to course correct in a storm, we'd somehow managed to get ourselves hundreds of miles from the desired destination, with no fuel left to get back. In the end you caved and ordered a pizza.

Clearly, the party was off the cards. You suggested I go by myself, but there was no way I was doing that—I'd already cried half my makeup off and I was in no mood to fix it, or indeed spend the night explaining what my costume was because you weren't there to make it make sense. Besides, this didn't feel like just another fight. You finally said it out loud as you picked the last of my uneaten crusts back out of the box.

"Just to be clear," you asked, "are we ending things?"

"Well, we're not ending *all* things."

You gave me a limp smile.

"That's good," you said. "I was worried for a second there."

"I just think that would be a drastic response to our relationship not working out."

"Agreed."

I love that I can lob a joke like that at you, even at a time like this, and know exactly where it will land. I suddenly realised I was going to miss that about you. Then I realised that I'd already begun realising things I was going to miss about you and a pang of grief hit me, softly, like the first few bars of a familiar song.

"Is that what you want?" you asked, serious now, staring down at your lap.

"To end things?" I had to think on it a moment. "No. But I'm not sure it's about what we want anymore. It's about what we definitely don't want."

"Such as?"

"Such as these fights," I said.

You shook your head.

"They're horrible," you said. "I'm sorry."

"I'm sorry too. But that doesn't stop them from happening."

"I feel like all I do is let you down," you whined. "Like nothing I do is right."

This is my least favourite part, the part where you come

back to yourself and need me to soothe you. You make these broad, self-pitying statements that make you sound like a child, desperately trying to impress his ghastly, overbearing mother—which I suppose is me in this scenario—and that's not a role I wish to play. I don't want to reassure you in these moments. Or tell you you're a good little boy. I'm too angry to give you that.

"Like tonight," you continued, "I forgot the groceries. And I was late. And, okay, that upset you. But then I feel like such a piece of shit about it. Even though I know I was late because of the traffic. And I forgot to buy the food because— Oh, I don't bloody know. I just forgot. Sometimes I feel like there are too many plates and I can't keep them all spinning at once."

"I'm not a plate," I said, and you looked up.

"I know that."

"You make me feel like a plate," I said. "And anything I suggest right now will only make me feel more . . . platey."

"What would you suggest?"

"Couples' counselling, maybe."

"I don't want to do that." The words came out of you reflexively, like I'd just tapped your knee and been kicked in return.

"See?" I said.

You said nothing.

"You're right," I added. "I *was* upset tonight, but you flew into a fit of self-defence before I'd even said anything. It's like you're at red alert, ready for a fight at all times."

"Because you would have said something," you insisted.

"I don't know." I sighed. "Probably. And all you had to do was say sorry. 'Sorry I'm late. Sorry I forgot the groceries. My bad.'"

"You make it sound so easy."

"It is easy! But instead you end up shouting and slamming doors and slinging insults."

"You slung a few yourself," you said.

"I know!" I snapped, and then I took a breath. "I know."

What I wanted to say then was that your anger scares me. And that my instinctive response—to shrink back and pacify you—only makes me feel smaller and therefore more vulnerable. So I make myself bigger; I meet you where you are even though I don't want to, just so I can feel less afraid. Lately, I've noticed myself slipping into that space more and more easily—at the first sign of a fight I bristle like a bird puffing up its feathers, but underneath I'm still a bony little chick. If I'm honest, I'm disappointed that the feathers ever fooled you.

But I didn't say any of that. Because I knew from experience that if I mentioned your anger, you would, funnily enough, get angry. And I am tired to my core of its hold on you. I'm no longer saddened or even afraid of it. Just tired.

Half an hour later, we were on the sofa sharing the leftover Mars bars and comforting each other while we tried to figure out what to do next. Outside, fireworks exploded intermittently, filling the living room with spurts of pink and green and purple light.

In the movies there's always one final blow. A death blow.

One person says or does something so horrific that it just hangs there, unforgivable, irretrievable, until the other one tells them to leave, or walks away themselves. But you never see the part after that, where they remember that they live together and so must sit down and discuss the ungainly logistics of disentangling. And you don't see, either, how courteous that can be.

That's how we were last night, on the sofa, eating chocolate. We were courteous. Except, more than that, we were caring, we were loving, we were kind. At one point you offered me the end of your last bar, knowing that's my favourite bit. It was such a sweet gesture that instead of basking in the moment, I could already feel it unfurling on the page; I was writing the end of us before it had happened.

We always fought. Even when we were friends. But it was different then. Heated. Hot, even. We'd debate constantly. Bicker over every little thing. Our friends would joke how like a married couple we were, just without the sex. And then we had sex, and everything changed; we went through an extended period of honeymoon bliss. That is, until the fights crept back in and became much uglier. This past year we've barely recovered from one before we find ourselves in another.

Last night was the final straw, we both felt it—our proverbial backs breaking under the weight of it. At one point I zoomed out and saw us as a child might, standing half-hidden in the doorway, roused from sleep by the racket, watching us scream at each other. That's when I made up my mind.

"You still haven't told me what you want," you said.

"What do *you* want?" I deflected, hoping you'd say it first.

"I want us to be happy together."

When I didn't answer, you said, "You don't want that."

"I do want that," I said, "more than anything."

"But . . ."

"But I think we missed the exit for 'happy together' a few miles back. And now our only options are to stay on this road, which I would call 'unhappy together,' or take the exit for 'happy apart.'"

You bit your lip and bobbed your head a little, the way you do when you're biding your time. I watched your eyes dart around the room, coming to rest on the four cardboard boxes in the corner, full of things we had yet to unpack. I knew what you were thinking. I was thinking it too; *we just moved in here in August.* Our first place together, and we had only made it three months.

"Happy apart," you repeated, as though answering a question you had silently asked yourself.

I think, if I'd asked, you would have been willing to keep trying. But that's exactly the reason I didn't ask; I'm sick to the back teeth of trying. That's all we've been doing for I don't know how long now—not living, not loving, not growing, not moving in any direction at all, just trying. Friends ask how we are, and I say, "Oh, you know, we're trying," and they nod sympathetically and change the subject, and I want to reach out, grab them by the collar, and scream, "Please, please make us stop. Please make me leave!"

If I'd asked, you'd have given it one last chance—another in a very long line of last chances. And I almost did it, I almost let you let me step back from the edge. Almost suggested we give it one more go. But before I could speak you said, "I'll move out."

"That's not fair," I replied. "This is your home too."

You looked around to emphasise your point, that this is more my home than it is yours. Which is fair, I suppose; the furniture is all mine, but that's only because I brought the entire contents of my previous flat—one I'd spent years decorating—and your only contribution was a broken patio table. We bought some new cushions and lamps, but I chose them without you because, despite your insisting that you wanted input into the decor, when it came down to it this house was just another plate. And in the meantime, we needed a fucking lamp.

"Still," I said, "you shouldn't have to move again so soon. Where would you even go?"

"I don't know," you admitted.

"Besides, I can't afford to live here alone."

"Me either," you agreed.

We were talking like a couple deciding which movie to watch. And what's weird is how not weird it was. How completely pedestrian this conversation about changing the course of our lives felt.

"We could both go," you said.

"We've got three months left on the lease," I reminded you.

I remember when the estate agent offered us a six-month starter lease, he made some jab about this being handy "if it all goes tits up." We laughed. But maybe he could tell. Maybe he sees enough couples come and go to know which ones will and won't last. I did note as he showed us around the second bedroom, he made no comment about it being a nursery one day.

"Sorry," you said, rubbing your eyes. "Yeah. Of course."

You were tired. We both were.

"Let's sleep on it," I offered.

We didn't have sex. That's how I knew it was over. All the other times we broke up we had sex. "One last time," we'd say, knowing full well it wouldn't be. You startled me when you spoke. I was sure you'd fallen asleep.

"Let's both stay," you said. But I didn't understand.

"Not together," you added. "You have the place one week. I'll take it the next. And we'll alternate till February. It'll soften the blow. Give us both time to figure things out."

Silence while I tried to decide if this was genius or madness.

"That's twelve weeks," I said, counting on my fingers. I felt you nod.

"Do you think we can manage it?" I asked.

"I do," you said, and the poignancy of those particular two words was not lost on me.

I held an accidental vigil over you all night; unable to sleep, I just lay there, pretending we were back at the beginning, feeling the moment swell with possibility, and crying quietly for every version of us that might have been, the potential we never quite reached but were always, and still are, painfully aware of; when we're good, we're very, very good, and when we're bad, we're horrid.

I savoured every heartbeat, every rise and fall of your chest under my hand, not allowing myself to drift off in case I missed even a moment of this night, which I knew would be our last. I stared at you, your profile vaguely backlit by the pale glow of a waxing moon outside, and I tried to memorise the topography of your face: tired eyes tracing your chin, your nose, your forehead, the peaks and troughs of this terrain I've come to know as home.

By the morning my body was stiff, one arm numb beneath me, and my jaw sore from resting on your shoulder. I had been afraid to move, afraid you'd pull away from me, afraid to lose your embrace, or the view of your face, which I held the whole night through as darkness deepened and then dawn bloomed behind you. Like a long-exposure photograph, I tried to burn the image onto my mind in the hope that every time I blinked or closed my eyes, I'd see you imprinted there. It didn't work, of course; it lasted a few moments and was gone.

When you woke up, we discussed the terms of our arrangement. We would alternate weeks, as you'd suggested, vacating the house on Sunday afternoons and coming back the following Sunday evenings to avoid any overlaps, then we would meet back here on February first to pack up and move out. Until then there would be no talking, no texting, no communication of any kind. We were officially breaking up, that much was clear; but we would move through the next phase carefully, as though traversing a frozen lake in tandem, arms outstretched, fingertips grazing each other's.

You showered, shaved, packed some things, drank your coffee, and left. And the urgency with which you moved gave the impression you were keen to get gone. Even the goodbye happened fast; a few niceties and a quick hug—awkward hands unsure where to be or what to do with themselves. That strange transition as we pulled apart, faces lingering instinctually in anticipation of a kiss that never came. Last night we threw around "I love yous" like we'd never run out of them, but this morning, neither one of us said it. I could feel the words floating between us like a rain cloud ready to burst.

In the few short hours since you left, I've become restive, roaming the house like a neglected pet. I float from room to room, watching the clock, side-eyeing time like it's the enemy. Earlier, I took a shower just for something to do, and when I spotted your razor on the shelf, part of me hoped you'd use it as an excuse to come home, while another part of me prayed you'd have the good sense to buy a new one and leave me the fuck alone. The two thoughts entered my head at the exact same moment, with such volume and velocity that I experienced a sort of emotional whiplash. Already, these conflicting voices—the one that wants you here and the one that needs you gone—clamber for space inside my busy brain.

Even now, I want to use your mother's call as an excuse to

talk to you. I compose several text messages: The first is angry—
why is she calling *me* about Christmas? The second is logistical—
what *are* our plans for Christmas? Just out of interest. Should
we get a tree? And the third is casual—your mother called, just
passing on the message. I delete them all. Because we're not
talking. And if I message you about this, then you'll message
me about something else and then we're talking again.

"We're not talking," I say to the empty room. Then I write
it on a Post-it note and stick it to the wall next to my desk.

We're not talking.

The first words I've written all day.

This wouldn't usually be a problem, but today is the day I
planned to start writing my book in earnest. It's marked there
on the calendar. November first, *WRITE A BLOODY BOOK*,
it says, and underneath that, an afterthought, *Please.* I find it's
best to be kind to my future self, otherwise she'll get nothing
done out of a warped sense of defiance. That future self, though,
the one my past self wrote the request to, is now my present
self. And she does not want to write a bloody book.

To be clear, no one *wants* to write a book; they want to
have already written one—it's the difference between wanting
clean teeth and wanting to have them cleaned. Anyone who
tells you they want to write is either lying or not doing it properly. Oh, they're probably putting words on a page alright, but
then you might as well be jotting down a recipe or a shopping
list. Writing, for me, isn't about putting words on a page; it's
about putting myself on the page, leaving so much of myself
there that I go to bed wondering if perhaps, this time, I gave
too much away, if I've kept enough to get by on.

I'm staring at the blinking cursor when the phone rings again. This time it's my literary agent calling from New York; she must have marked today on her calendar too.

"Well? Is it finished?" she jokes.

"Just sending you the final draft now," I retort.

She's not actually from New York—this is apparent from her sickening Midwest optimism, which at first I couldn't stand and now I cannot live without. Alexis Snow. That's her name. Imagine. Going through life with a name like that. No wonder she has such a positive outlook on things. You used to write little jingles about her, then sing them to me whenever she called, like Roger Radcliffe taking to the piano to sing about Cruella de Vil. I catch myself smiling at the memory.

Alexis is the reason I'm still writing at all. Having spent years on my first novel—the manuscript was turned down by every publisher I approached, the catch-22 of this industry being that you can't get a publisher without a good agent, and you can't get an agent without first being published—I had all but given up hope of becoming an author, when Alexis called me out of the blue. My manuscript had somehow found its way onto her desk through a friend of a friend, and she had literally just put it down. She was still crying.

She cries a lot actually. She cried when we sold the US rights. She cried at the launch party. She even cried when the book was translated into Russian. She calls me every time something good happens and says, "I need you to understand what a big deal this is." She's said it so much that last Christmas

I had the phrase sewn onto a ridiculous frilly cushion, which I sent to her office.

Unfortunately, Alexis hasn't had cause to say her catch-phrase for a while; the hype around my book has fizzled out and last time we spoke she gave it to me straight like a doctor delivering bad news.

"You need to do it again," she said. "I'm sorry."

I knew she was right. It was time. I needed to write another book.

Damn it.

"I gave all I had to the first one," I protested.

"You did. But that was then. You'll find more now."

"How?" I asked.

"Magic," she said.

The sad part is I believed her.

I've spent months since that call trying to decide what to write about, rifling through the reams of notes I've made over the years, poring over diary entries, even my half-incoherent scribblings from therapy sessions. I found plenty of morsels but nothing meaty enough to warrant writing a book about. Every few days I would pick a new nugget and sit with it, waiting for it to lodge like an embryo in the lining of my mind and grow there. Thus far, though, my mind remains barren, infertile to inspiration.

The elephant in the room, of course, all along, has been my mother. I could write about her, *should* write about her, I suppose, and yet I never have. I wrote *to* her, come to think of it, after she died. I wrote to her just as I'm writing to you now, and told her thousands of things I knew she'd never hear. But I stopped doing that a long time ago, demoting her from mother to dead mother to an old pen pal whose address I've misplaced.

Just start, I told myself. *Just pick a day and start. Sit with the page and see what happens.* And so I picked today and marked it on the calendar, not knowing of course that this would be the day you left or that your departure would render me incapable of writing about anything else. I explain all this to Alexis now, expecting it to ruin her chirpy attitude, but it hardly makes a dent.

"You couldn't write it," I say to her.

"Technically, you could."

"No, I mean, it's so ridiculous, you couldn't write it."

"I know what you meant," she says, "but what's stopping you?"

"From writing about this breakup?"

"Yes."

"Well, okay, first of all, my last book was about a breakup."

"You're right," she says, deadpan. "No other writer has ever explored the same theme more than once."

"Fine," I say, "but everything that comes out of me is addressed to him."

"And?"

"And . . . this poses two problems."

"Libel," she says, without missing a beat.

"Libel," I repeat.

"We can get around that," she says. "Just focus on feelings, not facts."

"Okay," I say, "but how do I write a whole book in the second person?"

"It's been done. I'll send you a couple examples," she says, and I can hear her typing the email already.

I tell myself I'll pop down to the bookshop tomorrow, after we've had breakfast, then I catch myself. The grief glitch, I call it: those little lapses—usually between sleeping and waking, or when you're fully focused on another task—when you forget that someone is gone and you're forced to remind yourself. It's like receiving the news all over again. Alexis must sense the shift in me.

"Just be gentle with yourself," she says. "I don't need to tell you how rough breakups can be—you literally wrote the book on it."

⌿

A lot of people think I wrote that book about you, but we both know it's actually about Charlie—poor, stupid Charlie. He wasn't a bad guy. Just an idiot. You and I had been together almost a year when I started writing it, but it took so long to get published that we'd already been through a few of our own mini-breakups by then and so you seemed the most likely candidate.

I've never written about you. It's not the done thing, is it? Writing about people when they're still around?

You wrote about me once. Well, you composed the score for that short film with me in mind, the one they screened in Temple Bar. You were beaming all night, introducing me to the cast and crew, proud to have me on your arm. The film itself was fine, but my God, your music soared above the images on-screen. This was back when you were still doing films. Now it's mostly commercial work, which doesn't allow for much personality.

I go to the shelf to look for that CD and realise another thing I'll miss: the way you still keep all your work on CDs and make little homemade covers for them. I take the disc out of its plastic case—holding it by the sides like you asked me to—slide it into the stereo, and hit play. When it's over I play it again. Then I play it again. And again. Until I'm sitting on the sofa, sobbing into my fifth glass of wine, wishing I could tell you how beautiful this is, and how—while I never had any aspirations of being someone's muse—I always loved hearing myself between your notes. I type all this out in a text, then delete it when I catch sight of my Post-it on the wall: *We're not talking.*

I prepare for bed slowly, half dreading, half welcoming the onset of grief, which I've kept at bay with vast amounts of noise and light. But as night engulfs the day I feel the first tendrils of it reach under the door, searching for a place to wait until darkness and silence fall.

That's the difference between panic and grief: panic rushes in regardless of where you are or what you're doing—panic is the crazed gunman who bursts through your door in the middle of dinner and drags you away by the hair, while grief is the quiet caller who sits in the corner and watches wordlessly while you finish your meal. Grief waits for you to notify the necessary people and organise the funeral, pick the hymns and pay the priest. Grief waits for you to tidy up and say goodbye to the last guest. Grief is patient. Grief waits.

When I climb into bed, there it is, lying beside me in place of you, and the emptiness is more than I can stand, the flat sheets too much like a home that has been levelled. Time lurches, like a train coming to a sudden stop. It catches and drags and now I'm nine years old again, and painfully aware of being *in* time, just like being *in* water. I can feel it pressing in on me, skewing my vision and warping my perception of things, making each movement laborious and slow.

I grab at the duvet, furiously tossing it into a haphazard pile, throwing a pillow in for good measure.

There. That's better.

Eventually, I fall asleep next to this lumpy imitation of you.

The rest of the week passes in much the same way. Days rise up before me like great waves, threatening to drown me if I can't surmount them. So I kick until my legs are heavy and my lungs burn from the effort, and each night, somehow, I crest the wave, sliding down the other side of it into a meagre sleep, only to wake the next morning to the sight of another wave gathering on the horizon.

I move only from the bed to my desk, to the sofa, and back to bed again, ignoring everyone and everything outside these walls. I don't even watch the news because on Wednesday I saw there'd been a major accident in Cork involving a truck and a passenger train, and even though I'm fairly sure you're not in Cork, there was no way of knowing for certain that you weren't on that train. I wanted to call you. Just to check. But that would set a very weird precedent, wouldn't it? Calling you every time there's an accident anywhere in Ireland? Best to just assume you're fine and not watch the news, I decided.

I wondered if you'd seen it too and wanted to call me. Maybe, I thought, if something happened a bit closer to home you *would* call me. And then I found myself going down an especially dark rabbit hole wherein I sort of hoped for a large-scale disaster in Dublin City Centre.

By Sunday I'm exhausted. All I want is to stay here, hiding, but it's your turn to have the house. I'm just done packing when there's a knock at the door. I open it and see Fran blinking wearily back at me.

"So you *are* alive," he says.

"Welcome to the jungle," I reply, then I step back and Fran sidles straight past me towards the kitchen.

"I'll pop the kettle on, my babe."

We sit facing each other on opposite ends of the sofa—standard crisis formation—sipping on coffee while I fill him in. Fran nods sympathetically throughout.

"You're not surprised," I say when I'm done.

"No," says Fran, a firm kindness in his voice. "This has been a long time coming."

He glances around. I see his eyes land on the Post-it by my desk.

"Do you think this is really your last breakup?" he asks, and I throw him a withering look even though it's a perfectly fair question. Fran was there when we met; he's been with us through all the highs and lows and heard me say "it's over" a hundred times before.

"Yes. This is it. This has to be it."

Another sign that you and I are really over—Fran doesn't argue or crack some cutting joke.

"Is sharing the house a good idea?" he asks.

"Christ no," I say. "But I don't see an alternative."

Fran lets out a resigned sigh.

"And where will you go this week?"

"My dad's."

"Your dad's!?" he shrieks. "In Colligeen?"

"Yes."

"No," he says.

"No?"

"No. I won't have it. I won't have you moping about that dark, drab house all week. Miles from civilisation. You're coming home with me." And with that Fran is up and gathering my things. He points to my backpack. "Is this coming?"

"Yes. But—" He's already putting the bag on his back. "You don't have a spare room, Fran."

"There's a sofa. You'll be fine," he says, carrying our mugs to the kitchen.

"Won't Jay mind?" I ask, following him around like a frantic child.

"Jay loves you."

"Jay hardly knows me," I say, but Fran isn't listening; he's halfway out the door, shouting back at me to hurry up.

I rinse the mugs, taking one last look around to make sure I've left everything tidy, and I'm struck by how sterile this house is; a tacked-on end-of-terrace with no soul to speak of. It might as well be made of plywood—a temporary set built especially for us, the staging for our final scenes. They could rip it all down when we're gone. It would be like we were never even here.

THE GHOST IN
THE GARDEN

I fell in love with you arms-first. But that's not where our story starts. We were friends long before we were lovers, and before we were friends, we weren't much of anything. Truth be told, the first time we met, I didn't actually know I'd met you—I found out months later while visiting Fran in hospital.

That detail always confuses people, until I tell them the story. Our story. The one I recite to new friends at dinner parties—women, usually, who look on with their chins in their hands, elbows on white tablecloths, wan smiles, practically cooing.

I'm telling it to Jay tonight. I hope you don't mind. Why would you, I suppose. It's just that it feels so odd telling it now. For starters, it's better when we tell it together—with me taking the lead and you interjecting at all the right moments. But more importantly, the ending has changed; it's decidedly more difficult to inject a sense of whimsy into a love story when you know that they break up in the end. Now this is just another sad tale about a couple who thought that for some reason they'd be different. Silly them.

Still, Fran's at work tonight and Jay and I are hanging out alone for the first time. We're on the balcony sharing cigarettes and stories, and he's asked to hear this one. So I begin, knowing that this is perhaps the last time I'll tell it.

⠇

It was seven years ago, almost to the day. I'd been invited to a party by my friend Jenna, who knew a girl who was the second cousin of the guy hosting it. A tenuous link but I agreed to go anyway—Charlie had cancelled our plans at the last minute and a stranger's house party seemed more appealing than a night in on my own.

Jenna sent me the address and said she'd meet me there after work, and so I found myself taking two buses and a tram only to wind up on a doorstep in Cabra with a bottle of wine and no clue whether I was at the right house. When the door opened, I was met by the unmistakable reek of cheap weed and the distant thud of music I would never willingly listen to. This was the place alright.

The guy who opened the door was wearing a hula skirt with a pair of tan cowboy boots—it wasn't a costume party— and he'd pinned an antique cameo brooch to his Guns N' Roses hoodie. A thick stripe of metallic blue paint stretched across his eyes from temple to temple, shimmering in the streetlight as he looked me up and down.

"I'm Fran," he said, dragging deeply on a short, fat spliff.

"Kate," I said.

He nodded for a beat too long, running one hand through his unruly curls and squinting at me as if deep in thought.

"Welcome to the jungle, Kate," he said finally, then he turned and stalked away down a long, dim hallway.

"Wipe your feet," he called over his shoulder, and I obliged, following him to a windowless room at the back of the house. The whole place throbbed with people and noise, and on instinct I held my breath as Fran took my hand and pulled me through the door behind him. We dived into a sea of bodies undulating to the music, each one bathed in pale violet light, which seeped through a thick layer of smoke and came to settle on their skin. The whites of their eyes shone, moonlike, from their heads. They all looked dead and beautiful.

Someone had installed a disco ball, which hung precariously from an old light fitting in the centre of the high ceiling. Another smaller disco ball was also doing the rounds. Currently, it was being held aloft by a woman in a turquoise sari. She was swaying her hips from side to side, smiling with her eyes closed. I couldn't not look at her.

"That's Kashi!" shouted Fran, when he caught me staring.

"Cassie?" I screamed.

"No, Ka*shi* . . . like *she*." He exaggerated the "sh" sound, and when he did his teeth glowed bright yellow.

"If you think *she's* hot you should meet her boyfriend. Those two need to do the world a favour and start procreating. I'll introduce you when she's"—he waved one hand towards her with a lazy flourish—"done."

When we reached the kitchen—and by kitchen, I mean there was a broken sink and a bucket full of ice and beer—Fran clamped his joint between his teeth and got straight to work opening the bottle of wine I'd brought.

"Is Jenna here?" I roared over the music. Fran shrugged. He was trying to clean two dirty wineglasses with an even dirtier towel.

"Do you even know who Jenna is?"

He looked up from what he was doing and shook his head.

"Right," I shouted. "It's just, she's the only person I know here."

"You know me!" Fran grinned.

"Well, yeah, I suppose so. It's just . . . I wouldn't usually turn up at a stranger's house and—"

"Here, have a cookie, my babe. You seem stressed."

Fran handed me a chocolate chip cookie, which I was pretty sure he'd just produced from his pocket, and I reluctantly accepted—I'd rushed straight from work and neglected to feed myself.

"Thanks," I said, gobbling down the cookie. It was surprisingly good.

≡

This is the part where you tell me I'm taking too long. And I say, "Leave me alone, I'm telling the story." Then you say, "Get to the good bit," and I reply, "If by 'good bit' you mean the part where I meet you, that's debatable." And anyone who's listening laughs and tells you to shut up so I can get on with the story.

That's exactly what happened when I met your parents for the first time. We were walking to that French restaurant your mother still insists on going to, even though the food is subaverage and overpriced—I think she fancies the manager. Anyway, she and I had fallen behind, and she asked me to tell her how we'd met. You turned and interrupted, as you always do at this exact point in the story, and I remember how she shushed you and shooed you away, linking her arm in mine and asking me to finish. Such a small thing, but it caught me off guard and my eyes welled up. I tried to keep talking but I got flustered and had to stop.

"What's the matter, love?" she asked.

Your dad noticed and called back to us, "You two alright back there?"

"Just doing a bit of window-shopping," she said. He rolled his eyes good-naturedly and you both kept walking. Then she turned back to me.

"Sorry," I said. "You reminded me so much of my mam just then."

"Finn told me," she said with a knowing tilt of her head. "I lost my mammy when I was little too." And then she hugged me, rocking me gently side to side in the way only mothers can.

I wonder, when you do tell your family we broke up, which version of events will you give them? Probably the "Kate's always sad" narrative. Definitely not the "I'm always angry" one.

I notice Jay staring at me, eyebrows raised in anticipation. I'm so used to you interrupting here that I've inadvertently stopped anyway, and now I've lost my flow.

"Where was I?" I ask.

"The cookie," says Jay.

"Oh yes. The cookie."

Suffice to say the cookie was laced with drugs. Although, in Fran's defence, he wasn't secretly trying to drug me. In fact, when I told him I was worried someone *had* drugged me, he said, "God, I hope whatever they gave you doesn't clash with that cookie."

The high didn't kick in for a while, so I got to work on my bottle of wine and then it all hit me at once. If that night were a film, this is the part where the screen would go blank and the words "some footage missing" would appear.

Jenna says that by the time she arrived, I had stripped down to my underwear, climbed up on some man's shoulders, and was trying to "catch" the disco ball attached to the ceiling. Eventually, the host, Aidan, whom I had befriended at this point, lured me down using the smaller ball I'd seen Kashi with earlier. Once in possession of that ball, I reportedly danced for a solid hour, at the same rapid pace regardless of the tempo of the music playing. I looked like "a frog on hot coals" according to Jenna, who lost track of me for a while after that. The next time she saw me I was covered head to toe in gold glitter, and she's fairly certain I had eaten at least one more of Fran's cookies.

I was back on the dance floor when Charlie rang. I could barely hear him over the music, but he sounded upset. It was 3 a.m., he told me.

"Is it?" I asked.

He assured me it was.

"Shit."

I'd forgotten to tell him I was going out. And I hadn't seen any of his calls or texts. I tried to set things right, but everything I said came out wrong on account of all the drugs.

"But *you* cancelled on *me*," I told him.

"What? So this is some kind of punishment? You really are a child sometimes, Kate."

"No, no, I'm just trying to tell you."

"Tell me what?"

"I had some cookies, Charlie, they were really good."

He hung up on me then. I was shoulder-deep in dancing bodies, and suddenly all the purple faces around me grew ghoulish, their yellow smiles turning sickly and strange. One man tried to dance with me—his eyes a pair of ominous orbs glowing in their sockets—and I could no longer shake the sensation that these people were not living, never had been, that they, we, were all just skeletons in shrouds of skin.

My flesh felt heavy. I needed to leave. I needed to breathe.

I stumbled off the dance floor, out the back door, and into a starless night, gulping down the raw November air, and welcoming the way it burned my throat and lungs. My skin prickled against the cold as I looked into the murky void looming

ahead of me, staring for so long that shapes began to emerge
from it in varying shades of black, all of them vaguely human.
I thought I could feel their eyes on me. Here was a hunched
old man; there, a child with arms outstretched. And over here,
three women swaying together, like the Fates quietly scheming.
Eventually, my eyes adjusted to the gloomy garden, and the shapes
revealed themselves for what they really were: wheelie bins and
bushes, mostly. But still I had the sense of being watched.

When I turned around, I saw one final figure standing near
the door, backlit by the party's purple glow. The tiny orange
tip of a cigarette blazed gently in its hand, and although I
couldn't see the creature's eyes I could feel their gaze on me,
stinging my skin just as the cold air had moments ago. I was
sure it was a ghost, and I was about to speak to it when Jenna
appeared at the door, sweaty and flustered.

"There you are!" she said. "Jesus, where are your clothes?"

I looked down at my half-naked body, golden and goose-
fleshed.

"We need to go," urged Jenna. "I've got a cab waiting."

I hesitated.

"Come on, Kate!" shouted Jenna, before storming off.

"Goodbye, then," said the ghost as I followed her inside.

Fran arrives home at this point. Jay and I can hear his boots
come clomping up the thin stairway to their apartment. Have
you seen their place? They moved in around the same time we
did, despite having only been together a few months. I was
sceptical about how fast it was moving, I think I told you so at

the time, but being here now, I can't deny how happy they seem. The place is small. Cosy. Part of the living room is set into the eaves so you can't fully stand up in it, which sort of adds to the charm. Fran's clearly been busy doing what Fran does best, making things beautiful. It's all woollen throws and thick, scented candles, hanging ivy in macramé planters and the odd piece of provocative art offsetting the kitsch vibe. When I got here this afternoon there was a coffee-and-walnut cake cooling on the counter—Jay bakes on Sundays, apparently. I instinctively started decorating our place in my head, thinking of ways I could make it more homey, and I was once again hit by the grief glitch.

Fran flops onto the couch, one arm landing with a thump across his face, and groans a greeting at us. Without a word Jay is up and untying Fran's boots, pulling them off one by one while I pour him a glass of wine.

"Rough day at work, honey?" I ask.

"Two of my ushers called in sick," he grumbles from under his arm.

"Poor baby," says Jay unironically as he sits back down with Fran's feet in his lap, rubbing them tenderly. Fran groans again.

"I was led to believe that running a theatre would be the height of glamour and sophistication," says Fran, sitting up as I hand him his wine. "Thank you, my babe. But I spent half an hour tonight picking chewing gum off a vintage velvet seat."

"I told you to buy the cheap seats," says Jay, "literally," and Fran lets out a weary laugh.

"I know, darling, but I just couldn't bring myself to do it."

Fran says this as though asking his audience to sit on anything other than vintage velvet is like asking them to sit on broken glass. And while I don't entirely agree, I do admire him for his conviction. Fran may not be an artist, but he is a facilitator of art; he understands the conditions necessary to appreciate beauty to its fullest, which I suppose is an art form in itself. If Fran had his way, every film would be experienced in a cinema—with a compulsory intermission—and viewing movies on phones, or indeed tiny screens built into the backs of airplane chairs, would be criminalised. Books would be banned from screens altogether and remain in paper form. And music, all music, would be played by a live orchestra. The logistics of this last one are especially complicated, but I get where he's coming from.

Remember when Fran helped move us in? And you two spent hours setting up your studio in the spare room? I know you thought he was being finicky, but he honestly wouldn't have been able to sleep that night if he hadn't found a way to get your desk chair exactly equidistant from both speakers, and your electric piano facing out the window—because heaven forbid you be stuck staring at a white wall while composing. He did the opposite with my desk in the living room, pushing it right into the corner and insisting I close all the curtains while I write. "Musicians look outside for inspiration," he said. "Authors must go inwards." Most people would have rolled their eyes at that, but you just shrugged and handed him a beer.

Fran knows he isn't "the talent." He's not the one baring his soul onstage every night, but he respects the hell out of anyone who does, which is why he's named his theatre the Arena, after a Theodore Roosevelt speech called "The Man in the

Arena." There's a plaque by the box office window with an excerpt from the speech, which Fran recites for us now, by way of proving his point about the chairs.

"'It is not the critic who counts,'" he begins, as Jay and I drop our heads to our hands.

"You've done it now," I grumble at Jay.

"'Not the man who points out how the strong man stumbles,'" continues Fran, in his best impression of a thespian, "'or where the doer of deeds could have done them better.'"

"No," I say.

"Indeed not," adds Jay.

"Not at all," says Fran, with an aggressive shake of his head. "'The credit belongs to the man who is actually *in* the arena, whose face is marred by dust and sweat and blood!'"

At this, he stands, wielding his glass like a Shakespearean skull.

"Oh, he's up," says Jay.

"'Who at the worst, if he fails, at least fails while daring greatly, so that his place shall never be with those cold and timid souls who neither know victory nor defeat.'"

Fran takes a bow as Jay and I applaud.

"Bravo," says Jay.

"You missed a bit in the middle," I tell Fran as he collapses back onto the sofa.

"Did you two have a nice evening?" he asks.

"We did!" says Jay. "Kate was telling me how she and Finn met."

Fran winces at me as if to ask if I'm okay talking about it and I laugh. "I'm fine, Fran."

"Right so," he says. "Where did you get up to?"

"We've just left the party in Aidan's house," says Jay, "the one where you drugged her."

Fran nods, smirking, then leans back, cradling his head in his hands. "Good times."

"Actually, this next part involves you," I say, but I can see he's already nodding off.

"Shall we reconvene tomorrow?" asks Jay. "I need to be up early for my normal grown-up job."

Jay manages a hedge fund, I think you knew that, but here's something you probably didn't know—Jay can't go to sleep without watching walking-tour videos on YouTube. He admits this to me as though confessing to some filthy kink and I tell him I've got no idea what he's talking about. Apparently, there's this whole community of people who film point-of-view perspectives of themselves walking around, and an even bigger community of people who watch them. By way of explanation, Jay puts one on, and next thing I know I'm watching a complete stranger walk around Tokyo at night. It's weird at first. A little voyeuristic. But after a few minutes the ambient noise and monotonous footsteps lull me into a state of calm. Eventually, Jay slumps off to bed and a very drowsy Fran returns with a blanket and pillow for me. He hugs me and says, "Well done on today."

"What do you mean?" I ask into his shoulder.

"I know you're just about holding it together, my babe. And I think you're doing a very good job of it."

Earnestness is my kryptonite, as well you know, so all I can manage is a quiet, "I'm okay."

I'm not okay. Obviously. Despite being exhausted, I can barely sleep. Not because of Fran and Jay's lumpy sofa, although it is extremely lumpy, but because somehow the only thing worse than sleeping in our bed without you is knowing you're sleeping in our bed without me. And by sleeping, I mean sleeping. Not tossing or turning or making me-shaped mounds out of the duvet. In all likelihood, you're sprawled in the centre of our bed like a horizontal Vitruvian Man, mouth open, snoring softly.

I've always hated that about you, the way you can sleep through anything. Through flights and fights, no matter the turbulence, literal or figurative, you can just shut down. Like a machine with an off switch. Sometimes, and I'm not proud of this, I'd make noise just to wake you up. Well, not to wake you entirely, just to rouse you enough that your arms would reach out and find me. Like a sleepy child searching for his favourite teddy, you would scoop me up and pull me into you again. Because in sleep you always love me. In sleep you seem to remember me. I wonder if your arms will reach for me tonight, or if they already know better.

In the morning Jay is gone and Fran is here. I try and fail to write until it's dark, then Jay comes home and Fran goes to work again. I feel like they're taking it in shifts to monitor me.

When evening comes, Jay and I make dinner together and he asks me to tell him the rest of the story. I turn it back on like a tap.

Not long after Aidan's party, I tell him, I met up with Fran for dinner, and we quickly became regular fixtures in each other's lives. It was that simple. Like shaking a Polaroid picture and watching a friendship develop before our eyes.

"This next part, I don't usually tell people—I skip to the hospital instead.

"But since it's you," I say to Jay, "I can give you the uncensored version."

Around six months in, Fran said he was going abroad and might not see me for a while. He was reticent about the details at first, but the next day he called me and said, "Fuck it, we're either friends or we're not." He told me he was flying to Belgium for his first gender reassignment surgery. Chest masculinisation, he called it, which I knew meant a double mastectomy. I also knew this wasn't a simple in-and-out procedure—not long after my mam died, her older sister, Kathy, had both of her breasts removed following a cancer scare and was bedbound for almost a month.

"Thank fuck I'm only a B cup," joked Fran over the phone, but I didn't laugh along with him. I knew he was trans. And he knew that I knew. So why had he been so afraid to tell me this?

I asked Fran that very question, and when he made an excuse to get off the phone, I knew I'd fucked up. He didn't speak to me for a few days after that. Couldn't, he said, when

I finally showed up at his flat—unannounced and extremely apologetic. Fran explained, with more than a little frustration, that his reaction had nothing to do with me and everything to do with the people he'd told before—his parents being the worst offenders. It all came pouring out then. How he'd told them he was trans on the same day he was accepted into Trinity College—thinking these two pieces of news would balance each other out. How they "simply couldn't bring themselves to watch their little girl turn into a boy." How they'd "rather she was dead." All along Fran thought he was the one who was changing, but that day he saw his parents become two totally different people. He realised then that he would go on being who he was—it was only his whole world that would change.

Fran's parents paid him off and kicked him out. Asked him to leave for college right away, to spend the summer anywhere but in their house. He graduated three years later with a first-class honours degree and they weren't there to see it. All he got was another cheque in the post.

"Not even a card," he said. "Not even a fucking card."

I remember Fran showing me the bandages around his chest, the raw red lines under his arms from where they chafed his skin, the box full of discarded needles and broken testosterone vials, which he had to regularly inject into his leg to help regulate his hormones—all the ways in which he hid himself from the world. That was why, he said, he was using his parents' "blood money" to pay for his surgeries and to set up a theatre for queer and trans artists: a place for them to be seen, instead of feeling like they had to hide.

I notice a tear slip down Jay's cheek, and suddenly I'm worried I've revealed something I shouldn't have.

"No, no," he says, placing a hand on my knee. "I just hadn't heard it put quite like that before."

We take a moment before I go on.

"I still think about it sometimes and cringe," I confide. "I should have been a soft place for him to land. Last thing he needed was more concrete."

"We're all just figuring things out as we go," offers Jay. "But dare I ask, what has all this got to do with you and Finn?"

"Well, Fran's surgery went exactly to plan. After he flew home, myself, Jenna, Aidan, and a few of Fran's theatre friends took it in turns to pop round and check on him. He had a set of spare keys cut for us all, which, by the way, were colour-coded based on our birthstones."

Jay laughs and shakes his head. "Of course they were."

So one morning, I let myself in and the flat was empty. Fran's bedroom was a mess; a bunch of things had been knocked off his dresser, including a mirror, which was smashed all over the floor. But Fran was nowhere to be seen. I called him but his phone rang out. Then I started calling his friends. Finally, Aidan picked up and explained that Fran had phoned him in the middle of the night from the Mater Hospital—absolutely off his face on morphine, apparently. It took Aidan a while to understand what had happened, but eventually he pieced it together; Fran had slipped on the way to the bathroom—probably woozy from all the painkillers—and ripped his stitches in the process. He'd passed out from the pain, but when he came to, he managed to call himself an ambulance. Aidan had been to see him first thing and said he was stable, but they were keeping him in for observation.

"Oh, and before I go," said Aidan just as I was about to hang up, "the hospital will only let family in, so you'd best tell them you're related."

"Who did you say you were?" I asked.

"His brother," said Aidan.

I thanked him for the tip and headed straight to the hospital, where I told them I was Fran's fiancée—I'd even had the foresight to stick a ring on my finger—and was allowed straight in. I had to traipse down several seemingly endless corridors before reaching Fran's ward, where I finally found him in a bed by the window, propped up on a stack of pillows with his eyes closed. I placed a hand lightly on his arm to let him know I was there, and as I did his head rolled slowly towards me and his eyes lolled open, lids still heavy. He tried to speak and then winced, so I leaned in closer.

"Are . . . the badgers safe?" he whispered.

"The badgers?"

Fran nodded sombrely. His pupils were fucking enormous.

"Oh, the badgers!" I said. "Yes, of course they're safe. I saw to it myself, darling."

"Good girl," he said, his features softening.

"How are you feeling?" I asked.

"Wonderful," said Fran. "Really just . . . great. Have you

seen my lovely button?" He lifted his hand slightly to show me a white plastic box with a big blue button on it, which I could only assume administered morphine.

"That is a very lovely button," I said, and Fran smiled wanly as his eyes fell closed again.

I made myself comfortable in the chair by his bed and got to work on the grapes I'd brought for him—he certainly wouldn't be eating them anytime soon—then I took out my book and read for a while.

Most people don't like hospitals, but I find them quite peaceful. Especially the bright, clean wards full of people quietly healing. That particular day, a June sun was streaming through the window, warming the back of my neck while a shy breeze danced with the hem of the curtains. I could hear the commentary of a football match come faintly floating from a portable radio, and the soft click-clack of knitting needles in a pair of unseen hands. All the while a dumpy nurse drifted from bed to bed, like a bumblebee, doing her rounds. I was almost dozing off myself when Fran's doctor came by to check on him. She looked from me to his chart, then back to me.

"You're the fiancée?"

"Yes," I said, standing up and straightening myself.

"Mm-hm."

She fussed about, taking measurements, jotting them down, and was just finished explaining the next steps to me when another friend of Fran's arrived. He was tall, but he didn't act tall, which is to say that most tall people stoop to compensate. This man, who I guessed was somewhere in his late twenties, stood perfectly straight with his shoulders pulled back and entered the room like he had something important to say. If he hadn't been carrying a bunch of flowers and a small teddy, I'd have assumed he worked at the hospital.

"And who are you," asked the doctor, "the mother-in-law?"

I had to stifle a laugh.

"Cousin," he lied.

"Of course," she said, as she turned back to me. "I take it the patient's family aren't in the picture, then?"

"No," I admitted.

She nodded, with a resigned expression that seemed to suggest this wasn't rare.

"So will you two be looking after him?"

"Oh," I said, catching the newcomer's eye. "No. We've never actually met."

"Yes, we have," he said.

"Nope."

"Yep."

"I haven't met you before."

"You have."

"I haven't," I insisted, a little irritated now.

"Kate, isn't it?" he asked.

"No," I said, though for the life of me I don't know why.

"Oh." He was very confused now.

"Yes," I admitted, "I'm Kate."

"Then why did you—?

"I don't know. It's been a weird day, okay?"

Here's how I knew we'd never met. The man standing in front of me was objectively beautiful. So much so that my first thought when I saw him was, *Fuck,* because I was still with

Charlie at the time and being attracted to another man was, at the very least, an inconvenience. There was no denying, though, that I was attracted to this man, whose black hair landed messily around his frankly ridiculous cheekbones and whose wise brown eyes sat in stark contrast among the rest of his babyish features. There was something at once innocent and worldly about him—it wasn't hard to imagine him as a student running late for class, but at the same time I could easily picture him descending the steps of a private jet or addressing a room full of world leaders on the perils of climate change.

"I'll leave you two to . . . get your story straight," said the doctor, before rushing off to something undoubtedly more important than this.

"Look, I'm really sorry, but I don't remember meeting you."

"It was a while back, to be fair," he said. "At Aidan's party? I was smoking in the garden, and you came outside. And then your friend came and got you."

I searched my memory while he searched my face for a hint of recognition.

"You were sort of . . . naked," he added, "and gold." Then it clicked.

"Oh my God, I thought you were a ghost!" I blurted without thinking.

"Yeah, I get that a lot," he said as he reached his hand across the foot of Fran's bed. "I'm Finn."

And then it happened: I took his hand in mine intending to shake it, but as soon as we touched, we froze. Time hardened around us like rock around bone and we became, for one brief, spaghettified moment, two fossils holding hands across a hospital bed, gazing down at our intertwined fingers as though trying to scry our future in a crystal ball.

"Finn!"

We heard her before we saw her, and instinctively we dropped our hands as she came gliding towards us, a vision in the bright June light. Kashi. The girl with the disco ball. And the gorgeous boyfriend. And suddenly it all made sense.

"Sorry I took so long, sweetie," she said, lifting onto her tiptoes and planting a kiss on Finn's mouth. "Parking was a nightmare. How is he?"

"He's good," said Finn, wrapping an arm around her waist and nuzzling the top of her head. With that, Kashi clocked me, and straightaway I knew she knew me too.

"Well, if it isn't the Dancing Queen!" She beamed.

"Oh Christ," I said, wincing. "Yeah, I was a tad out of it that night."

"That's one way of putting it," said Kashi with a warm laugh. "Well, for what it's worth I thought you were great fun!"

She kept talking, all the while snuggling herself under the crook of Finn's arm. I needed to leave.

"Shit," I interrupted, "I just remembered. I have to go."

"So soon?" asked Kashi. She seemed genuinely disappointed.

"Yeah, I'm supposed to meet my boyfriend for lunch."

Charlie wasn't even in Dublin that day.

"No worries," said Finn, as he nodded towards a still-sleeping Fran. "We'll make sure this one gets home safe."

I'd made it all the way to reception when Finn came running up behind me.

"Wait!"

I turned, worried he might want to discuss what had just happened, but then I saw him waving my book in the air. It was my mother's copy of *The Lord of the Rings*, and to say that it was well loved would have been something of an understatement; the page edges were all worn and frayed and the once vivid cover—blues, greens, and golds—had faded to a muted mess. The whole thing looked like it had been repeatedly dipped in tea.

"You forgot this," said Finn, examining the book as he handed it over. "Although I don't know how; it's bloody massive."

Of course he didn't want to discuss what had just happened. Because nothing *had* happened. We shook hands. I imagined the rest.

"Looks like it's been through the wars," he said as I tried to shove the book into my bag.

"Yeah, it's sort of a comfort read. I come back to it whenever I need . . ." But I trailed off.

"Comforting?" asked Finn, with the kind of crooked grin that renders the receiver incapable of not grinning back.

"Well, yes. Although . . ." I was looking more closely at the shabby cover. "The state of this particular book would seem to suggest I'm in a perpetual state of anguish."

"Are you?" he asked.

"Isn't everyone?"

Another moment passed in which we both stood, motionless, staring at each other while the world whizzed by.

"By the way," he said, snapping out of it, "Kashi wanted me to tell you we're having a few people round for dinner, once Fran's on the mend."

"Oh. Lovely."

"And she'd like you to come."

"Right."

He was staring at me with such intensity that I returned my attention to the tome I'd been squeezing into my bag.

"Sure," I said, "I'd love to."

I had zero intention of going to that dinner party, or ever seeing Finn again.

"And she never did see him again," declares Fran from the front door, dropping his bags and shrugging off his coat.

"Welcome home," says Jay.

"Hello, darling," says Fran, kissing Jay on the head as he passes round the back of the sofa, where he once again lands with a thump.

"Instead," Fran continues, "Kate found herself a nice, stable man. A librarian! A quiet, well-endowed librarian, who rarely speaks, save to compliment her, of course. And now she's a happy, healthy, well-adjusted adult with a country cottage and two cocker spaniels."

"The end," I say.

"BOR–ING!" says Jay, faking a yawn. "I want the *real* story."

"The *real* story is, unfortunately, quite boring," I say. "I did go to the dinner party. But while the writer in me wants to tell you that Finn and I fucked in the bathroom and eloped the next day, we actually spent the whole night squabbling, and then I went home to Charlie."

"That's it?" asks Jay, visibly disappointed.

"That's it," I say. "We're so used to hearing stories where an initial spark leads to an immediate explosion, or the introduction of a handsome new character spells the end of a relationship, or, worse still, an unrequited attraction drives someone to madness. But the truth is that every day, people find other people attractive, and most of the time nothing comes of it."

But Jay is still sulking.

"What was I going to do?" I ask him. "Leave my partner of four years—who, by the way, I loved dearly at the time—because of a completely superficial crush on some boy I'd just met?"

"Yes!" says Jay.

"And then what?" I laugh. "Go and ask said boy if he'd like to leave his stunning girlfriend for me? And what if he did, and we didn't even get along? What if we had nothing to say to each other? What if the sex was awful?"

"It wouldn't be, though," he says with a smirk.

"Fair," I admit. "But that's sex. It's not love."

"But what if it waaaas?" whines Jay. "What if it was love at first sight? What if Finn was your soulmate?"

"Okay, firstly, I think we've proven he wasn't. But secondly,

I don't believe in love at first sight. And I don't believe in soul-mates. I believe that with seven billion people knocking about, there's bound to be at least a couple hundred you could happily spend the rest of your life with. Some of whom you'll never meet. Some of whom you'll meet at the wrong time. And some of whom you'll meet and never even know you met."

"Don't listen to her, darling," says Jay, covering Fran's ears and dramatically peppering his face with kisses. "You're my soulmate forever and ever and ever."

"I dunno," says Fran, pulling away. "She raises some interesting points."

"Oh, you bad bitch," mocks Jay, shoving Fran playfully before turning back to me. "So how on Earth did you end up together?"

Like I said, Finn and I fought all night. I still found him physically attractive—I was aware of him squeezing past me in the kitchen, passing me a cigarette, hugging me good night—but it started and ended there. We disagreed over everything, and this never changed; he kept inviting me to parties and we kept finding ourselves debating in some corner, shouting to be heard over the music. And yes, I was aware that these fights were probably caused by sexual tension, and yes, I sort of liked fighting with him. But I knew nothing could happen—not only was I not trying to break him and Kashi up, I was actively rooting for them. I was surprised at how upset I was to hear they'd broken up, actually—she was offered a place at some dance school in Oklahoma, and after a few months of long distance they realised it just wasn't going to work. So that was that.

Meanwhile, Charlie and I sputtered along until one evening he announced he was leaving me. Things hadn't been right between us for a long time—I sometimes wondered if they ever were—but still, the breakup hit me hard. It was like being stabbed in slow motion; I could see the knife coming, but that didn't stop it from cutting me. And it cut deeper than expected too. Two months later I felt like I was still walking around with an open wound, flesh jagged and seeping and unable to heal. It was my "first big breakup," as everyone insisted on reminding me, but it shouldn't have hurt that much for that long. Should it? I couldn't sleep. I'd dropped two dress sizes. And I'd been avoiding my friends. But worst of all, I couldn't write. Each time I picked up a pen, it just hung flaccid from my fingers till I gave up and put it back down again.

I decided to throw a party. I was still living in the city centre flat that Charlie and I had shared, waiting to find a new tenant, and in the meantime, I decided, a massive party would help cleanse the place. I invited everyone I knew and bought way more booze than I could afford—I even got a disco ball to hang from the ceiling. Sad, I know, but sadder still, the day beforehand, I came down with the flu and had to cancel. And so I found myself lying on the sofa under that bloody disco ball—which I was too weak to take down—staring at the TV for two straight days. I hadn't showered. I could barely get up to make myself a cup of tea.

That evening I ordered myself a pizza, but when I heard a

knock on the door, I opened it to find Finn standing there with a bottle of wine.

"You're not pizza," I said.

"Yeah, I get that a lot," said Finn. I just stared at him.

"You look like shit," he said.

"Thank you, I'm aware."

"Sorry, I meant, are you sick?"

"Yes. Didn't you get the text?"

"No," said Finn. "What did it say?"

"That I'm sick."

"Right."

"So the party's cancelled."

"Oh," he said, but he made no move to leave.

"Look, I'd invite you in, but this is a pretty nasty dose."

"I don't mind," he said, then, realising how strange that sounded, he added, "Kashi's in Dublin. And she wants to see me. And I want to see her. But I don't think I should."

"Right. So you're asking me, a sick woman, to distract you so you don't go fuck your ex."

"Bit harsh," he said, "but, eh, yeah, basically."

I rolled my eyes as I stood aside to let him in, perhaps knowing somehow that I would live to regret it.

Inside, I collapsed onto the sofa and Finn got cosy in an armchair at the other end. It amazes me now that I didn't mind him seeing, or indeed smelling, me like that, but at the time I was too sick to care. Besides, sex was the furthest thing from my mind; I'd been with Charlie for five years and the thought of another man even touching me was enough to reduce me to tears. In the meantime, I was aware through the grapevine that Finn was handling his breakup quite differently: he'd slept with no less than six different women since Kashi left him, which I didn't judge him for; I just had no interest in being number seven, or eight, or whatever number he was up to on his list of rebounds. We relaxed in silence for a few minutes, me sprawled on the sofa, coughing occasionally, and Finn with his head tipped back and hands clasped across his belly. He reminded me of my dad in the tattered leather armchair back home.

"Sorry about you and Charlie," he said, breaking the silence.

"No, you're not."

"No," he admitted, "I'm not. You can do better."

"What, like you?" I teased. It was just a joke. But his answer surprised me.

"Christ no," he said. Then he really thought about it. "No. You deserve someone who'll be nice to you."

I got up on one elbow to look at him.

"Would you not be nice to me, Finn?"

"In all likelihood, no."

He didn't appear to be joking.

"Anyway," he said, "you seem sad. So, I'm sorry that you're sad, is what I think I mean."

"Well, thank you."

When the pizza did arrive, we shared it—I could only manage two slices anyway—then, without saying a word, Finn put *The Fellowship of the Ring* on, as though our conversation in the hospital had been just yesterday, and not over a year ago.

It was a long time since I'd thought about that day, and longer still since I'd asked myself if Finn thought about it too. Now here I was with proof that he remembered at least part of it. I must have been staring at him, because he looked back at me, his thick brows furrowing.

"Is this okay?" he asked, suddenly self-conscious.

"Sorry. Yeah. This is great."

Finn beamed proudly and turned his attention back to the TV. He then proceeded to talk the whole way through the film, mostly about its score, which he said was one of his favourites. I didn't mind. I knew every line by heart. And I'd spent so many nights alone that I was happy just to hear another voice in the room. After the film, Finn helped me tidy up, then he saw himself out.

The next morning he called to ask if I wanted to watch *The Two Towers* that night, which I did, of course. He came over again, this time with a pot of chicken soup, and took up his spot in the armchair like he'd been sitting in it for years. By the third night I was feeling much better and didn't really need a babysitter, but Finn seemed keen to come over and finish the trilogy. I assumed he still needed distracting, but just before we started the movie, I asked how much longer Kashi would be in town.

"She left yesterday," he said casually, then asked if I was ready.

"Ready," I said, and he hit play.

I fell asleep before the hobbits even made it past the gates of Mordor. When I woke up, the TV was off and the room was dark, save for a blue streetlight that bounced dimly off the disco ball overhead, scattering stars all over the walls. It was freezing cold; I was surprised I couldn't see my breath, which came and went in little shivers. My body shook and my face was wet with tears. Finn was kneeling in front of me, his features twisted with worry.

"Hey," said Finn. "It's okay. You're okay."

"Hi," was all I could manage.

"Hello." He smiled.

"Is it cold?" I asked.

"Not particularly," he said, placing the back of one hand on my forehead. "Do you have a fever?"

"Maybe," I lied. "Can you stay here a sec?"

"I'm not going anywhere," said Finn, taking my hands in his. And as soon as he did, it happened again. We froze. Time stretched. And as Finn brushed his thumb across the back of my knuckles, it stirred something in me. It wasn't a sexual feeling. I cannot stress enough how unsexy this all was; I was still blubbering—a stream of snot and tears was flowing freely down my face—and I had no desire whatsoever to be touched in *that* way. But I did want to be held. All I wanted, in fact, was to be held. And with that, as though reading my mind, Finn climbed around me, lay down behind me on the sofa, and collected me up in his arms. When he did that, I came undone. The tears fell faster. And my body shook even harder. I hadn't realised how much I'd missed the feel of someone's arms around me. I even said so out loud, but Finn said nothing in return. He just squeezed me tighter, his grip firm but delicate, like he was holding a glass statue instead of a girl.

We fell asleep this way, but somewhere in the night I woke up and realised that we had moved. Finn was now on his back, one arm still pulled tight around me, and I was facing him. My head was on his shoulder, my hand resting on his chest, and I had draped my left leg across him. Before, he was a friend comforting another friend, holding her while she cried. But this felt different. This felt intimate. Our faces weren't far apart now. I could feel his breath, his heart, which was beating too hard and too fast for him to be sleeping.

"Do you want me to move?" I whispered.

"Not really," he said. Then: "Do you want to move?"

"No."

I tell Jay we kissed that night, but I leave it there; suddenly, recalling it all out loud doesn't seem very appealing.

The part I leave out entirely, as always, the part only you know, is that I didn't have a fever that night. I'd had a nightmare; I have nightmares. It's a difficult thing to admit. It sounds silly, like something a child might say. Which is why it wasn't till we began regularly sleeping in the same bed that I told you about them. I remember needing to look away while I explained—that I'd started having them after my mother died, that my father would wake me, night after night, screaming and weeping and soaked with sweat, reduced to a quivering wreck over some variation of the same bad dream. I never did tell you what that dream was, and I was grateful that you never asked.

The nightmares subsided while I was with Charlie, but they crept in again after he left, and that night on my sofa was one of the worst in a long time—I don't think you understood what a relief it was to see you there when I woke up. I felt safe with you in a way I hadn't since my father scooped me up as a child, rocked me to sleep, and stayed with me till morning. When you wrapped your arms around me in the dark, I felt myself unfurling, like a flower blooming not by choice but by design. I fell in love with you that night, Finn. I fell in love with you arms-first.

The details keep trying to swim up towards me, but I push them down until Jay and Fran have gone to bed. Now, alone on their sofa, I let myself imagine you're here with me, like that first night is happening all over again.

"Do you remember that day in the hospital?" I asked you.

"Yes."

"What do you remember?" I pressed, and you hesitated.

"I'm not very good with words," you said.

"Then show me."

Your right hand found my left hand on your chest, slowly lifting it and, at first, simply holding it there. Then you placed your hand flat against mine and slid your fingers down across my palm, my wrist, and back up again. Like a tiny, unrehearsed dance, our hands moved and swayed against each other's, pushing and squeezing, bending and folding, fingertips exploring every line and dent and dimple and bone. I could just about make out the callouses from where you'd learned to play guitar, now hardened and part of you. And I could feel you find the faint scar on my palm, running your fingers along it, reading my past in braille.

Just the touch of your hand made my whole body hum, like some new instrument you'd just picked up and instantly knew how to play. I tried to hide the quickening of my breath, the slight stiffening of my hips, but you felt it. You let go of my hand and reached across to find my shoulder, then my neck, your thumb softly stroking the skin right behind my ear. I sighed as your fingertips slid across my jaw, then stopped beneath my chin and, with no force at all, lifted my face to meet yours. The tips of our noses touched. Your lips grazed mine.

"Is this okay?" you whispered. I smiled. And felt you smile back.

The first time we made love we did so hurriedly, hungrily, both of us desperate to know the answer to the question we'd been silently asking ourselves all year: If that's how it feels when our hands touch . . . ?

The answer was, perhaps, not what we expected—less an Earth-moving, mind-blowing explosion and more a quiet tremor of the soul, a sudden epiphanic understanding that our bodies were made to do this, and maybe only this. The belief I had in that moment, that I was exactly where I was supposed to be, that events would unfold as they might and that I was helpless to stop them, is the closest thing to faith I've ever known.

The second time had all the intensity of the first, only it

was heightened even further by our measured, almost languorous pace. With you, I felt time stretch in a new way, no longer unpleasantly drawn out but pleasurable almost to the point of pain. I found myself trying to make each moment linger, but I might as well have been grasping at smoke.

Every couple thinks that they discovered love. Invented it, even. I only claim to have known love that night. To have known it. And to have lost it. I should have seen this coming, I suppose, when the first word you ever said to me was "goodbye."

INTERLUDE

I wake up at home. And by home, I mean my father's house in Colligeen. It takes me a moment to adjust to my childhood bedroom: the imposing brown wardrobe and dark wood floors, the sky-blue wallpaper dotted all over with little white m's—faraway seagulls in flight. My mother used to ask if I thought they were coming or going, and I always said they were going.

"And where are they off to today?" she'd ask. The answer was always the same.

"Somewhere nice," I'd say, and she'd laugh. God, I miss her laugh.

Today, the gulls are coming this way, and their approach unsettles me. In the distance, they are screeching—one bird in particular more raucous than the others, his strained cries almost portentous in their urgency and tone. There is something oddly human about the sound, which is, of course, coming not from my bedroom walls but from the beach below; my single bed is pushed right up against the draughty window, and I can hear the birds out there, their caws mixed with the sound of the stubborn sea. Dord mara, we call it—the sea's murmur. But there's another sound too: a soft, unrhythmic thumping, like a stick being dragged along a fence. And I can't tell where it's coming from.

It feels late. Dad must have let me sleep in. I think he feels sorry for me.

What time is it, anyway?

Barefoot on the landing, I have the sense that I'm alone. All the doors are ajar, casting shadows at odd angles. And here's the beach again: an enormous oil on canvas that my mother painted the year I was born. In it, a vermilion sunrise is mirrored in the water below, like the ocean itself is aflame, and a lone figure stands looking out at it from the shore, minuscule against the scale of the sea beyond.

Descending the mahogany stairs, I find our front door flung wide, held in place by a strong breeze bursting through.

It isn't like Dad to leave the door open.

In the living room, stale yellow light seeps through the curtains, which are all drawn shut, giving the house a moribund air. The TV is on but muted. Images of kids playing football in the rain. A mother worriedly scrubbing grass stains out of bright white shorts. I'm beginning to worry when I hear the sound again, that dull thud, louder this time and more persistent. So I follow it, head cocked, through to the kitchen.

On the floor I find a pool of dense red liquid that I can't discern. It's slowly expanding across the tiles and running in rivulets along the cracks in between them.

"Dad?" I yell.

No answer.

I edge towards the puddle, stomach clenched, teeth pressed tight together, fearing the worst. But the colour is all wrong, I realise—not bloodred but molasses brown—and just like that the smell of coffee registers, acrid and sharp, and I spot my mam's old silver Moka pot sputtering on the stove, spewing hot, dark goo on the counter and down onto the floor.

In my haste to take it off the heat, I sear one palm on the metal handle and, clutching my hand close to my chest, I call out to my dad again.

Silence.

Then the banging resumes and I jump back against the sink, frightened now, eyes wide and tearful. That's when I notice the pantry door opposite me—the wind has picked up again, causing the door to rattle aggressively on its hinges.

The clangour stops the instant I open the door, only to be replaced by music blaring from the basement below. The Carpenters. "Yesterday Once More."

I call down. Still no response.

But they're back again.

And now my mind trips through every possible outcome, like flicking through the pages of a book in search of a particular passage.

Just like a long-lost friend.

I descend.

All the songs I loved so well.

But the basement is empty. Just shelves full of tins and tools, quietly gathering dust, and a pile of blank canvases stacked in one corner next to an assortment of wooden easels in all shapes and sizes.

Every sha-la-la-la.

I notice a thin window high on the back wall is flung open and now the wind is pouring through—replacing the familiar odour of paint and turpentine with that of a beach at low tide, littered with the sea's unwanted things.

Every whoa-oh-oh-oh.

As I slide a chair beneath the window and climb up to close it, the cellar door slams shut behind me. The music stops. And at the same moment a bird flies at the glass, scraping and screeching, flapping violently.

"Look!" it seems to shout. "Look! Look!"

I spin round. And that's when I see her.

My mother is standing in the centre of the room, her black hair hanging limp and wet, like streams of hot liquorice melting down her shoulders. She wears a thin grey nightgown, soaked through and clinging to her skin, which is itself a shade of purple-grey. Water drips down her rotting body and pools around her bare feet, moving in the same slow way that time does, inching sickeningly forward.

And her face. Is not her face.

My eyes fix upon it in terror now and I can't look away. It's as though someone painted a portrait where her face should be, then smeared it all in one angry stroke before the image had a chance to dry. I can just about make out the bloodshot white of one lopsided eye, a scrape of beige that was once her nose. Here and there clumps of paint hang, protuberant and close to falling free, with strands of oily hair clinging to them.

I feel bile rise in me as I step towards her, one hand reaching out, like I might still be able to save her, and then I notice the figures all around me, different versions of my mother, all with different clothes, their faces smudged and incoherent. All of them her, and not a one of them her at all.

The one in the centre moves now, her head tilting sideways in a shuddering motion as the paint just above her jaw begins to crack and split and a hole appears like a wound tearing open, forming a hideous mouth from which spills a stream of stagnant liquid, and a stench so foul I can taste it. Black liquid pours out as her one visible eye widens in terror. The room begins to fill with water. It's up to my neck within seconds. And then a sound emerges from my mother's not-mouth, an unspeakable shrieking somewhere between a scream and a wail and a seagull's moiling caw.

I wake up on Fran and Jay's lumpy sofa, thrashing and gasping at the air like a fish on a carpet. I sit up, still panting, and grab my phone. It's 3 a.m.; 10 p.m. in New York.

Alexis picks up after two rings.

"It's a horror," I blurt.

"What is?"

"The book," I say. "I think it's a horror."

LIFE'S ILLUSIONS

Coming back to our house feels like returning to the scene of a crime; I half expect to find yellow tape across the door, chalk outlines on the kitchen floor. As I round the corner onto our street, I imagine a team of people bustling about with notebooks in hand and those little blue booties over their shoes. All desperately trying to get to the bottom of it. Of us.

What I find instead is much worse: stillness, silence, everything precisely in its place—bed made, pillows fluffed, carpets vacuumed—there isn't so much as a rogue crumb in the kitchen or a bit of stubble by the bathroom sink. My first thought should be *How kind*, but instead I think, *How dare you.*

You were here.

You lived a whole week here.

And I have nothing to show for it.

I go so far as to check the bins, but you've emptied them—of course you have—and now I'm a bit suspicious actually, because (work aside) you've never been this thorough in your life; when you're left to your own devices, plans get half made, birthdays get forgotten, sheets get put on sideways, and surfaces get—at best—a cursory wipe. This is why your mother asks *me* about our plans for Christmas, by the way, not because she "doesn't want to bother you"—the official line we've all for some reason agreed to go with.

So, what is it you're trying to hide? A mountain of beer cans and cigarette butts—evidence of the ferocious all-nighter you threw in celebration of your newfound freedom? "Ding-dong, the witch is gone," that sort of thing? Or was it a pile of takeaway boxes, empty whisky bottles by the bed, proof that you've spent every night alone and pining? Maybe it was neither. Maybe it was both. Or maybe, I tell myself, you lived a completely normal week, and then you cleaned up like we said we would.

I sit with a thump on a kitchen chair, still in my coat and woolly hat, bag still on my back, and I finally admit what I've been keeping from myself all day. I wanted a fix. A hit. A tiny little taste of you. Instead, I feel like a spider in an empty web, waiting for vibrations that never come. A single strum on one silk strand would do. A gentle hum in the gossamer. But all is quiet. All is still. And another lonely week looms large.

Fran was surprised by how keen I was to get back (if only he'd known it was my inner junkie talking); he even told me I could stay another week if I wanted.

"I think Jay was enjoying your little chats," he offered.

"I was too," I said. But the truth is that I didn't just enjoy our chats, I relied on them; telling Jay about the beginning of us allowed me to feel—albeit fleetingly—like you and I were happening all over again, instead of something that had happened. Past tense.

I fucking hate the past tense.

I remember at my mam's funeral, a cellist played "Both Sides Now" as the coffin was carried from the church. It was beautiful. But it bothered me because Mam had always preferred the Carpenters to Joni Mitchell. I told my dad as much after the burial. We were standing outside a pub, doling out handshakes to a long line of sour-faced adults.

"Joni Mitchell is only her second favourite," I announced to the hunched black bulk of him stood next to me.

"Huh?" He was only half listening.

"Sorry for your loss," said a young man in a wool coat before offering us both a straight-lipped smile.

"Karen Carpenter is her favourite," I explained.

"Thank you," said my father, then, without looking down at me, he said, "Was."

"Was what?" I asked.

"Karen *was* her favourite."

My little child brain whirred trying to make sense of it. Surely, I thought, death doesn't change who your favourite singer is. If anything, rather than altering things about you, death cements them there forever, like a gnat caught in amber.

"No," I concluded aloud, "Karen *is still* her favourite."

My father took one of those breaths he takes when I'm being bothersome, then he looked down at me and said, not unkindly, "Mam died, pet. So we have to say *was* now. That's just how it is."

This was the moment I lost it.

In my defence, I'd conducted the day in fairly stoic fashion for a nine-year-old. I didn't object to the itchy black dress Aunt Kathy bought me, or the patent leather shoes that cut into the backs of my heels. I didn't cry once, not in the church during all those sad songs, or even in the graveyard when they put my mother's body in the ground. But this latest demand, that I start referring to her in a different tense—one that I'd been taught was exclusively used for things that had already happened, things that had passed, things that were effectively *gone*—this was too big an ask.

"You're wrong," I grumbled, with tiny fists clenched at my sides, clutching tufts of rough black tulle.

"We can talk about this later," said my dad, shaking the hand of some spindly blonde woman. She looked from him down to me, two beady blue eyes glaring out from darkened sockets, then spoke with a lipsticked smile.

"You must be Katie," she said. "God, you're every stamp of your mother. I knew her very well."

"Knew?" I sneered. "Have you forgotten her already?"

"Kate!" said my father, taking one of my hands in his. "That's enough of that now."

"But you're wrong!" I yelled, in that annoying child way that isn't louder, only squeakier. I never did learn to shout; I just get higher in pitch—a fact you love pointing out during arguments even though you know it only makes me angrier.

"She's not gone!"

I ripped free from his grasp and went tearing away from the pub and across the road, unsure where I was going at first until my feet took me up the hill towards the graveyard, those stiff black shoes cutting into my heels every step of the way.

I remember thinking of my mother's grave, deep and warm and inviting. I wanted to lower myself into it, to crawl inside the coffin and rest there under her arm, nestled forever in swathes of ivory satin. I wanted, more than anything, to sleep. But I couldn't find her.

Earlier that day, my mother's pale marble headstone had seemed to me to be the only one in the place. Now, grimy grey monuments stretched in all directions, like row upon crooked row of stalwart soldiers standing guard, weary sentinels of the bodies below. And as I traipsed down mossy pathways in search of her, I was suddenly five years old again, trudging up and down the brightly lit aisles of our local supermarket, frantically searching for a glimpse of my mother's long dark hair, or the cornflower-blue skirt she was wearing that day. I had lost her. That's what I thought. *I* wasn't lost. I knew *exactly* where I was. But I had lost my mother and with every second that passed I grew more convinced that I might never find her again.

In the end I heard her laughing and followed the sound to the frozen-food aisle. She had run into an old friend and seemingly forgotten all about me; those panic-filled five minutes I'd endured were merely a blip to her. Rage and relief filled me as I bleated into that blue cotton skirt, one hand clutching it for dear life, the other thumping feebly at her hip. She dried my cheeks and kissed my forehead, then continued her conversation like it was no big deal that I had almost lost her.

And so it was that I found myself standing stock-still in a graveyard that day, eyes closed, and listening. Of course, there was no laughter to lead the way this time—only birdsong and the first pitter-patter of rain. In hindsight, this may well have been my first experience of the grief glitch, and the realisation—not only that I wouldn't hear her bright, melodic laugh today, but that I'd never hear it again—was nothing short of a cannonball to my little belly. I doubled over, folding forward at the hips, and would probably have collapsed entirely had I not been struck by the upside-down image of my frilly ankle socks, once white, now turning bright red. Like a cartoon animal who doesn't fall until they notice that the ground is gone, the sight of my own blood made me suddenly aware of the searing pain in my heels. I tore off my shiny black shoes and peeled the blood-soaked socks from my feet before righting myself and continuing my search barefoot.

The rain intensified, and by the time my mother's headstone finally came into view, my dress was soaked right through. Soggy black tulle clung to my legs like a thousand tiny claws as I limped the last few feet towards her grave, filled with a familiar mix of anger and relief at what I saw: in place of the womb-like chamber I'd imagined, a mound of wet, uneven earth, as dark and fresh as my own grief. I collapsed on top of it, coming to rest roughly six feet from where she lay.

I had lost her. For good this time.

Aunt Kathy found me sleeping on the muddy soil. She lifted me up onto her hip and carried me all the way to her car.

"I lost my shoes," I confessed into her ear.

"Never mind about that," she whispered.

On the drive home she offered to run me a bath when we got back.

"Your mam would've been fond of a hot bath," said Aunt Kathy, smiling at me in the rearview mirror.

"Would she?" I replied.

The Irish, it seems, have found a loophole in the language of loss; the conditional tense with no conditions. No ifs or buts. She just would.

After she'd tucked me into bed that night, my fingertips shrivelled from soaking for so long, Aunt Kathy tiptoed out of my room, leaving my door open a crack.

A loud knock makes me jump to my feet. Something, or someone, just banged on the window. I stand motionless, still in my coat and hat, and let my bag slide from my back as I wait for another sound.

Nothing.

Did I imagine it?

I inch towards the back door and look out. There's no one there. Obviously there's no one there, I think. But then I see it, by the leg of your plastic patio table: a dead crow. At least I think it's dead; the bird's long wings are fully extended—like they've been nailed to an invisible cross—and its onyx eyes are open and fixed.

As I step outside, I can't help but glance skywards, shoulders squeezing towards my ears like I'm bracing myself for the sight of more falling birds, a plague perhaps, of which this was just the first. But there's nothing up there. No birds. No plague. No answers. Just the dusk sky, purpling like a bruise.

I want to take a closer look at it, but when I try to step forward, I imagine the bird's stiff little body bursting back to life. I see it launching itself towards me—flapping and scratching and screeching—and my feet refuse to move. When a strong breeze ruffles its scruffy black feathers, giving it the illusion of life, I run back inside, quickly pulling the blinds down and praying for some wild animal to take it overnight.

You would usually deal with this sort of thing. Not because you're a man and I'm a woman; there are plenty of things you're squeamish about that I have no problem with—like blood and gore and illness, for example. Remember that time you passed out after getting a flu shot? And you can't even hear someone *talk* about being sick without feeling sick yourself. But that's okay. Because the trade-off is that you deal with all the creepy-crawlies. The spiders, and mice . . . and dead fucking birds.

Dealt.

Dealt with.

Here we go again.

It's even more difficult to talk about you in the past tense because you're technically still here. Here as in alive, obviously, not here in this house. Although you so easily could be. If I called and asked you to come help me, you would. I know you would.

And this, I've just now decided, is maybe harder than death. With death there's no option to call someone, to hear them laugh, to see or touch or hold them again. There's no decision to be made. No temptation to resist. Choosing to be apart is its own special kind of torture. It means making that choice over and over again. Every moment of every day. And some days the choice doesn't seem as clear.

I take out my phone and let my finger hover over the little green call button beneath your name. I won't push it, I tell myself. I just want to tiptoe up to the edge. Take a look at what's down there.

I see you dropping whatever you're doing to come here. I see your arms around me, your body next to me in bed, your warm voice filling the silence. I see grief loosening its grip, receding under my door and out into the world to besiege some other sorry soul. I see comfort. Respite. A full, deep breath.

Just a hit.

Just a fix.

Just a little taste.

But I know how this actually goes. I call. You come over. We fuck. It's spectacular. We relax into a rhythm and three weeks later we're hurling cutlery at each other's heads.

I turn my phone off and throw it across the sofa.

"We're not talking," I remind myself out loud.

And with that, I remember the note I stuck to the wall.

Shit.

Did you see that?

I hope you didn't see that.

I run to my desk to check if it's still there. It is. Oh God. But there's another note underneath it. I snatch the second note off the wall as though it's a mirage that might vanish before I get there.

BIT HARSH, is all it says, in the same blocky lettering you use on envelopes and birthday cards. You've drawn a small smiley face at the bottom too.

Tears and laughter come at the same time. There it is. A hit. A rush. A brief blessed tug on the gossamer.

≡

Years after my mother's funeral, a therapist told me that being asked to change the way I spoke about her meant facing the reality of the situation. The request was like a threat to my denial, she said, and this elicited an extreme response in me (by extreme response one presumes she meant running to a grave with the intent of crawling inside it and never getting back out).

Well, I didn't agree then and I don't agree now.

What she didn't understand, and what my father has never seemed to grasp, is that I wasn't sad or confused or afraid; I was fucking furious. Not because I was being asked to face the truth, but because it felt like I was being asked to lie—to partake in some collective falsehood, a cover-up of my mother's very existence, wherein we all pretended that she had been nothing more than a body, a walking, talking flesh sack without which she simply ceased to be. It's true that my father sometimes sat up with me all night, but during the day we didn't speak of the nightmares, or their cause. We didn't talk about my mother, his wife, our loss. It felt like he was relegating her to the past at a time when she had never felt more present. After all, a body can exist in the next room, but absence fills a whole house. And our house overflowed. The floorboards practically creaked for want of her.

My mother was there alright. I saw her waving from the empty doorway as I left each day for school and crouched over the dwindling flower beds when I returned home in the afternoon. I saw her in the puffy crescents underneath my father's eyes, and the hesitation in his hands as he reminded them, for the hundredth time, to set the table for two and not three. I heard her in the murmur of his TV late at night, the songs we never played, the records that he threw away. She was there in the beds and sandwiches and memories that went unmade, the lightbulbs that blew and didn't get replaced, the disused fireplace, and the spikey green weeds that crept up between thick grey paving slabs. Every stilted laugh. Every silence. Every crack and gap and negative space. My mother slipped between the substrate of our lives and took root. And we pretended not to notice.

I make it all the way to bedtime subsisting on nothing but a bowl of noodles and your little note (which I briefly consider taking to bed with me). Then I turn out the light and wait for sleep.

All is quiet.

And then.

A motorised churning sound.

Which eventually stops.

Replaced by . . .

A tinny whoosh.

Dripping.

Clicking.

Was it always this loud here?

I conduct several futile investigations; the sounds all stop whenever I get out of bed, and the only one that continues—a low drone, like that of an engine idling—appears to have no source. Eventually, I return to bed and lie there listening to the clicks and drips and ubiquitous hum, which are soon joined by a gathering wind outside. As it sighs past my window, my thoughts turn to the bird in the back garden—the black wet mass of it being bashed this way and that. I wish I had just dealt with it earlier; now every tiny bump or thump unnerves me, and I have to bury my head in a pillow to muffle the noise.

Sleep comes bearing dreams like fruit. They bloom behind my eyes, ripening, then quickly rotting, sprouting mounds of furry flesh and twisted little feelers that reach unseeingly towards me before finally succumbing to putrefaction. How quickly the dreams shift. Each one a time lapse of decay. A summer's day that turns to night. A once bright room plunged into shade—the light switch broken, or gone. That sinking in my stomach when it won't turn on and I know deep in my bones that I will soon be set upon by some terrible version of her, drowned and dripping wet, faceless and yet seeing, silent and yet screaming out of one dead lung. You'd think by now that I could wake myself, but the closest I can come is to thrash my sleeping limbs about in bed, hoping that you'll notice, but in my state of dread I forget that you're not here to see. And I wonder from the dreamworld why you're not waking me.

Tonight, it's a double act, *My Mother and the Broken Bird*. A duet so absurd that I'd laugh if it weren't utterly obscene. They find me in my bedroom. In the basement. On the beach. By her grave. With dirt under her fingernails. Always reaching out for me.

I'm up before sunrise. Exhausted by sleep. I boil a kettle. Make some tea. And check outside. Relief. The bird is gone.

The stories were the first to go. Before her clothes. Before even her makeup on the bathroom shelf. The stories were all quietly boxed up and put away.

One day, maybe a week after the funeral, a neighbour came around to help with dinner. Mrs. O'Donohue I think it was. She was kind like that. Anyway, she commented on a ceramic bowl on the kitchen windowsill—a gorgeous yellow bowl with tiny gold flecks.

"Where did you get it?" she asked, and from my seat at the kitchen table, I instinctively looked to my father. Only instead of launching into the story about my mother randomly deciding to take up pottery; instead of laughing, as he always had, about the stack of failures that had come before this beautiful piece—the wonky, leaky, half-baked, vaguely bowl-shaped objects that she brought home week after week and tried and failed to find some use for; instead of him reminiscing about her determination to get it right, segueing assuredly into her perseverance in the face of any difficulty, and then arriving at the conclusion, the same conclusion he always arrived at, that it was this calm, resolute quality that made him fall in love with her in the first place; instead of all that, my father simply said, "I'm not sure, Mary," and carried on peeling the spuds. He threw a sideways glance at me as he said it, and perhaps sensing my dismay, he added, "I think it was Abigail's."

He knew full well it was hers. He just didn't want to talk about her.

Anger flared in me and turned quickly to guilt. Isn't that strange? I felt guilty just for bearing witness to his denial.

She wasn't much of a talker, my mam; she always said she communicated better with paint than with words. Like you with music, I suppose. There were rare occasions when we'd get her going on a topic she loved and then she wouldn't stop. We used to call it "pulling her string." Anything relating to the human condition would do it; art, science, literature, language—we'd set her off and then sit back and marvel as facts and fascinations came tumbling out of her like great big hay bales careening joyously downhill. She'd take you on tangents that she never returned from, leave you stranded without resolution while she confidently bumbled down yet another path, likely getting lost along it. I learned this at an early age and, some nights, right before she'd switch out the light, I'd bring up something like faeries or photosynthesis, knowing that my mam would stay and talk, and I'd get another twenty minutes out of the day.

Most of the time, though, she didn't say much, especially in big groups. People assumed she was quiet because she was shy, distracted, rude even, but they were wrong; she was just observing—if life were a meeting, then my mother was the one taking minutes. And while she was watching the world, I was watching her, noting her half smile and the graceful tilt of her head, like the Earth on its gentle axis. Sometimes she'd catch me staring and wink at me. I felt like I was being let in on a secret, though what that secret was I'll never know.

My dad was the real storyteller, a proper seanchaí, like his father before him. He would pause to collect his thoughts before he spoke, and when he did speak, he did so slowly, mindfully, constructing sentences like sturdy little houses, brick by careful brick. Listeners could be forgiven for thinking that he'd dropped a brick, sometimes, or at the very least misplaced one, but they soon learned that he'd put it precisely where he meant to. He was soft-spoken, his voice just loud enough to be heard, and his audience would lean in to listen as he carried them from one end of a story to the other, like baby ducks in a pair of cupped hands. When he was done talking, silence fell as people collectively held their breath, and his words settled over them.

He was our very own historian, the custodian of our family's lore, retaining and reciting back the mundane moments that made up our lives. Stories of birthdays and weddings and funerals alike. Stories of mistakes made and lessons learned. Stories with no apparent moral or conclusion. But always an abundance of love. I missed them. I missed the stories he told only once, the ones that broke his heart to relive, and I missed the stories he told so many times that they'd been altered by the telling.

Stories are like memories in that way, you know; they change with each remembering. No memory is set in stone. They are fluid, pliant things, easily rewritten. When we remember something, it's not even the scene itself we see, but the version of it we called to mind last time, and with every recollection the image shifts; details are distorted by our current mood or mindset, shaped by the things we've experienced between the event and the moment we recall it. In other words, the very act of remembering a memory alters it. It's like looking at a photo of a photo of a photo of a scene, all shot on different cameras, in different places, at different times of day—a light flare added here, a corner cropped off there. *Something's lost, but something's gained*, as Joni once said.

Eventually, any resemblance to the original fades, leaving only a vague impression of what was. Which begs the question . . . are the moments we remember most actually the moments we remember least?

It's life's illusions I recall.

There's a photograph I keep on my desk, of my mother in her early thirties. She's sitting at a dressing table in a room that I don't recognise. It might be a hotel room. The photographer—presumably my father—is just behind and to the left of her and has caught her reflection in the mirror. She doesn't know her picture is being taken; her face is soft, vacant, lips parted, eyes staring out of frame, fixed on nothing in particular. She looks lost—to us at least, if not to herself. A shock of ink-black hair is caught across one shoulder, leaving the other exposed. Her right hand is lifted, one finger resting loosely on her chin, while her left hand clutches a towel wrapped tight around her chest. The towel could be yellow or green or brown, its colour muddied by the dim lighting and the passage of time.

I found the photo a decade ago, in a box in my father's attic—the one marked, simply, ABIGAIL.

There were hundreds more; clearer, brighter images, taken outside on sun-drenched beaches and at back-garden barbecues. But I was drawn to this one. Perhaps because the woman in this picture feels more akin to the mother I knew, her subdued mien more familiar than any posed, smiling versions of her. Or maybe it's because, if I hold the photo at arm's length and soften my gaze, the woman at the dresser could easily be me—a fact that has become truer with each passing year, and that will eventually become untrue as I grow older than she ever did.

Sometimes I like to look at it. Sometimes I find myself thinking about it, remembering it even, as though I were there, which is of course impossible since I hadn't even been born yet; my mother didn't have me until she was forty-two, an unexpected-bordering-on-impossible surprise for a couple who'd been told they couldn't have children. A miracle, she called me, a "noisy little miracle."

My mind has filled in the rest of the room—the maybe

hotel room in the photograph I definitely wasn't present for—placing a shuttered window along one wall, a double bed in the corner, and a wooden bureau opposite. I could describe to you the particulars of this room down to the detailing on the antique door handles, the scent of hairspray and Chanel No. 5, and the font on the room service menu (green, cursive, faded in places). Sometimes I see it all from the perspective of a child, resting on the bed, watching the photo being taken. Sometimes I am the photographer. Sometimes the subject. I recall the click of the camera, the whirr of its little motor, and a sudden self-awareness as I return, blinking, from my reverie of this room I was never in.

Life's illusions indeed.

Monday is a write-off.

On Tuesday I make it to midday without crying. Then a bouquet of flowers arrives, and I stupidly let myself believe you sent them before realising that they are in fact from Alexis. This is enough to send me straight back to bed for the day.

Wednesday. I don't even want to talk about Wednesday.

By Thursday Fran calls to tell me that the two ushers who were off sick have, in fact, eloped.

"With each other?" I ask.

"Well, they've hardly both eloped with two other randoms."

"That's fair. I just can't believe anyone eloped at all. Do people still do that?"

"Apparently," he says. "Their parents didn't approve of their relationship, so they upped sticks and moved to Holland."

"Why Holland?" I ask.

"Why not?"

"Well, fair play to them, I suppose."

"Fair play indeed," says Fran. "But while I'm all for fleeing the country for love, it has left me rather short-staffed."

"And?"

"And," he says, "you owe me."

"I'm busy," I tell him.

"Uh-huh," he replies. "See you at six. Wear black."

He hangs up before I can protest further.

It's incredible what Fran has managed to do with the place. I haven't seen it since we came to that one-woman show back in March—a fact that neatly demonstrates how caught up in our own bullshit we've been. The Arena is unrecognisable; what used to be a run-down dance studio with a makeshift stage and folding chairs is now an exquisite art deco theatre. From the carpet to the wood panelling—even the ceilings and staircase—every square inch is adorned in sumptuous golds and greens and deep cherry browns. A grandiose glass light fixture hangs from a domed ceiling in the foyer. It is both far too extravagant and entirely necessary. Much like Fran himself. And indeed, like the red velvet seats, which, by the way, he was absolutely right about. The whole thing is a somewhat spectacular two fingers up to his parents, I must say.

The production is a comedy about a bisexual time traveller whose past and future selves engage in satirically existential conversation whilst waiting for their present-tense self to arrive. He invariably doesn't show.

"It's like *Waiting for Godot*, but gay," says Fran, when describing it to me.

"Everything here is 'like something, but gay,'" I retort.

"Waiting for *Gay*dot," he muses, and I can't help but smirk as I hang my coat up in the staff room. Fran nods approvingly—at his own joke or my black outfit, I'm not sure.

"To be fair, there's nothing especially gay about our new opening act," says Fran. "Well, except the performer, of course."

"Of course," I say, half wondering if I should run out for coffee now or wait till the interval; I can already feel the effects of last night's sleeplessness. I realise Fran's still talking.

"Wait till you see it, my babe. Just wait. It starts next week and it will fuck—you—up." He emphasises each word in staccato fashion.

"Because Lord knows what I need is to be more fucked-up."

"You make a good point," says Fran, thoughtfully sizing me up. "Maybe don't watch it."

Except now I'm intrigued.

≡

I'm put to work on front-of-house duty, which means pointing people to their seats or the toilets. Standing in the foyer, I can hear the audience laughing uproariously at tonight's performance, and I try to listen in a few times but my thoughts keep wandering to other things. Like you. Like what you're doing tonight. Who you're with. How you feel. Whether you're thinking about me too. Then I think about my father, no doubt settling in for the nine-o'clock news in his same battered slippers and threadbare robe, a cup of green tea in hand. I really should call him. But I can't bear the conversation about us. Not that it would even be a conversation; you know what he's like.

"Right you be," he'll say, and that'll be that.

After the show, Fran asks if I can bring some costumes down to the storeroom before I head home.

"Absolutely," I tell him. "But I'm charging overtime."

Stepping into the lift feels like stepping through time—from an old-world theatre into mid-eighties machinery; dented metallic walls, large plastic buttons, and a broken overhead light, which at once emits a sickly hum and a dense green glow. The doors close and I see my face reflected. Wan. Waxen. Like I've just seen a ghost.

Or I'm about to, I think, before quickly dismissing the thought.

Still, when the lift begins its descent, a queasiness overcomes me, my stomach tensing further as the steel box lurches to a stop and a loud ping announces our arrival. After that, a guttural grinding begins, metal on metal, and the lift doors shudder open onto a pitch-black corridor, at the end of which is a doorway outlined in stark white light. No part of me wants to step out of this lift.

You're just tired, I tell myself, *and severely sleep-deprived.*

But this does little to ease my nerves as I drag the rickety clothes rack down the dark hallway, one wheel squeaking the whole way like a frantic little sidekick mouse trying to warn me of the danger up ahead. When I reach the door, I'm quick to grab the handle and swing it open, blinking against the harsh glare behind it. I quickly pull the rack inside and deposit it in the nearest corner.

Job done, I think. *Now, let's get out of here.*

The first thing that strikes me when I turn to go is the sheer size of the room—cavernous; this whole place is a veritable Tardis. The second: a huge stack of blank canvases, and beside them a collection of wooden easels.

No, is the only thought I'm capable of, as my eyes adjust and the other canvases slide into focus, some thirty or more enormous white slabs, all standing side by side against the far wall, like rows of teeth.

Or gravestones.

The hum of fluorescent lights high above me becomes audible as their flickering intensifies. Somewhere in the distance, there's a faint thumping sound. And I could swear that I hear seagulls squawking outside.

"Look," they seem to say.

I leave before my mother can appear; like the titular Godot, her arrival feels somehow inevitable in this scene, and I pray that, like him, she won't show. That I won't be faced with the sight of her tonight.

Within seconds I'm slamming the door behind me and scrambling up the long corridor, flooded by that same dream dread I know so well. Not similar. The same—I might as well be sleeping now, my real body thrashing about in a bed somewhere, trying to wake itself up.

Back inside the lift, I pound the square button with the flaking number 1 on it, willing the doors to slide shut as I stare straight ahead, gaze transfixed on that bright white rectangle of door in front of me. I imagine it opening, light spilling out around her sodden silhouette as she reaches for me, seeking me out with her one lidless eye.

Seconds stretch. Nothing happens. I hit the button again, ramming it with my fist now, tears in my eyes as a sound blasts out from the storeroom, a hollow, bone-rattling-teeth-chattering sound, like a thousand talons landing on a tin roof.

I could scream. In fact, I'm about to when the steel doors clang mercifully shut and the lift climbs shakily upwards with me still shuddering inside; she may be trapped down there, but my fear ascends with me up into the night.

Worth noting: trauma is an exception to that rule about memory, the one where memories change with each remembrance. Because a trauma memory gets stored incorrectly; like a folder put in the wrong drawer of a filing cabinet, it won't be where you expect it to be when you go looking for it. It might disappear altogether. Or reappear when you're not looking for it. It might even fracture and show up in several different drawers—strange fragments of it spliced in among other files. Each piece you do remember comes at you with razor-sharp, pinprick, paper-cut accuracy. And no matter how often you look at it, no matter how much time has passed, no matter how little sense it makes, a trauma memory will never change. Because you don't recall trauma. You relive it.

This is why I know that the thesaurus in my dad's study was blue, that my nails were painted glittery pink, that the lining of the coffin was a rich ivory with delicate folds, like the ice creams we got from the van by the beach. Except I don't *know* all these things. I *see* them. I see the dark, paisley wallpaper in my principal's office—where they made me wait for my dad to come deliver the news—and the small square of crisp winter sky outside the window. I can still hear the squeals and shrieks of kids playing in the courtyard below. The smack of a ball against concrete. And the tick-tick-tick of the oil radiator by the principal's desk. I can smell the fake heat wafting up at me. I can even taste the banana I'd just had with my lunch. Which is why I've never eaten a banana, or anything banana flavoured, since.

"Not even ice cream?" you asked me once.

"No."

"What about a banana milkshake?"

"No," I said. "What are you not getting about this?"

Maybe what you weren't getting is that I don't dislike bananas—I actually enjoy the taste—but eating one would send me straight back to that room, to exist there again with those sights and sounds and scents and my father's stooped and sorry presence. His eyes-down, mouth-flapping delivery.

"There's been an accident."

I could be eighteen or twenty-three or sixty-eight years old and it wouldn't change. I'd still feel fear simmering in my stomach, that grief-steeped bile rising in my throat (a half-digested ham sandwich threatening an encore), and the taste of banana in my back teeth.

I don't eat ham sandwiches anymore either. They got stored wrong—along with bananas, pink nail polish, paisley wallpaper, and many other items—in a file labelled THINGS YOU OUGHT TO BE MORTALLY AFRAID OF.

Death itself, images of death, descriptions of death, funerals, morgues, coffins, and the like, have very little effect on me. Offer me a banana, though . . .

The basement eludes me. It is neither memory nor trauma.

There is a basement in the house where I grew up. And my mother used to paint in it. There were easels and canvases and jars of murky water with long thin brushes poking out like river reeds. She even had a small CD player that she blared music out of as she worked.

But I never met her dripping corpse down there. Never saw her smudged, unknowable face. Or heard that shrill cry, like a spirit wailing from the underworld.

The basement of my nightmares isn't real.

So why do I remember it? Why does it occupy my body like pain? Why do shards of it show up, slicing through the membrane between dreams and waking life?

Fran's outside enjoying his post-work spliff. He catches me
scurrying off and asks if I'm alright.

"Fine," I lie. "Just not a big fan of basements."

"How Jungian," he jokes, but then our eyes meet and his
face grows sullen.

"Those things in the storeroom," I begin, not knowing
how to ask what I want to ask. "Are they . . . there?"

Fran squints at me, just like he did on that doorstep in
Cabra.

"I'm not sure what you mean, my babe."

"Never mind," I say, forcing a smile. "Long day."

"You sure you don't want to stay at mine?"

"I'm fine. Really. See you tomorrow!"

I bark this last bit over my shoulder as I cross the street.

There were nights after my mother's death, more nights than
I can count, when my bedroom ceiling creaked and I could
have sworn she was up there, in the attic. Flicking through
those photos. Insatiable for proof that she existed.

Maybe I was haunting myself. Maybe I still am. My way of
missing her.

When I get home I add another note to the wall, beneath
yours. *Just needed the reminder*, it says.

CURSING AT RABBITS

It begins as an itch. Not on my skin but at the very centre of my brain. I could reach it, I think, with a straightened coat hanger up my nose. Or a white handkerchief stretched taut between my ears, yanking it back and forth like some goofy magician, crossing my eyes to emphasise the side-splitting comedy of it all. It's a feeling not unlike the impulse to yawn, or sneeze, or stretch upon waking. To bite a broken nail or pull a rogue hair from your tongue. Once noticed, the urge to write is just as physical and can quickly become just as bothersome.

You took me to a magic show once. Remember? Though he didn't do the old handkerchief-through-the-head routine. I'm not sure anyone does anymore.

It was in the basement of that pub with the giant mechanical trout above the bar, the one that sang "Come On Eileen" on a constant loop. We arrived late and had just found our seats at a table in the back as the lanky magician ascended the stairs, tripping over his own feet and sending himself sprawling onto the stage.

"I'm alright," he announced, though no one seemed to care. Two people clapped half-heartedly as he dusted himself off and began setting up his props.

The magician's limbs appeared to act independently of him, swiftly knocking over his little stool and the glass of water he'd placed on top.

"Shit," he said. Then: "Sorry," when he noticed a mother with her young son right up front. He grimaced at her and then at the room. "I'm not quite— This was sort of a last-minute booking. Bear with."

He continued to set up, throwing his top hat at a nearby coatrack and missing completely. The hat rolled off the stage and landed at the little boy's feet.

"Shit," he said again, and instantly looked to the mother in fear. "Terribly sorry, madam."

She scowled this time. The boy giggled.

Moments later, the magician accidentally revealed a bunch of plastic flowers from inside the lining of his coat, and as he awkwardly shoved them back in, a couple at the table next to us glared at each other in disbelief: *Is this guy for real?*

He wasn't, of course. It was all part of the act.

You flashed me a conspiratorial smile just as the magician retrieved his empty glass and placed it back on the stool. He then walked away to fix another prop that had fallen over, and as though remembering something, he returned to the glass and casually filled it with water, which he conjured out of thin air. As he gulped it down, the mood in the room tangibly shifted from annoyance to mild awe.

They were in on the joke now.

People like to be in on the joke.

After that, the magician reached for his hat, which he soon realised was not on his head. He began looking around for it just as the little boy plucked it off the floor and walked to the front of the stage, offering the top hat up to the magician, who accepted it with effusive gratitude, then put it on and let out a loud yelp. The startled boy stared up as the magician snatched the hat back off, revealing a fluffy white rabbit sitting atop his head, twitchy pink nose and all. He handed the hat back to the smiling boy while he removed the rabbit and placed it gently in a wooden box. At the same moment the boy squealed in delight. There was another bunny! he said. Inside the hat! Another one? asked the magician, scratching his chin now, like this wasn't the plan at all.

Once that rabbit had been dealt with, another one appeared. And so on and so on. Unwanted bunnies everywhere. And the audience chuckled and cheered as the increasingly baffled magician rounded them all up with the help of the little boy, who had unwittingly become an eager assistant.

The entire show was a polished, pristine mess, a simple set of classic tricks performed in increasingly complex ways, culminating in a crescendo of clumsiness that at no point appeared complicated. People looked on, their faces frozen in dumb delight as they were given only what they needed in order to be wowed.

By the final trick, all I could see was what the magician wasn't showing us. Not just onstage tonight—the sleights of hand and nylon thread—but all the days this ordinary man spent figuring out how to seem magical; the early mornings and late nights, the injuries and failed attempts, the hair-pulling-teeth-grinding-back-breaking hell of it. The tears. The fits. The tantrums. A full-grown man alone in a room, spilling water on himself for the tenth time that day, cursing at a box full of rabbits. The excruciating effort that goes into making something seem effortless.

That's what writing feels like sometimes—cursing at rabbits. I spend entire days berating sentences for not being better. As though it's their fault and not mine.

But even when I hate them, I still love them. Just as a painter has to love the smell of paint, or a sculptor the feel of wet clay between their fingers, a writer must love sentences. All of them. Because every sentence written, no matter how mediocre, brings us one step closer to the elusive perfect sentence, that rare beast we spend our whole lives hunting—not to keep or to tame, just to find, to say we have found it. Like a butterfly between cupped hands, we hold each perfect sentence close, allowing ourselves to peek in and marvel at its precious form before setting it free, knowing it was not meant for us alone. This is the secret—to write not for the page or even the paragraph, just the next good sentence. And once it's been found, to let it fly.

I didn't find any today. The hunt proved fruitless. And

while you'd usually leave me to it on days like this, Jenna doesn't know better; she keeps offering me cups of coffee, asking if I'm hungry, if she can help in some way. She sees me sitting quietly and starts chatting to me, taking my silence as an indication of inactivity when it's exactly the opposite; the stiller I seem on the surface, the deeper I'm diving inside myself for treasure.

I remember the day you walked into the living room and found me staring out the window.

"What are you doing?" you asked.

"Writing."

"Oh," you said, and left.

Two hours later you came back to find I hadn't moved.

"Still writing?" you asked.

"Yep."

"Okay."

Another three or so hours passed before you gently suggested I should move my body. In case the wind changed, you said, and I froze that way.

You were joking, of course, but that's the fear, isn't it? That I'll freeze this way, forever trapped in the act of trying to write. I often wake up in the dead of night, suddenly afraid that I've written my last good sentence. That there are, in fact, no good sentences left. I imagine a weary, aproned lady sweeping the floor of my mind, wiping her brow, pulling the shutters, switching the sign on the door from OPEN to CLOSED. *Sorry,* her expression seems to say, *we're fresh out of sentences.*

I asked you once if you ever worry you'll run out of melodies.

"Of course not," you said, laughing. You actually laughed.

"Why worry," you added, "when there are endless possible combinations of notes?"

Such a logical way of looking at it. And I know that words, too, can be arranged in infinite beautiful ways. But my fear is less about the existence of good sentences and more about my ability to find them. To continue to dive for them day after day.

There are days, rare, hallowed days, when writing feels less like dredging my depths and more like ambling along the shoreline of my psyche, collecting all the gleaming gems conveniently scattered there. I gather them up, rinse away the silt and sand, and arrange them in pretty formations for people to enjoy.

But most days I go under. I dive and dive, barely coming up for air until I find myself deposited once more on the slow, wet sand, exhausted but empty-handed. On these days, I haul my tired body up and trudge begrudgingly homeward, all the while convincing myself to never come back here again.

But I do.

I always come back.

If only someone had prepared me for this, told me what writing really was. If only I had seen just one film in which writers weren't depicted as a busy bunch, always frantically typing, or scrawling, or balling up pages and discarding them in frustration.

Or, my personal favourite, suddenly struck by an idea and desperate to write it down—at once! That never happens. Which isn't to say that inspiration never strikes. It does. You know it does. But for you it's different, the phases of it are all separate, lively, loud—there are the initial notes, usually hummed, then the first fumblings at keys and chords; a line becomes a phrase becomes a melody. So much of the process happens outside your head. But for a writer, having an idea looks an awful lot like developing an idea, which looks an awful lot like choosing to scrap one; they all look exactly like a person, sitting alone, in silence, staring into space.

Besides, those lightning-bolt ideas are never good. Oh, they seem brilliant in the moment, but given time and a little distance they reveal themselves to be too dark, too dumb, too saccharine. Coming back to them feels like waking up next to someone you thought was attractive the night before. No, the best ideas are usually the slow burns. They require stillness, patience, time. You don't go out and grab them; you set up the ideal conditions and wait for them to come to you. If writing were a sport, it would be fishing.

Is fishing a sport?

Jenna's letting me stay with her this week. In the room that should have been a nursery. It might still be a nursery, I suppose, but the last two rounds of IVF treatment "didn't stick" (Jenna's words, not mine), and she's not optimistic about this current attempt, since her egg numbers seem to be decreasing. Her psychic, Sandra, told her to stay positive. And to wear green—the colour of fertility, apparently. So she's sitting here now in a green blouse, green skirt, green cardigan, and green socks. Even her hair band is green. She looks like a salad.

"Sandra accurately predicted my manager's hernia," Jenna offers, by way of explanation.

Sandra also told Jenna that she'd meet the love of her life in Brisbane, Australia, and now she's seriously considering moving there. I can't even begin to fathom the causality loop on that one.

What breaks my heart is that Jenna already met the love of her life. Aidan absolutely adored her. He still does, actually; even though he's dating what's-her-name now, I can tell he's still head over heels for Jen. But he doesn't want children. That's it. The one box—in maybe a thousand—that he didn't tick, and it just so happened to be the most important one as far as Jenna was concerned.

The trouble with these boxes is that most people don't even know they need ticking till it's too late. You meet someone and suddenly your heart has bolted out the gate without a single thought for the Big Stuff. I'm beginning to think every couple should be forced to have a comprehensive conversation on their first date: how they feel about marriage, money, sex, religion, veganism, vaccines . . . where they'd like to live, whether they want kids, who they voted for in the last election, how they want to spend Christmas—whether they even celebrate Christmas! I'm telling you, it would save an awful lot of hassle. And legal fees.

Jenna and Aidan did not have that chat. And then one day

they found themselves in the incredibly unenviable position of being madly in love and on very different pages. I'm just grateful that he loved her enough not to lie, enough even to let her go.

And I know you struggled with her decision to leave him—maybe she should wait and see, you said, maybe he'll come around—but, Finn, you are blessed with a body that doesn't know the constant subatomic sensation of time rushing steadily towards it, like an invisible avalanche hurtling down a nearby mountain. Jenna's thirty-eight. And she's sure that this is what she wants. I just worry after all she's sacrificed, she might not get it.

"A pair of barren bitches." That's what she called us when I told her that I can't write. Ordinarily, I'd agree. But lately I feel more impotent than barren; not a naked winter tree, but one laden with ripe summer fruit that refuses to fall, its long boughs bent and sagging from the weight. Losing words feels a lot like losing a loved one, actually, in that I'm increasingly aware of their absence; instead of dissipating over time, the words seem to multiply, filling me up, sloshing around inside me as I go about my day. I wake up thinking *I should write today* and go to bed thinking *I should have written today* and at every moment in between I'm thinking *I should be writing today*, only I'm not writing because the mere thought of opening my laptop fills me with a paralysing dread akin to that of my worst nightmares; the thin black cursor might as well be a dead bird blinking back at me.

Why is a raven like a writing desk?

They both scare the living shit out of me, that's why.

And along with this constant awareness comes constant anger—some days I can barely see straight I'm so angry. With myself, mostly, for not doing the one thing I'm supposed to do. Being the one thing I'm supposed to be. A writer. Realistically, how many days can I go without writing and still call myself one? If a week passes, that's fine. Maybe a month. Even six months is acceptable. That's a break. A hiatus. But a year? More? We're coming up on two now and I haven't squeezed out a single chapter.

Oh, I've got notes. Tens of thousands of words' worth of notes. Written on buses and park benches and in the backs of cabs, or curled up in bed at some point after midnight and before dawn, sobbing into a pillow, wracked by vicious thoughts about you or her or something much less specific like the general sense I seem to have, every waking hour of the day and night, that nothing is okay, that the world is hurtling steadily towards annihilation with nobody at the wheel, and we're all riding shotgun with our hands clamped over our eyes like children, too terrified even to scream.

I don't blame us. It's pretty fucking grim. And there's no point in writing about it because (a) no one wants to hear it and (b) if they did they wouldn't want to hear it from me—a mid-thirties Irishwoman whose expertise on the topic amounts to a deranged amount of doomscrolling and give or take two hundred articles I've made it halfway through and then bookmarked to "come back to later." As though I ever will. Articles on deforestation, natural disasters, climate refugees, the meat industry, and the 150 million metric tons (and counting) of plastic in our oceans. Articles with headlines like HUMANITY AT RISK OF EXTINCTION and PAST THE POINT OF NO RETURN. And even if, IF, we can somehow fix all that (we can't), we're still left with the rise of the far right, the looming threat of AI, and a fucking patriarchy to dismantle.

I'm just not sure I have it in me.

Maybe the next generation will. Maybe they'll have the drive and the compassion and the common sense to do right by the planet and by one another. Or maybe that's far too heavy a mantle to pass to them. Maybe, given the magnitude of the mess we've created, there shouldn't even *be* a next generation. Maybe we should read the room. Accept we've overstayed our welcome. And see ourselves out, as it were.

You know, there's a very calm and rational part of me that finds comfort in the thought of an extinction-level event. A nice asteroid, maybe. Or an especially powerful solar flare. Nothing too horrific, of course. Something quick. And relatively painless.

The only problem is, that would take out all the animals too. And I've got nothing against the animals. They don't poison or pollute or pass laws denying anybody's reproductive rights. They just get on with things. In fact, I'd love nothing more than for animals to inherit the Earth. I frequently fantasise about the planet rewilding; our cities and airports and factories collapsing over time, the bones of buildings exposed like prehistoric rib cages, stripped of flesh and overrun with thick, curling vines. Skyscrapers becoming giant moss poles for enormous flowering plants, the roots of which dig deep beyond the sewers and subways below. Ancient office blocks and banking districts, now habitats for creatures big and small. Whole new species we will never see, or document, or endanger.

I looked it up, by the way. Fishing is a sport.

On the wall of the room-that-might-still-be-a-nursery are four vaguely square-shaped splodges of yellow paint. Jenna put them there during IVF round one, back when science was still on her side and her main concern was getting the room finished on time. She wrote the name of each shade just below it, in pencil: lemon sherbet, honeysuckle, summer straw, and pale daffodil. To my eye they are all the same colour. Though I'll concede honeysuckle is a touch darker than the rest.

I'm lying here now trying to read my book (it will come as no surprise to you that I'm once again revisiting my fictional friends in Middle Earth), but my eyes keep wandering to the wall, and my thoughts to the future. I find myself questioning why, given the circumstances, Jenna's trying so hard to have a baby at all. God forgive me, I even go so far as to question the morality of it. Is it fair to create a life now, knowing what we know?

There's no right answer, of course—these are unprecedented times—but the mere fact that this is now a reasonable question to ask is devastating in itself.

With that, Jenna pops her head round the door. She's wearing lime-green pyjamas.

"I'm making a cheese toastie," she says. "Do you want one?"

"It's 1 a.m."

"So?"

"Yeah, go on, then."

We sit on the sofa, with a plate of sandwiches and a huge packet of crisps between us, our legs bundled up together in a chunky wool blanket Jenna knit herself. There's a nature documentary on mute in the background. Briefly, I am happy.

Jenna licks buttery crumbs from her fingertips as she rants about why she's up so late—she's usually in bed by 9 p.m. these days. She had to write a firmly worded email to a client who's been causing her no end of trouble, and, as well you know, confrontation is not Jenna's forte (remember that time she ate a practically raw lasagne to avoid telling the waiter?), so it took her hours to get it right.

"I fucking love writing angry emails," I tell her.

"Well, next time I'll get you to do it," she says, shuddering. "That was horrible."

"Maybe I could offer my services to passivists for a small fee. Little side hustle."

"And another excuse not to write the thing you're actually supposed to be writing," teases Jenna. "How's it going, anyway?"

"Never ask a writer how it's going."

"Fair."

A moment passes and I see something shift. She's thinking about that customer again.

"What pisses me off," she announces, "is that I went to all

the bother of setting up my own law firm so I could choose which clients to take on. And I've still ended up dealing with pricks."

"Can't you just drop him?" I ask.

"I need the money. This baby-making malarkey doesn't pay for itself, you know."

I hadn't even thought about how much this must be costing her.

"Do you think you'll try again?" I ask. "If this one—"

"Doesn't stick?"

I nod.

"Maybe. I haven't decided yet."

Our eyes wander to the TV, where a camera pans majestically over a snowy tundra. In the distance, a windswept polar bear and her cub make their way dolefully towards us. Cut to a glacier breaking away.

"Jen."

"Mm?"

"Do you ever wonder if the world is so fucked that having a kid would be cruel?"

"Wow," she says, almost laughing as she turns her attention to me.

"Sorry," I say immediately.

"No, it's a fair question. And yes, of course I worry about that. Especially since it's the main reason Aidan doesn't want children."

"Really? I didn't know that."

"Yeah," says Jenna, fidgeting with the fringe on her wool blanket. "He's convinced we've already passed the point of no return and our governments are keeping it from us to avoid mass hysteria."

"Fuck."

"Yeah."

"And what do you think?" I ask.

"I think it's hard to see past something you're in the middle of. If I'd been alive during World War II or the Cold War or even the fall of the Roman Empire, I probably would have thought that was the end of the world too."

"This one is different, though. Before it was civilisations at stake, now it's the planet."

"Look, I'm not denying things are bad. Or that they might get much, much worse before they get better. But I do believe they'll get better. Mostly because the tipping points will become so catastrophic that we'll eventually have no choice but to act. Which isn't ideal, but that's the only way humans seem capable of growth: amidst destruction. And in the meantime, I'll protest, and donate, and sign petitions, and cut out meat, and buy recycled fucking bamboo toilet paper. But I won't stop living my life."

"You make a good case," I say. "Speaking of that toilet paper, though, it's ripping my arse to shreds, babe."

Jenna just nods and shrugs, like this is the price we must pay.

"I presume you saw that video of the cow running after her calf?" I ask.

"Don't," she says. "I'll start crying again."

We go back to staring at the silent TV. Now a troupe of blue-faced monkeys are swinging deftly from branch to branch along a misty mountain ridge.

"Jen?" I say.

"Mm?"

"What if it's all over in thirty years?"

"What if it's not?" she replies.

There are two kinds of people in the world.

For what it's worth, I hope she's right. Of course I do. Because the part I'm wilfully overlooking in my utopian fantasy—the one with the moss-pole skyscrapers and abandoned office blocks—is the complete erasure of laughter, and friendship, and cheese toasties at 1 a.m. Without people there'd be no creation, exploration, or art for the sake of it. We'd leave behind us a world of empty stages and unplayed pianos. Sunsets unseen and dreams undreamed. Songs unsung, words unwritten and unread. A place bereft of hope and grief and yellow paint splodges on would-be nursery walls.

These things wouldn't even be forgotten; since there'd be no one left to forget, they'd simply cease to be.

But what's the point, is what I'm trying to say.

What's the point in creating anything now, when every creative endeavour, be it a book or a baby, is just a thinly veiled attempt to outlive ourselves? We make things more permanent than our brittle, breakable bodies so that we might somehow live on in the collective consciousness after the speck of time we've been allotted here has elapsed. We leave our DNA in our children and our stories set in ink. We leave ideas and inventions, bridges and buildings, behind us. All evidence—no less inelegant than graffiti on a bathroom wall—that WE WERE HERE.

With nobody around to read what we've scrawled, why bother?

≣

And look, it's possible I'm overreacting. But it's more likely that everyone else is grossly underreacting. I see people going about their lives—buying houses, having kids, working towards that promotion—acting like nothing is wrong, and I feel like I'm the only sane one in a world gone mad. It's like I'm being gaslit by society itself.

Should we all just get drunk? Eat? Fuck? Travel? Do shrooms? I mean, obviously the ideal course of action would be, well, any kind of action, really. But since no one seems to be taking any (no one who could actually make a difference anyway), wouldn't we be better off just enjoying the precious time we have left on this rare, beautiful rock?

I asked my therapist this—back when I could still afford one—and she offered an interesting perspective; she said that there has always been a subset of people who live on the periphery of society. The ones we used to call weirdos but who we now know are just hypervigilant, highly sensitive, anxious types—people whose senses are keenly attuned, usually as a result of trauma, to subtle shifts in the world around them. Like canaries down a mine, they can predict an impending attack or a storm building beyond the horizon, and though they often seem cut off from their community, they are in fact integral to its survival because they are the ones who raise the alarm.

My therapist posited the theory that a lot of climate activists are more than likely modern-day canaries. And not just the people who chain themselves to trees, but the journalists and politicians and teachers and scientists and everyone else who senses the iceberg ahead and is trying desperately to steer the ship in a different direction, or who at least is horrified by the people who don't seem to care if we hit it or not.

"What if we've already hit the iceberg," I asked, "and I'm sitting around writing books?"

"Then I suppose you're like the musicians who played as the ship sank."

Lovely as that sentiment is, though, it all just feels so futile.

She assured me that mine is not the only profession that seems suddenly fatuitous in the face of impending disaster; she had at least a dozen clients—ranging from a postman to a marine biologist—all constantly questioning whether they should bother getting up for work the next day. And she and the other therapists (I imagine a council of elders round a large oak table, cloaks, candles, etc.) had been getting together to discuss how best to serve these patients; apparently, the emerging data on the decline of humanity had thrown quite a large spanner in the works.

"Circumstances being what they are, should I encourage people who want to sack it in to just go ahead?" she asked me. "Or do I advise them as I always have, to exercise and eat well and go to therapy, to do the work to heal themselves and those around them, because there are reasons to do so even if the world is ending?"

"Such as?"

"Well, let's start with you," she said. "You're faced with a choice between spending your days alone in a room, creating a piece of art for a society on the brink of destruction, or using your time here to experience everything the world has to offer. The answer seems obvious, does it not?"

"It does."

"And yet you choose to write, despite complaining, almost every week, that it's"—she literally checked her notes—"'seriously soul destroying on every level.'"

"I do."

"Why?" she asked.

I didn't have a satisfactory answer. I still don't. And as far as I can tell, no one ever has—countless writers throughout history have been asked why they do it, and though their answers differ, there seems to me to be this one common thread: they just can't help themselves. Byron even went so far as to claim that *not* writing made him ill: "If I don't write to empty my mind, I go mad," he said, blaming his deteriorating mental state on his inability to write, and not the gnarly syphilis coursing through his body. Gloria Steinem said that writing was the only thing that made her feel that when she was doing it, she didn't need to be doing something else. Meanwhile, Isabel Allende described it as "an obsession," comparing each story to a seed that grew and grew inside her, like a tumour that inevitably had to be dealt with.

Like. A. Tumour.

Joan Didion alluded many times to being incapable of understanding herself or the world around her without access to a typewriter, as though writing weren't a choice at all but a necessity. "Had my credentials been in order," she once said, "I would never have become a writer. Had I been blessed with even limited access to my own mind there would have been no reason to write."

And everyone knows Ernest Hemingway's famous quote: "There's nothing to writing, all you do is sit down at a typewriter and bleed," which I love not for the melodramatic allusions to the long-suffering artist but because people don't just sit down and bleed, do they? By omitting the means of injury, Hemingway's words work in the same way magic does: forcing us to fill in the gaps, imagining for ourselves a writer causing himself harm, literally cutting himself open to get to the good stuff.

I'm voicing these thoughts on a call with Alexis and her new boss, Phil, when he completely cuts me off.

"Don't quote Hemingway in the book," says Phil.

"Why not?" I ask.

"It's pretentious."

"So, I should leave out the Michelangelo quote too, then?"

"You're being facetious," he says.

I'm really not.

"And so is writing about writing," he adds. "It excludes people."

"Only people who don't understand the concept of writing, to be fair."

"Can't you just make your protagonist something else?" insists Phil.

"Like what? A neuroscientist? Surely then I'll be excluding people who don't understand the concept of neuroscience."

With that a text comes through from Alexis: "Be nice."

"Look, I appreciate the suggestions, Phil. I'll see what I can do." But Phil obviously doesn't know this is writer-speak for "go fuck yourself," because he thanks me for seeing sense. Then he hangs up, leaving me and Alexis on the line.

"I really like Phil," I say. "Please can we schedule more calls with him?"

She begins to laugh, but it devolves into a sigh.

"Kate, you've no idea. He's insisting we all push our authors into 'broader territory.' And stop giving them extensions."

"Good luck with that," I say.

"Seriously, though, he wants something more concrete. And I hate to have to tell you this, but he's right; if you don't deliver something soon, the publisher could rescind the advance."

"They can't do that."

"They can," she says. "It's in your contract."

"Yeah, but nobody reads those."

"Listen," she says. "I can keep them all at bay, but I'm gonna need more than batshit notes. No offence."

"None taken."

In her defence, the notes I've sent over so far are absolutely bonkers. There's nothing even remotely resembling a book in there.

"So, what can I give him? Is it definitely a horror?" she asks.

"I don't know."

"Any idea when you will know?"

"Not really."

"It's just, I thought you said it was going to be a love story," she says.

"It is."

"But horror and romance are very different things, Kate."

"Are they?"

I'm saying goodbye to an understandably exasperated Alexis when Jenna enters the kitchen in a flurry. We stayed up talking well into the wee hours and now it would seem she's late for work.

"Who was that?" she asks, only half paying attention. She's looking for her keys.

"Alexis," I tell her. "Apparently they're expecting me to actually write this book."

"The one they're paying you to write?"

"Yeah."

"How rude," she says, stopping to scrunch up her face in mock disgust. "Anyway. I'll be home late tonight. I've got an appointment at the clinic."

I offer to go with her, but she refuses, saying she needs to get used to doing things alone. As if my heart weren't breaking enough already.

Despite all I've said about the fate of the planet, I spend the whole day hoping for good news on Jenna's behalf. But as the evening wears on with no sign of her, I start to suspect it hasn't gone well.

I'm in bed reading again when she gets home. I hear her kick off her shoes in the hall before her face appears in my doorway, pink and puffy from either the cold or crying or both. She slumps towards me like a child after having a bad dream, and crawls in beside me. I keep reading while she flicks through the pile of books on my bed, finally settling on *The Writing Life* by Annie Dillard—I brought it with me thinking I might be able to handle something other than my comfort book one night. How wrong I was.

Jenna's been reading for a while when she gets to a quote I've highlighted, probably years ago while I was writing my first novel.

"'Write as if you were dying,'" she reads aloud. "'At the same time, assume you write for an audience consisting solely of terminal patients. This is, after all, the case.'"

We both sigh, taking it in. Then come the tears.

Jenna folds over and begins to cry into a pillow. I wrap myself around her like a shield against the world, stroking her hair until she's ready to speak.

"They think I should try again," she mewls.

"That's good, isn't it?"

"I thought it would be. I thought that's what I wanted to hear. But after I left the clinic, I realised what I really wanted was for someone to tell me to stop. To put a hand on my shoulder and tell me it's over. No more. No more appointments. No more injections. No more sobriety. No more disappointment. No more fucking hope. And I'm not supposed to feel this way. I'm supposed to want it so bad that I'd break if they told me to stop trying, but God help me there'd be a comfort in it. I think I'd be relieved."

I get it. Jenna's not afraid of letting go or moving on. She's afraid of being stuck here forever. She's afraid the wind will change and she'll freeze this way. She has just put to words a fear I've never voiced: that maybe it would be easier if someone told me to stop, that there were, in fact, no more good sentences for me to find.

We lie spooning for a while, both staring at the wall ahead, and the four yellow patches that a past version of Jenna painted there.

"They're all the fucking same," she says eventually.

"Honeysuckle is a bit darker," I offer.

She regards them a moment longer, then says, "Imagine the hardest thing I had to do was choose between four basically identical shades of paint."

"That would be nice," I agree, as another wave of grief wracks her body and then subsides.

"I know you're not okay, by the way," she sniffles, and I squeeze her tighter. "You haven't mentioned him once this week."

"Mentioned who?" I ask, and she laughs.

"Is it possible, do you think, that you've become preoccupied by the end of the world because it's easier to think about mass extinction than your own problems?"

"Doesn't sound like something I'd do," I joke, and I feel her relax in my arms, like a block of ice thawing.

"What will you do now?" I ask.

"I'll try again," she says. "I don't know how to not."

Once again, I understand perfectly. Immortality was never on the table; this is all returning to dust eventually. But if there's even a chance that I'll have one more good day. A day when the words do come. When they spill from me like so many kept secrets bursting to be known. If there's any hope at all of a day like that. I'll keep going.

I don't know how to not.

Michelangelo once said, "Every block of stone has a statue inside it, and it is the task of the sculptor to discover it. I saw the angel in the marble and carved until I set him free."

And maybe he was right. Maybe there is another Angel in me somewhere. Maybe there are countless angels inside me, waiting to be set free. But it's all well and good when you have a block of marble at your disposal. I have only myself to hack away at.

THE MOURNING MOON

I just got home and the place smells like fish.

You don't even like fish.

And there are dishes draining by the sink. Two of every-thing: two knives, two forks, two plates, two whisky glasses. I call Fran to tell him.

"They're the nice Waterford crystal ones I got him for his birthday," I say.

"So?"

"So, Finn had someone round. And he went to the bother of unpacking the good glasses."

"It was probably just Aidan," says Fran.

"Aidan doesn't drink."

"He didn't have a date round, if that's what you're implying."

"He might have," I insist.

"Okay, he might have. In which case you can be even more sure that you're doing the right thing by leaving the prick."

"Do you think she slept in my bed?"

"Kate!" shouts Fran. "Cop on to yourself."

"Fine!" I shout back, then, realising how pathetic I sound, I start to cry. "I feel like the world's saddest detective."

"Oh, honey, no," says Fran. "Batman is way sadder than you."

I laugh through my tears. "Do you think?"

"Absolutely. Sure didn't *both* his parents die?"

Would you do it? Would you have another woman over, knowing I'd be back the next day? I suppose we didn't set any rules around dating. I just assumed you wouldn't be ready that fast because I'm not. But then, men are different. And this *is* how you typically deal with breakups. If anything, it was probably naive of me to think you *wouldn't* see anyone for a whole three months. But to bring someone here. To our house. That would be a new low.

This is the most I've wanted to call you since you left. I need to ask. I need to know.

But what if it *was* one of the lads? I don't think I could handle the embarrassment.

No, I tell myself, we're not bloody talking! At which point I am reminded once again of the notes on the wall. I rush to check on them, and sure enough, under my last note telling you I needed the reminder is a new one that reads, simply, *So did I.*

WHAT DOES THAT MEAN?

I scream the question at an empty room.

Do you miss me? Are you desperate to talk to me? Do you

keep instinctively picking up your phone to call me? Have you typed and deleted a hundred messages to me at all hours of the day and night? What did they say? That you love me? That you can't live without me? Or that you're happy it's over? That we did the right thing? Can you tell that I'm suffering? Is this note your way of being polite? Are you just offering me a morsel of hope while you fuck around with someone new?

Wait.

Surely you didn't have a date here with these notes on the wall. And I'd like to think you'd at least *try* to hide the evidence if you had. But then, maybe you didn't see it as evidence. It's entirely possible you assumed we would see other people, in the same way I assumed we wouldn't. And that bringing a date here would be okay. I mean, it's not. And it must have been weird for her given the house is full of my stuff. But once again, you are a man. And men do all sorts of weird, inexplicable shit during breakups.

I skulk through the house, trying to distract myself from this maddening line of thought, but everywhere I look bare walls glare back at me. It has begun to feel like a waiting room in here. I consider lining all the chairs against one wall. Fanning out magazines on the coffee table. Playing instrumental versions of Burt Bacharach songs through shitty speakers.

I eventually find a few more clues that betray your presence here: a stack of CDs by the sofa—Death Cab, the xx, Beck—no more melancholic than usual; a suit jacket slung over the back of a chair—nothing in the pockets; and in your studio, the bright red keyboard is noticeably absent, as is the metal stand it usually rests on. There are, however, several Wispa wrappers by the leg of the piano stool and two quarter cups of coffee on the window ledge opposite.

You've been writing.

Which makes me angry.

I wonder if there's anything I could find right now that wouldn't make me angry. Then I open the fridge and see the bowl of pasta salad you left with another sticky note attached: *Made too much. Hope you like it.*

The pasta salad doesn't make me angry.

Somehow, this is worse.

I grab a fork and sit at the table, but as soon as I begin picking at my food, I notice grief sidle into the seat opposite. I move to the sofa but it joins me there, watching me and not the screen, its doleful eyes boring into me until I get back up again. I take a bath. Grief sits cross-legged on the floor. I take a walk. It follows me, always one pace behind. And when I finally go to bed, I find it there in place of you again.

In the morning there's nothing but a blade of sunlight on your side of the bed. Relieved, I slink down to the kitchen, only to find grief waiting there, drumming its nails against the countertops. Time ticks along like it's got all day.

I need to get out.

I take the DART to Howth, and the shuddering of the train carriage sends me to sleep. When we get there, a young woman with two kids in tow gently shakes me by the shoulder.

"Last stop, love," she says, and for just a moment it's my own mother's hand on my shoulder. Her voice in my ear. It's a dark December morning right before the Christmas break and I must drag myself from the warm cocoon of bed and go to school. She's leaning over me to open the curtains, even though it's pitch-black outside; we're up before the sun today. She smiles down, and I sit up with a start, scaring the poor woman who woke me.

"Thanks," I say, frowning out the window at Howth Harbour. It takes me a while to remember where and when I am.

≣

I get myself an ice cream despite its being close to freezing outside—this is the only country in the world, after all, where ice creams are acceptable year-round—and I walk to the end of the pier. A trio of seals are jostling in the water, their shiny grey heads like massive sea-smoothed stones bobbing in and out of its slick green surface. We came here on one of our first dates—which weren't really dates since we'd already been friends and lovers by that point. Still, we tried to treat them as such, to get to know each other anew. You brought me bowling and ice-skating and out for endless walks around Phoenix Park. You took me to gigs and museums and even, once, to a pottery class, where my botched attempt at an ashtray reminded me so much of my mother that I cried afterwards. We walked the head of Howth that first biting January, when "us" was still a bright, giddy thing, wide-eyed and dumb. The weather was Baltic, but we got ice creams then too, only yours was plain and mine was covered in chocolate and sprinkles and strawberry syrup.

"It's like dating a toddler," you said, taking it from the vendor and handing it to me.

"Says you!" I clapped back. You had brought tea in a *Jurassic Park* flask your mother gave you that Christmas—a fact I refused to let you live down but secretly found adorable. We sat right here, at the end of the pier, while I tried to squeeze inside your coat with you. Then we got fish and chips in the Bloody Stream and found ourselves in a lock-in late that night; we'd stayed talking for so long that we didn't even notice the doors being shut, or the band switching from classic covers to old rebel songs. Soon enough you were up at the piano, drunk as a skunk and still perfectly able to play, and I was standing on a table with a woman I'd just met, bawling through each and every line of "Grace."

Yet, all I want in this dark place is to have you here with me.

An elderly man has been idling on a bench nearby.

"Looks like rain," he says, gazing out at an angry, smoke-coloured cloud. Beneath it, I can see the opaque shadow of rainfall in the distance.

"So it does," I say.

"I used to come here with my wife," says the man, "Lord rest her soul." He blesses himself, and though it means nothing to me anymore, I bless myself too.

"You've lost someone yourself," he says.

"My mother," I say, surprised that my mind went to her, when you're the one I came here to mourn. The man blesses himself again.

"Fifty years we were together."

"Fifty years," I echo.

A lone seagull broods nearby.

"It'll be five years this Wednesday since I lost her," he says. Then: "You?"

"Twenty-six."

"It never gets any easier," he says. It's not a warning or even a complaint, just a statement of fact.

"No, it doesn't."

Peeking out from behind the rain cloud is a milky moon, almost full, but not quite. There's a white cúr—a thick foam—on the tide. And the sky near the horizon is crayon blue. The whole scene could so easily be a child's drawing.

"Right so," says the man, as he leans his hands into his thighs and pushes himself up to stand with what seems like considerable effort.

"I'll light a candle for you," I say as he walks away. Something my mother would have said. She was always lighting candles for people. "For good intentions," she'd say as she nipped into a parking space outside the church. Inside, I'd stand beside her in the cool brown gloom and she'd hand me an old punt to put in the offering box. Then she'd light three candles: one for me, one for Dad, and one for herself.

"Not that I need one," she'd say, pulling me in close. "I've got my noisy little miracle right here."

I'm still sitting with my eyes closed, watching those three flames dance on the dark of my eyelids, when the first drops of rain hit me. I hurry to the train station, but it's much too late; I'm soaked through by the time I get there and I have to sit in a pool of water the whole way home.

It's evenings like this I want to turn the key and hear the

sounds of loved ones from behind the door. Smell stew simmering on the hob. Have someone slip my wet coat off and give me a welcome-home hug. I want to sit in front of a roaring fire with a mug of tea and hear footsteps through the ceiling while I sip on it alone. I want the convenience of missing someone from one room away.

Instead, I step into this husk of a house, and my breath turns shallow and shaky as I move from room to room, turning on the lights, the radio, the TV, anything to drown out the silence.

I find ways not to be here—a Hitchcock double bill at the Stella, a trip out to the waterfall at Glendalough, and a long walk around Phoenix Park, where I spot a herd of wild deer and wonder if this might be the same herd we saw years ago. One of them, a brown doe dappled with spots like dollops of fresh cream, wanders over, regarding me warily. She stands close by, slightly separate from the rest of her kin, and I'm grateful for the company. When she glances at me and then bolts out of the blue, I wonder if she saw the stranger sitting next to me, whether grief's presence scared her off. I'd run from it too, if I could.

Don't laugh, but Jenna invited me to a full moon ritual tonight. It's a night swim from the Bull Wall, organised by none other than Sandra the Psychic. I told Jenna it's not really my thing, but she pulled the "I'm sad because I can't have a baby" card. I tried counteracting with the "I'm sad because my mother died and I'm going through a breakup" card, but it backfired.

"Actually, that's perfect," she insisted, "because this full moon is the mourning moon, and the whole ritual is about remembering and releasing."

Christ.

"I can hear you rolling your eyes," she said. She was right, I was.

"Look, I know you don't believe in all this woo-woo shit, but I do. And at the very least it's a bit of exercise."

She had a point. A swim before bed might tire me out and help me get some sleep.

"What does one bring to a full moon ritual?" I sighed.

"Swimming gear, warm clothes, a big towel, and an open heart," she said.

I rolled my eyes again, promising to bring three of those things. And now, several hours later, I'm in the back of a cab, bouncing down the wooden bridge towards a darkened Dollymount Strand. I can already hear shrieks of laughter from the women's bathing shelter as I step out of the car, its headlights sweeping cinematically across the pale yellow structure as the driver turns around and heads back the way we came.

Inside, the shelter is lit by a dozen votive candles in glass jars of varying sizes. The flames flicker in the brisk breeze, casting a party of dancing shadows against the concrete walls, where coats and bags and towels are hung. Over twenty women, most of whom are properly kitted out in wetsuits, bathing caps, and swimming socks, are gabbing noisily with one another as they ready themselves. I feel suddenly self-conscious about the slinky black swimsuit underneath my clothes—the one I bought for our weekend in Malta, a last-ditch effort to add some fun to our floundering relationship—but my summer clothes have vanished in the move, and this was all I could find. I just hope no one notices.

The full moon, our guest of honour, has yet to make an appearance. Most likely hidden behind a wall of coastal cloud.

"Late to her own party," jokes one woman.

"Probably wants to make a grand entrance," replies another, and as laughter ripples through the group, Jenna spots me and squeals.

"You came!" she says, wrapping her arms around mine and squeezing me tight. "This is my friend Kate, everyone."

"Hi, Kate," they echo in unison, before carrying on their conversations. One of them, a burly grey-haired woman, hands me a purple glow stick. I must look utterly bewildered, because she chuckles and fastens it around my wrist for me.

"First time?" she asks, and I nod.

"Welcome to our circle!" she booms, clapping me hard on the back before going about her business.

"That's Mary," says Jenna in my ear. "She swam the English Channel twice last year to raise money for her daughter's chemo."

"That's incredible," I say, genuinely amazed. "How's she doing now?" But Jenna shakes her head.

"She passed last April."

You wouldn't think it to look at Mary—with her broad shoulders pulled back, chest out, chin up, and a warm, bright smile billowing across her face—you'd never know grief had slipped so recently under her door. The woman she's talking to is almost comically different in stature; half Mary's height, and borderline skeletal—wizened skin pulled taut across protruding shoulder blades. Her whole body seems to want to curl in on itself like a dry leaf. Mary's laughing so hard at whatever this woman is saying that she has to wipe a tear from the corner of one eye. Jenna catches me staring.

"Jess," she says fondly. I find out later that Jess has multiple sclerosis and an absolutely filthy sense of humour.

I'm taken aback by the age range of the women here— Jenna introduces me to a spry lady named Nancy, who tells me she just turned seventy-eight last week.

"Well, you don't look a day over sixty, Nancy," I say, and I'm not lying either; the woman's skin is immaculate, her long silver hair caught up in a high ponytail and her blue eyes full of mischief.

"This one can stay," she says, beaming as she pinches me by the waist.

On the other end of the spectrum is aspiring chef Jude—a sullen no-nonsense old soul in a twenty-year-old's body, which is covered head to toe in intricate tattoos—and a teenager named Holly, who glances up from underneath a thick ginger fringe as she speaks and tries to cover the acne on her chin by constantly touching her fingers to her lips. There's something instantly disarming about Holly and the way she asks questions like the answers mean the world. She's here with her mother, Simone, a nervous slip of a thing who fusses over her daughter constantly.

Across the harbour I can just about make out the two Pool-beg chimneys, black against the city's twinkling white and yellow lights. Evening traffic makes its way up and down the causeway above. And here I am, for reasons beyond my comprehension, about to get in the icy sea.

I'm still finding my bearings when the first swimmers make their way down the slippery stone steps to the water below, their gasps and yelps nigh on beatific as their flesh meets the water. I mentally prepare myself as I take off my jeans and pull my chunky navy jumper (well, your chunky navy jumper) over my head.

"Skinny jeans," says Amber, Nancy's glamorous, much younger girlfriend, "that's brave."

I look at Jenna, not quite understanding, but Holly chimes in from under one hand.

"Good luck getting back into those when you're all wet," she says.

"I really didn't think this through," I admit, just as Jess notices my plunge-line swimsuit with its crisscross straps and silk bodice.

"Would ya get a load of this one in her sexy lingerie?" she jeers, tilting her head towards me.

"It's all I could find!" I protest, covering my face in mortification.

"Jesus, Kate." Jenna laughs when she sees it. "Are you here to swim or seduce us?"

"Admit it, love," says Amber, deadpan, "you were hoping to nab yourself a girlfriend at the full moon ritual."

I'm giggling so hard behind my hands that I can't speak. Jenna's rubbing my silky stomach in hysterics.

"It's alright, there's no shame in it," adds Amber, and we all cackle.

"Sure that's how we met!" exclaims Nancy, provoking more laughter.

"I think we'd all better go cool off," says Jess as she fans herself, feigning hot flushes. Then she links Mary by the arm as they start to carefully navigate the steps. Jenna and I share a look before we head off: hers says, *I can't bring you anywhere*, and mine says, *I know*. Our giggles dissipate as we leave the pool of light cast by the candles to follow the others down into the dark. I'm briefly blinded by a stark blue torch in someone's hand. Then it's gone, and I'm plunged into a kind of sightlessness I've never known.

It's hard to grasp these next few minutes, which slip by like tiny villages from the window of a speeding train. First, the darkness; not the grainy humming dark of old film, or the backs of closed eyelids—flecked by specks of dancing blue and green—but a pure, sharp dark, thick and absolute. Lightless, like the singularity that looms eternal in some soft crevice of my mind, this void stretches out before me, thick as tar, swallowing the bodies of the women I've just met. Down here, where the sea meets the steps, there is no shape or form, no distance, no edge to things; the inky air and water might as well be one. When my feet find the gelid surface—skin screaming from the shock of it—I bypass my senses and sink further, to my knees, to my waist, to my chest (this step is the hardest), then all the way under, diving and coming back up, afraid to take a breath in case I'm still somehow beneath the salty sea. When I swim, my body doesn't seem to travel—I might as well be tethered to the shore—and submerging feels no different from surfacing. It's like waking in a dream to find that you're still dreaming.

I could be anywhere, in this place. And nowhere at all. I could be unborn, floating still inside my mother's womb. Or I could be dead and drifting through the afterlife. The nothingness of this moment is at once dreadful and sublime.

Then I turn, unsure which direction I'm facing, and am met with a surreal sight: a shoal of phosphorescent sea creatures, radiant and strange, undulating in the high tide like a cluster of amethyst crystals lit from within. They remind me of a storybook my mother used to read to me—a square-shaped hardback with tattered corners and this exact image on the cover, an illustration of violet ghost lights in the fuzzy dark.

"Comfy?" asks my mother, as I settle back into my pillows. Then she reads to me of the will-o'-the-wisp, a race of wretched spirits shut out of heaven and hell, forced to wander forever in limbo. They would roam the land, floating above the bogs and marshes of old, leading wayward travellers astray, off the beaten track and into treacherous terrain. One of the purple creatures glides quickly back and forth, dragging streams of light behind it like smoke. It calls out to me.

"Kate," it says. "Come back, Kate."

It's Jenna, waving her arm at me, the glow stick on her

wrist becoming clearer as my salt-stung eyes begin to finally adjust. All around her are the oscillating outlines of women wading, their heads and shoulders alien-like in tight swim caps. I make my way towards them, both grateful and sad to be oriented now.

We float, soundless in the soft belly of Dublin Bay, drinking in the night around us, until the clouds pull apart like great wads of celestial cotton to reveal the mourning moon, hung against a sable sky, a lantern on the world.

"Grand entrance indeed," comes a solemn voice from nearby.

The giddiness has worn off the group, and a quiet reverence moves in now like a low fog as we gaze up awestruck at the fat, round moon. Her creamy white surface looks soft to the touch, her craggy shadows like the gentle dimples of a woman's thigh.

There's an Irish word—beacht—that can mean many different things: a circle, a ring, a certainty, but also perfectly, entirely, forever. This moon is what that word was made for.

Soon, the sweet, sorrowful sound of an Irish lament drifts down, siren-like, from the bathing shelter above, and we are drawn up towards it—travellers to phantom lights. The air feels colder now than the sea did before, so I climb the stone steps quickly and wrap myself in a big beach towel, holding it close around me as I attempt to wriggle free from my stupid swimsuit. When I look around, I realise that once again I'm the odd one out; there's no shame in nudity here, no shimmying awkwardly inside towels, gripping on for dear life—all around me, breasts and bums and bushes are on show as their proud owners gracefully disrobe. I drop my towel and let my wet togs fall to the ground, noting as I do the sense of shedding, of letting go.

Some of the women have brought back handfuls of seaweed and are rubbing it into their legs, their arms, their torsos. This calls to mind a memory of Aunt Kathy and my mother, standing at the water's edge on some halcyon morning, smearing seaweed on themselves, but it's gone as quickly as it came. Jenna hands me a fistful of the stuff and I copy the others, massaging it into me in what becomes a sort of moving meditation; I'm acutely aware of the odd, oily texture of the seaweed, the feel of my hands on my body and my bare skin exposed to the night, the quick flicker of the candles, and the mournful drone of an ancient dirge. I don't understand all the words, but I don't need to; something, or someone, is gone. Lost forever, by the sounds of it.

Sandra's haunting voice trills dancingly through streams of notes, like water tripping lightly over stones. And as I dry myself and slowly dress, I could cry for all the times I've rushed from the shower into the rest of my day, slapping on some lotion, never stopping to notice how sensual and self-caring an act this can be.

Once dressed, we settle ourselves, silently passing round hot-water bottles and flasks of steaming tea. Mary pours some whisky into her cup, then sends it clockwise around the circle. I take a drop and give it to Jenna, who briefly considers before passing it straight on.

I am swaddled now in blankets, palms cupping a mug of

tea, eyelids heavy as the last few bars of Sandra's soporific ballad wash over us like frothy waves breaking on the shore.

"Faoi sholas na gealaí," says Sandra after a long pause, "by the light of the moon."

Sandra is not at all what I expected, sitting with a slight slouch in blue tracksuit bottoms and an oversized hoodie, the cuffs of which hang loose around her hands. She hugs one knee into her chest and occasionally fidgets with her hair, which falls across her shoulders in a heap of tight chestnut curls. Her doughy face is open and soft, and the edges of her eyes and lips are creased in a permanent smile. She looks like she belongs here. She looks like she could belong anywhere.

"The mourning moon is upon us," she says in a sweet, sing-song way. "Thank you all for being here tonight to honour the occasion. This is the last full moon before the winter solstice, and as the days grow shorter and the sun grows weaker, it can sometimes seem as though that light will never return. This mourning moon is a reminder of the cycles of life, of waxing and waning, death and rebirth, the comings and goings of things. It's a reminder that while light sometimes leaves us, it always returns.

"Mourning is not simply about letting go," she goes on, "waving a bit of sage about, chanting a few affirmations and insisting that you're 'so over it.'"

This gets a knowing laugh from the group.

"No, unfortunately, mourning is a little harder than that. It's about fully feeling our grief, accepting that something is gone, and along with it, the life we thought we might have."

Around the circle, tears drip down the faces of several

women. Mary weeps openly while Jess rubs her back with the palm of one hand. Next to me, Jenna's head bows forward, her chin dropping to her chest, and I place an arm across her shoulders.

"In times like these we are like seeds in winter, alone in the cold, dark ground, not dead but dormant. Gathering strength for a new life in spring. Before we can begin anew, though, we must make room for our new life by lovingly releasing the one we'd hoped for. I'll begin."

Sandra describes a life in which her father hadn't abandoned her, and her mother had been stable enough to support herself and her family through the loss. A life in which, earlier this year, her parents had both been present for her wedding and helped her through a rough pregnancy and the birth of her first child.

"I release that hope now," she says. "I release the life I thought I'd have, to make way for a better one."

Not everyone speaks, but those who do describe the lives they'd imagined, none of them idyllic or unreasonable—simple things, like a country free from war, a family free from addiction, a mind free from anguish, or a body free from pain. When it's Jenna's turn, she takes my hand in hers as she talks.

"I hoped for boring things," she says, almost apologetically. "Night feeds and school runs and shopping trips. Little feet growing out of the shoes I bought just last year. Shitty drawings on my fridge of animals I can barely make out. Loose teeth, scraped knees, monsters under the bed. And maybe someone to discuss it all with, at the end of a difficult day."

Around the circle a dozen brows knit together in empathy.

"Boring things," she repeats, batting away tears with the backs of her fists. Jenna looks to Sandra, nodding that she's done, and Sandra smiles back at her. There's a pause.

"Oh," says Jenna. "I release that hope now, I release the life I thought I'd have, to make way for a better one."

She rushes through it, her voice cracking. And I can't help but be moved. By Jenna. By all of them. It's one thing to complain about the life you have and another thing altogether to describe the one you lost. There's more strength in vulnerability than there is in battling through.

When it's my turn, I don't speak. And it's not because I don't believe in all this woo-woo shit. If anything, I'm actually starting to understand it; these people aren't idiots, they don't think that the moon will literally heal them, but they do believe that there's power in ritual. Power in connection. Power in stories shared. In the invitation to reflect, to feel, to release. The moon is just an excuse to convene—like some heavenly hearth, we huddle around it as our ancestors did, gathering close on long, dark nights. And, yes, maybe some of these women also believe that they can charge their crystals by its glow. But there's as much harm in that as there is in an old man blessing himself when he mentions his dead wife.

I don't speak because, as seems to be the case in general lately, the words just will not come. I don't speak because I've no idea what to say; I've never really allowed myself to imagine a different life from this one—one that's not defined by loss. A life where my mother hadn't died, my father hadn't shut down, and I hadn't spent my whole adulthood hopping from one emotionally closed-off partner to another. A life where

I'm not plagued nightly by the brutal conjurings of my own mind. I'm overcome by the sheer scale of how much I have to let go of. And I'm not sure I'm ready yet.

Sensing this, Sandra deftly moves us along to the next portion of the evening, which she plainly dubs "the fun part." A crate of wine is produced from under a blanket, and two more naggins of whisky appear out of nowhere. Amber brought biodegradable cups. Jude brought her violin. And within minutes we're drinking and dancing and singing like we all go way back. This is what women do—we form everyday covens. We share, we mourn, we laugh. And my God, the laughter; we howl our way into the wee hours like a racket of drunken banshees. Eileen recounts the tale of last month's full moon, when Sheila forgot her pants. Apparently, Sheila had worn a skirt and had to ride her bike home. Amber doesn't get it at first. But she guffaws when it finally clicks.

"Say no more, Eileen," she says, one hand held up in front of her. "Say no more."

They lovingly joke about their husbands, describing them more like pets than partners. I picture them, dutifully waiting for their wives to return. And I think of my dad. I really should call him.

"They have their uses," says Jude, and we all murmur agreement.

"The other day mine cleaned the gutters and it gave me a fanny gallop." This is Jess. Mary is beside her in convulsions.

"Jesus, we really need to stop swooning for the bare minimum," says Sheila.

Becky, a twentysomething film student, is going through a breakup too. Although the more I hear about this relationship, the less I'm sure she was even in one. It sounds like some guy just strung her along for a bit and then stopped stringing her along.

A small group have gathered round to comfort Becky.

"I miss his body," she cries. "I miss his legs. They're so skinny. I just love them."

Sheila throws me a sideways glance and it's all I can do not to crack up.

"Hold on!" says Becky, taking out her phone. "I have a picture of him reaching for something under his bed. Don't worry, he's not naked."

At this point my shoulders are shaking trying to contain the laughter.

"Look at his legs!" she wails, all one note. Eileen gives her a hug.

Becky then takes us through a series of photos of her ex (is he even her ex?) standing in front of statues, replicating their poses.

"Look at all these pictures of him looking like statues!" she demands. "He's so good at matching them."

He is, to be fair. His Molly Malone is uncanny.

≡

There's something ancient and sturdy and safe about this circle. Something instantly familiar, like words engraved on my very bones. And for a brief moment, with my head full of wine, my ribs sore from laughing, and the flat white flower of moon reflected in the bay, I could almost believe the world's not on fire.

When we finally decide to go, there are only six of us left. Sandra packs all the blankets and cups and empty bottles into her car, along with the few remaining women, and Jenna and I walk back across the wooden bridge to the causeway. Right before we leave, though, while Jenna's busy hugging the others goodbye—and loudly declaring her undying love for them all—Sandra takes my hands in hers and smiles at me with her whole face. Nearby, a dozen seagulls are searching for scraps where we were sitting. They're either up much too early or much too late.

"Thank you for coming, Kate," says Sandra.

"Thanks for having me," I say. "I needed this."

She looks down at my hands then, and her features seem to sag, like she's noticed something concerning. I follow Sandra's gaze but see nothing of note. Then she runs one thumb along my palm, and I shiver.

"Can I offer you a message?" she asks. I have no idea what that means, but I feel myself nod.

"Listen to the birds," she says, and when I glance at the gulls clacking noisily nearby, she smiles again and adds, "Not those ones."

Sandra embraces me, holding me close like I'm family.

"They're trying to tell you something," she says in my ear before kissing me tenderly on one cheek, then she jogs back towards her car and the three remaining women still singing inside it.

I don't mind the walk back. I'm too smashed and too cold to feel my feet anyway. But I can't quite figure out what the hell just happened.

"Women are better," Jenna declares as we approach the causeway.

"We are."

"Why is that?" she asks.

"Because we've had to be."

"Maybe we were better anyway," she suggests, "and that's why they kept us down."

"Like the Irish," I say.

"Like the Irish," she agrees.

I tell Jenna to get in the first taxi we flag down, but, being the sober one, she refuses, forcibly bundling me into the back seat and screeching at me through the window to text her when I'm home.

I give her a thumbs-up as I pull away, and then spend the whole journey trying not to think about what Sandra said.

A few minutes from our house I text Jenna: "Almost home. That was so fun! Let's do it again soon." Only it's not Jenna who replies. It's you. With a solitary question mark.

"Fuck." I only realise I've said it out loud when the driver catches my eye in the rearview mirror.

"You alright there?"

"I texted my ex by mistake," I grumble.

"Fuck," he replies.

"Yep."

I reply to you like a teenager sneaking in the door late at night, gathering all my wits about me and desperately trying to seem sober.

"Sincere apologies," I say. "That was not meant for you."

"I assumed," you say.

I think that might be the end of it, but then you reply again.

"I hate to ask, but who was it for? Freaking out a bit here."

Freaking out? Why are you freaking out? I read back my first message and now I see it from your perspective; a drunken 3 a.m. text from me to some unknown third party saying that I'd had fun tonight and I want to do it again. Soon.

Oh my God.

You think I was on a date!

You're worried that *I* was on a date!

I won't lie, Finn. This feels good. This feels really good. Right now, I hold all the cards. And I like it. I like holding the cards. I like knowing that you're over there "freaking out," imagining me on an amazing late-night date with someone I'm excited to see again.

Then you reply, "Sorry. None of my business. Get home safe please," and suddenly I don't want the cards anymore.

"It was for Jenna," I admit. "She took me to a full moon ritual."

"You've changed," comes the reply.

"Haha," I say, though I don't laugh at all. I'm staring blankly at the letters wobbling about on my screen.

"Glad you two had a good night." Then: "Would it be okay if you let me know when you're home please?"

The taxi is just pulling up to our house, and though the thought of you still wanting to know I'm safe makes my throat throb, I reply and say, simply, "I'm home."

It's only when I stagger through the door, wincing as it bangs shut behind me, that I realise how absolutely plastered I am. Everything is suddenly too loud, too bright, and much too close. I leave the lights off as I bend to untie my boots, crashing against the wall and coming to rest there with one cheek mashed against the wallpaper as I wrench my shoes off and toss them down the hall. Stumbling forward, I unzip my jeans and peel them down my clammy legs, tripping as I go and then stopping at the foot of the stairs to tug my feet free. My toes are like tiny ice cubes. I can barely feel them. I need to be in a hot bath.

Making my way upstairs, I wriggle out of my coat and yank my jumper (your jumper) over my head, letting everything fall behind me as I go, a trail of cold, damp clothes like bread crumbs on my path to the bathroom. Once there, I turn the tap and wait in darkness for the tub to fill. The artificial warmth of the alcohol has completely worn off now, and I collapse onto the toilet with my knees pressed tight together and my arms folded around my shivering body, hands frantically rubbing at my own arms and shoulders like I am a small child who's just come in from the rain. I can hear my teeth chattering all the while, banging noisily together like a cartoon.

The water is only shin-deep when I get in, but I'm too cold to wait any longer. I sink into the tub, skin screaming just like it did when I entered the sea, and I watch as my gooseflesh dissolves and the water continues to rise around me. Soon enough, I can feel heat start to soak right through me.

Bliss.

I sink down, closing my eyes and opening them when the world starts to spin. Through the skylight above me, I can just about see a wisp of moon float glacially into frame, gleaming at the left edge of the window like silverware in an open drawer.

"You found me," I say to her, then I sigh and sink again.

I think about you. Those texts. How close I was to inviting you over. How much I still want to. I think about you being here with me. Then I pick up my phone and start typing.

"I miss you," I say. Then I wait. I'm shaking, but not from the cold this time.

"I miss you too," comes the reply, and the hit is so intense it might as well be your mouth on mine.

"Come over," I say.

"Are you sure?"

"YES."

"Give me half an hour."

This is dumb, I think. This is exceedingly dumb. And I don't care.

I'm woken by the smell of coffee drifting up from the kitchen, along with the sound of you clattering about. I have to shield my eyes from the midday sun blasting through the window— in our haste to rip each other's clothes off we forgot to close

the curtains. I smile. I shouldn't smile. But I smile. Your side
of the bed is a welcome mess.

Congratulations, I think, *I hope you're happy with yourself.*

I am! I reply to my own conscience. *Now, piss off.*

The aroma intensifies as I head downstairs, wrapping a
robe around me and giggling at the sight of my clothes drunkenly discarded en route. I'm still smiling as I enter the kitchen,
where you're stood by the stove, completely naked, stirring
milk into your coffee and sugar into mine.

"There she is," I hear you say, and I wrap my arms around
your waist, burying my sheepish grin in the warmth of your
back. "I figured you'd need a big breakfast after that."

Peeking around your body towards the table, I see that it's
set for two, with tea and toast and scrambled eggs.

Yes. I am very happy with myself.

I go to the fridge to get some juice, and when I look up, I
notice my mam's old silver Moka pot sputtering on the stove,
spewing hot goo on the counter.

"Finn," I say. "The coffee!"

Thick brown liquid drips down from the edge of the
counter onto the floor, forming a small puddle the colour and
consistency of clotted blood.

"Finn!" I shout, but you don't move. You just stand motionless as the steaming ooze inches towards your feet.

My mind lurches, my stomach sinking through my body
like a rock through water as the air rushes from the room and is
replaced by the stale dread stench of sea sludge and turpentine.
A clinking sound alerts me to the bird on our breakfast table;
the dead crow from our garden has come back to life and is

blithely picking at the plates of uneaten food, scraps flying in all directions. The more the bird consumes, the more its decaying underbelly bulges and bloats until finally it bursts open, releasing a clump of fat white maggots wriggling onto our table.

I become untethered. Unmoored from myself. I tell my feet to run but I have no feet to run with. And nothing to push off from.

"Look," squawks the crow, as if I have a choice; I am not in my body, I am merely an observer of this scene, watching, helpless, as you begin to turn around and I'm confronted with exactly what I expected to see—your naked body, the one I've known and held and loved for years, familiar as a playground rhyme, paired with an impossible face, blurred beyond recognition like paint smeared across a canvas. There's nothing of you here. Just the black of one nostril and a crudely drawn-on smile.

I inhale, ready to scream, but instead of air my lungs fill with saltwater. It spills from my mouth and nose as I choke, and I reach for you but you just stand there, unmoving, uncaring, as I sputter and cough my way back to the waking world, where I find myself still in the bathtub, taps still gushing and a deluge cascading over the edge and onto the bathroom floor. My knees and elbows squeak against the porcelain as I scramble to pull the plug from the drain and turn the taps off; then I clamber out of the tub and onto the sodden bath mat. Water sloshes across the tiles and out onto the carpet beyond, which squelches underfoot as I stomp across it to the hot press and pull out a pile of towels.

Naked on my hands and knees, I mop up what I can of the flood until, surrounded by a slurry of soaking wet towels, I drag myself to sit against the edge of the bath, legs sprawled and arms hanging limp with exhaustion. I can feel hot tears behind my eyes. They're about to spill over, when I turn and notice the tub is still full of water. There must be something blocking the drain, I think, as I reach in to unclog it. Only I can't find the drain, or even the bottom of the tub, and as I reach even further, shoulder-deep now in water as black as the sea I swam in just hours ago, something floats to the surface right next to my face. Tiny white pebbles. No. They're teeth. Followed by a clump of slimy liquorice hair.

I lunge backwards but it's too late. Her hand is around my arm and she's hauling herself up towards me. Her nails bury into my flesh, drawing blood as her grotesque face emerges next to mine. That nauseating cracking sound as my mother's dead mouth splits open, and a vile smell pours out.

This time I wake up stock-still. No splashing. No gasping. No flood. I look down at my body, paralysed in the tepid water, which is chest-high and no longer black but lit faintly blue. I look up, and sure enough the mourning moon is there, keeping quiet vigil over me. She hovers at the centre of the skylight now, her soft, sympathetic face like that of a parent at a child's bedside, gazing down as tears drip from my jaw onto my collarbones, which rise and fall with each quick, shallow breath that enters and escapes me. The moon stays with me, a steady, soothing presence, until my breathing slows and my body comes back to life. And the first thing that I reach for is my phone.

The last message, from me: "I'm home."

I haul myself out of the bath and crawl from the bathroom like someone escaping a car wreck. I'm trembling with the fear that I might not have surfaced, I might still be under, and at any moment I might still see my mother's bloated corpse, your distorted face, or, God forbid, that rotting crow pecking at my breakfast.

Listen to the birds, she said. But what the hell does she know? I don't want to look. I don't want to see.

I wrap myself in a towel and inch towards our room with one hand on the wall, steadying my jelly legs as I go, taking tiny baby steps. My eyes continue to dart around me, looking for a sign, any sign, that this might not be real. The veil is thin tonight, after all, and I can't seem to trust my own mind.

Leaving the lamp on, I come to lie curled up on my side, legs tucked into my chest and arms hugging them close. Your side of the bed is empty once again.

Have you ever noticed how our tears taste just like the sea?

GIVE US THIS DAY

We open on an auditorium. Exactly 115 vintage velvet seats. Two exit signs in neon green. And one pair of thick red curtains, tenderly framing a darkened stage. From the back row I watch as the last stragglers shuffle down the long, thin aisles to find their seats, and as the audience settles in, their discordant murmur like that of an orchestra tuning up, I can't help but feel as though we are the ones being observed, like the stage is some cyclopic god watching us through one formidable rectangular iris.

The illusion is broken when the house lights go down and a hush falls, soft as snow, across the crowd. Then suddenly, like the sun splitting the heavens, a stark white spotlight glares down on the centre of the stage. It creates a perfectly circular pool of light, in the middle of which stands a monolithic white canvas mounted on a thick pine easel. I've seen both of these objects before, in the storeroom below us. I thought I had imagined them, but here they are, as real as stars.

Standing in front of the canvas with her back to us—a tiny David facing her Goliath—is a waifish figure in black leggings and a loose grey shirt. She slowly pushes up her sleeves; rolls her shoulders, once, twice; catches her hair into a high pony-tail; and then stretches her neck from side to side, left ear to left shoulder, right ear to right shoulder. She reaches her arms high above her head, lifts up onto the tips of her toes, extends out long like a cat in the sun, holds there, and descends deli-cately, arms landing at her sides like wings.

She regards the canvas a moment longer, while all around her, arranged like ritualistic offerings on an enormous beige dust sheet, a selection of brushes, sticks, sponges, and spatulas await. Among them, twelve silver tins brimming with vivid shades of thick, shiny paint.

Ladies and gentlemen, may I present . . . *The Artist and the Blank Page.*

She selects a brush and begins.

Cue music. A second spotlight reveals a harpist stage right, long skirt hiked up and pale bare thighs gripping the enormous in-strument as though it were a wild beast that might at any mo-ment flee. Her fingers fly to the strings, and as they do, an Irish reel bursts urgently into the room. The melody is spirited and bright, the notes quick and intricate. The painter moves with them.

She spins and dives, lifting one leg high behind her, tilting impossibly forward in a standing split as she plunges a paintbrush into the first pot. Then she lands and twirls back towards the canvas, and with a flick of her wrist, a flash of fuchsia paint explodes onto the white cloth. Her first mark. Another spin. Another dip. Another twirl. Another splash. This time, electric blue. Then she switches tools, dragging paint across the canvas with a wooden stick before changing again to a thinner brush, which might as well be a wand; its bristles never seem to touch the page and violet lines appear as if by magic, like rivers of quick rain down a window.

The marks she leaves are vague at first, an indiscernible tangle of streaks, smears, and splatters. Occasionally, a shape seems to form, only to be lost again in the mire. Still she flows, never stopping, never pausing to consider her next move. At times it's less like she's covering the canvas in paint and more like she's drawing the colours forth from the cloth, raising them to the surface like a shipwreck.

I'm not sure how much time has passed—ten minutes perhaps—when a third spotlight comes to land on a sprightly fiddle player. He springs to life like a light-powered jack-in-the-box, weaving his bow furiously back and forth across the strings to create a melody that runs counterpoint to that of the harpist, who somehow picks up her already lively pace. The painter, too, increases speed, dancing with the canvas now like a matador with a bull. Her movement is at once balletic and feral—jabbing and stabbing at her opponent with machine precision and then leaning in close, smearing her hands, her feet, even her face across the image with all the tenderness of a lover. Watching her, I can practically feel the cold paint wet against my skin, the heat of the spotlight, a hundred pairs of eyes on me and beads of sweat trickling down my chest as my muscles burn to keep pace.

Suddenly, the thunderous sound of horses bolting; a woman with a huge bodhrán joins the chorus as a fourth and final spotlight reveals her, cradling the drum in one hand while she pounds its circular face with the other, head swaying and dark hair flying as she pushes the tempo even further. The fiddle player bends his knees, leaning his whole body into the beat as the harpist's fingers flit across the strings, hurriedly plucking them like hungry beaks at scattered crumbs.

The painter accelerates too, attacking her creation with both hands now, arms flailing like a crazed virtuoso as the image begins to take shape. She switches tools quickly, selecting one brush and then flinging it aside in favour of another—they can't quite seem to manifest her vision fast enough.

The music surges forth, an army's final ascent, and as the beat of the bodhrán drives the quartet relentlessly towards a sonorous crescendo, I become aware of the audience: the backs of their heads black against the stage, the sense of a collectively held breath for the painter, who can just about keep up. She moves feverishly, like a woman possessed. This is no longer a painting but a prayer, a frenzied dig for meaning, for purpose, for answers, for God. She is not creating but communing with something outside herself, outside us all, calling it forth like the colours from the canvas. Briefly, I feel it enter the room, as though a swarm of hummingbirds is hovering above our heads, their presence unseen but felt in the stirring of air all around them.

A few more strokes and suddenly the picture becomes clear. The music soars; the painter adds the final flash of paint, takes two steps back, and drops to her knees. As she falls, the music falls with her, and the lights go down on everything but the scene she's summoned . . .

Evening in a teenage bedroom; vivid pink walls adorned with posters, photos, sticky notes. Colourful clothes in a heap by the door. And a string of fairy lights dangling from a shelf. Outside the window a full moon peeks through the branches of a bare tree, casting dappled blue light on the young girl kneeling by the bed, head bowed in prayer. The image is detailed but loose in form. Clichéd. Mundane. We all know this room. And yet this particular moment feels important. Sacred, even.

There's an extended silence in which all I can hear is the painter's ragged breath returning to normal. Then a staggered applause moves through the crowd, slow and sustained, until the spotlight fades out and the house lights come back up.

The dust sheet is now a massacre of pinks, purples, blues, and blacks. The spell is broken. The band is gone. Only the painter remains, staring vacantly out at us. Instead of a brush, she now wields a pair of silver scissors in one hand. And something about the whole audience being lit, our faces visible to her, makes me feel complicit in what's about to happen.

She turns to face the canvas once again, then steps towards it, violently driving the scissors into the cloth. I hear someone gasp reflexively as she begins to cut, moving in a clockwise circle from the bottom of the canvas all the way to the top, creating a hole almost as big as the image itself. There's no music now. Just the sickly sharp snip-snip-snip of the blades as she unceremoniously carves the heart out of her own work, leaving jagged borders hanging limp from the wooden frame like broken skin around a wound.

The audience looks on, hands on chests and tears in their eyes as the massive disc finally falls away, landing with a damp thud at the painter's feet. She barely regards it before dropping her weapon, exiting the stage and leaving us alone with this carcass of creation.

Silence again. Much denser this time. Nobody moves. Nobody so much as breathes.

I feel the lady sitting next to me jolt when a disembodied voice announces there'll be a ten-minute break before the evening's main act begins. Then, one by one, she and the rest of the people present begin to stir as though waking from a shared hallucination. They file wordlessly back up the skinny aisles and out the door to the foyer. And I stay a while, staring at the scene with no centre till a small crew of stagehands rushes in to reset things for the next performance. Within a few short minutes order is restored, and all evidence of the painter is gone.

I've come here every night for the past six nights—I travel to work with Fran, sit in on the opening act, then head back home to Jay and the lumpy sofa. He usually has some leftovers waiting for me and, since I've been less chatty this week, a shit film we can stare at in silence. After that, Jay takes a shower while I clean the kitchen. Fran gets home, we all share a bottle of wine, and when he goes to bed, Jay and I watch our nightly videos until he starts to nod off.

I haven't been sleeping. Not at night, anyway. I try to sneak a few hours in while Fran potters about the flat during the day—the nightmares are less likely to strike then, and if they do at least I wake up to company, and light. I haven't been writing either. I hate admitting that to you. I hate admitting any of this. I wish I could tell you that I'm thriving, or at the very least healing, but the truth is that more and more now, days feel like something to be survived. It all seems to be getting harder, not easier. Like it's supposed to. Like everyone keeps telling me it will. I'm beginning to realise that time does not heal wounds. Time just adds more days in which to feel the effect of them.

On the plus side, I have no desire to see you. Not because I don't want to see you, I do, but because I don't want you to see me. Not like this. In fact, I wish I could make you unsee every ugly piece of me. I wish I could erase them from your memory and leave only the good bits—the bright, shiny, attractive bits. I hear people asking exes to delete their nudes. Fuck that. Keep them. Keep all the filthy debaucherous shit we got up to. Keep the time we fucked on the kitchen table and ate dinner off it without cleaning up. Keep the time you slipped a hand up my skirt and made me come in the Royal Albert Hall during Beethoven's 6th. Keep all the flesh and mess and moans and sighs and unflattering angles only you were privy to. But give me back my ugly parts, please.

Give back that night when my fever reached 102—a rare case of adult pox—and you tried to sponge down my blotchy inflamed body as I fervently fought you off; in my head your hands were huge crow beaks, pointed and pecking at my skin.

Give back the Christmas Eve I vomited a bellyful of mulled wine onto the back seat of your mother's brand-new car, and you mopped up the putrid crimson puddle while I slept off the booze in your childhood bed. Me hyperventilating in a crowded park. Me in convulsions at a Death Cab for Cutie concert during "I Will Follow You into the Dark." Me slumping to the floor of an elevator during our last breakup, begging you not to leave me. Me standing in front of you in a dozen fights, mousy and small and only making myself smaller.

Give it back. Give it all back along with that morning you found me by the banks of Lough Derg, delirious from lack of sleep. We'd rented a cabin for the weekend, and one night, when we went out for dinner, you left a window open and the light on. Do you remember? When we came home the bedroom was swarming with mosquitos, but you just stripped off and went to sleep, leaving me to deal with them. I woke you up and then we fought for hours—not because you'd done something that upset me, but because I'd had the gall to *tell you* you'd done something that upset me. Our speciality.

I have visions of you fuming, shouting, and then leaping about the room stark naked, swatting mozzy after mozzy with a rolled up towel until the formerly white walls were streaked red. You killed thirty-nine mosquitos that night—I counted them—out of guilt and rage and a desperate desire for both of us to get some sleep. Only I couldn't. I lay there with the duvet pulled all the way up to my nose, listening to the sounds of you snoring and the high-pitched buzzing all around me. Thirty-nine wasn't enough, apparently. There were more.

The reason I couldn't sleep, and I don't think I ever told you this, was not just the fear of being bitten; I'd been told that mosquitos intentionally buzz near our ears to make us lash out, to get our hearts beating faster so our blood pumps harder and is therefore easier to access. The thought nauseated me. And I was afraid to swat them away, for fear of giving them exactly what they wanted. So I lay there, trying not to move when they flew right next to my head. And somewhere in that paralysis, following yet another fight on yet another trip I'd planned to try to save us, a story crept in, simple but potent, that I would be better off dead. I chewed on this story for hours, giving it the credence I felt it deserved, candidly considering all the practicalities involved in no longer existing on this Earth.

Then I went down to the lake. I'm not sure what my plan was exactly, only that my feet took me there the same way they had taken me to my mother's grave. I wanted to be close to her, and I was convinced in that moment that getting to her wouldn't be hard. She was, after all, only a breath away.

I told you later that I didn't hear you call my name, but that's not true. I heard you. I knew you were searching for me. And I hoped you wouldn't find me. But of course you did, you saw me sitting there and you came barrelling down the slope, sending pebbles flying in all directions. It was like you couldn't wait to get to me, but when you did, you'd no idea what to do. You just stood there, hands on your hips, looking down.

"I don't want to be here," I said, and you offered me your hand.

"Let's get you home."

Did you really think I was talking about the lake?

Or, in the same way I pretended not to hear you calling, did you pretend not to understand?

＃

As it happens, mosquitos aren't quite as Machiavellian as I'd thought; the buzzing is nothing more than the beating of their wings, and aside from several theories, no one really knows why they fly so close to our ears. The stories we tell ourselves often cause us more pain than the truth ever could.

＃

I left the theatre in a blur tonight, making my way quickly through the crowd and out into a brisk black evening where the cobbled streets were slick with a fine rain, which floated more than fell. Shallow puddles all around me reflected the coloured Christmas lights in every shop window, and I tried not to see them, or indeed the endless stream of couples drifting arm in arm from brightly lit doorways, bearing gifts and garish smiles. If I didn't know better, I'd say there were more of them this year. And that they were put here specifically to piss me off.

Have you noticed them too? Or does your world look the same without me in it?

"Merry Christmas," chirps the bus driver as I shake off my umbrella and climb the steps towards him. I force a grin and take a seat.

Two weeks, I tell myself. Two weeks and Christmas will be over. But then it'll be happy fucking New Year. And I'm not sure which is worse, honestly. At least, come January, everyone will be broke and sad again and my misery will seem less out of place.

Two weeks. Jesus. It's mid–December and I haven't even got a tree. I've never not had a tree. Even after Mam died, especially after that, in fact, Dad made sure we had a proper Christmas. That's one thing he got right: special occasions—birthdays, Easters, Halloweens, even visits from the tooth fairy were well organised.

Acts of service. That's how my dad shows love. Home-cooked meals. Clothes washed and ironed. A hot-water bottle in my bed each night. And lifts everywhere. He could have added chauffeur to his CV by the time I turned eighteen. He even learned to sew.

You're a lot alike, you and my dad; you both gave me the sun, moon, and stars. And when I told you that wasn't enough, you gave me more. More of the same. More cups of tea, more breakfasts in bed, more lifts to the airport. It was like getting a million apples when what I really wanted was five apples and an orange. Because I wasn't asking for more; I was asking for something else entirely. I wanted you. I wanted access to you. To the honest-to-God-warts-and-all-wholehearted-fully-present version of you that I knew was in there, hiding behind a wall of anger or, in my dad's case, forbearance. That's the main difference between the pair of you; your emotions bubble up as rage and his never surface at all.

Sometimes I wish I could be more like him—silent and

stoic—and less like my mother, whose moods were as unpredictable as the coastal weather outside, and equally intense.

"I'm just having a cry" was quite a common phrase in our house. I'd walk in on her in different rooms at various times of day and find her crying. Not sobbing, not even particularly distressed, just crying, shedding tears, letting them fall. We'd be heading out the door, ready to leave for some event or other.

"Sorry," she'd say. "I have to nip upstairs for a quick cry."

Like she needed to use the toilet.

Dad didn't know what to do with her. He'd offer her things. Water, tissues, advice. I just left her to it. Sometimes I even gave it a go; I'd sit on the sofa and scrunch up my face, trying to think of something that would make me cry. But nothing came to mind. God be with the days.

After she died, I went from feeling not much of anything to feeling absolutely everything, all at once. I started crying at school, in the car, in bed at night, whenever I needed to. But what's strange is that I never felt I had inherited this trait; it was more like it had risen from her dead body and come in search of me, like a spirit seeking a new host.

Cut to us, decades later, an exact replica of my parents. You'd find me crying and seize up, unsure what to do. Then you'd disappear and come back with a huge wad of toilet paper. Not a hug. Or a kiss. Or some reassurance. Sometimes, it was like you'd forgotten entirely how to human, and I resented having to teach you while also soothing myself. That first night, when I woke up shivering and scared, you were there. In every sense of the word, you were *there*. But as time wore on that version of you faded; any display of emotion from me pushed you away instead of drawing you near, and I think that's because you became the cause of my tears. They began to represent something you had broken, instead of something you could fix.

On the train home from the lake that day, you told me your greatest fear was me ending my own life. But I've since wondered if, in fact, your greatest fear was people suspecting you drove me to it.

I sit on the top deck of the bus, right at the front, and I catch my reflection in the window opposite. There's a man sitting next to me. He's stout, square-headed, handsome, with a thick, well-groomed beard, and I notice if I lean just so, it looks as though we're travelling together—off to spend a Saturday night out with friends, maybe, or back home after a hard day's work, ready to curl up with our favourite show, the one we're not allowed to watch without each other. I could have met him, instead of you. I could be his wife by now for all I know. We could be happy, this stranger and I. I could be well, and he could be kind and decent, and we could be madly in love even after all these years.

He gets off at the next stop, ruining the illusion entirely.

Do you ever wish we'd never met?

Jay has made some sort of lentil stew tonight. It's good. And the film we watch is sufficiently pulpy. There are a lot of explosions and gunfire. Several limbs are severed in the first ten minutes. It takes my mind off things for a while.

"Fran said he's postponing the second surgery," Jay confides in me as the credits roll. "He wants to wait a little longer."

"How much longer?"

"Till the theatre's running smoothly without him."

I throw Jay a look that says we both know that day will never come.

"The thing is," he says, "I don't care if he ever gets the surgery. It's for him, not me."

"Then what's the issue?"

"He doesn't want to get married until it's done."

"I see. And you?" I ask.

"I think if you know you want to spend forever with someone, why wait for forever to start?"

I never once felt that way about you. I was waiting for something alright. But it wasn't forever.

I can tell Jay is worried about me. I don't blame him. I'm worried about me too. But I have no idea what's wrong. I miss you, yes. But that's not all. It's like I'm looking for something I didn't know I'd lost. Or maybe never even had. Like I'm searching for the question itself, rather than the answer. And the only time I come remotely close to finding it is in the gloomy womb of Fran's auditorium, somewhere between the lights going down and the audience filing out, when I find myself alone once again with the painter's mutilated canvas, the emptiness there like a weighted blanket across my chest, one that crushes and comforts me in equal measure.

No two performances are the same. The scene she paints is different every night—as well as the girl's bedroom I've seen a swimming pool, a classroom, a meadow, a car park, a kitchen, and a church, each one created and destroyed by her own hand. The music is different as well. Sometimes hopeful, sometimes triumphant, sometimes haunting, sometimes achingly sad. And unlike the magician we saw all those years ago, there's nothing that the painter isn't showing us. No tricks or illusions, no gaps left for the mind to fill in. She takes nothing with her at the end of the show, she leaves all she has right there on the stage, then she goes away to find more. And we come back like a bunch of eager Christians, jaws slack and tongues raised, ready to receive what someone died to give us. Comfortable with their sacrifice.

The stage, too, changes. Some nights it's a one-eyed god watching us watching it. Some nights it's a deep, unending tunnel. Once I saw the singularity; once it was my mother's grave, inviting me to dive in and sleep. But always, always, it's a portal to other worlds. Better worlds than this.

THE BACKROOMS

I saw a photo today that I'd really rather not have seen. I didn't know what I was looking at, at first—it took my brain a good ten seconds to make sense of the man at the altar and the woman opposite, both in profile, both teary-eyed and grinning—Charlie and his beautiful new bride.

The picture was posted by a mutual friend in an album of "Summer Highlights," which I'd been absentmindedly scrolling through on the bus back to our house, and it surprised me to realise that my first reaction—once the shock had worn off—was to smile. I actually smiled. Because Charlie, as we have established, is not a bad guy, just a bit of a fool. He had a tough run of it growing up, and his finding love and happiness—anyone's finding love and happiness—can only be a good thing. My smile quickly turned to tears, however, when I realised that one day I might be looking at a photo of you, in profile, grinning at a woman in a white dress.

And look, I know how this goes. I know that by the time

you get married I'll have healed enough that I can smile for you too. But this foresight barely makes a dent in the agony of imagining it now. Somehow, each fresh loss feels different, like a maze with shifting walls; I know there's a way out, but I'm fucked if I can find it.

Grief is full of these maddening discrepancies. Like knowing that the pain will pass and believing at the same time that it will never, ever go away. Like being certain we were wrong for each other and wondering, incessantly, if maybe we should try again. Like envying your next partner and pitying her in equal measure.

My feelings, too, are completely incongruous. Sometimes my body is so full of rage that I fear it will begin oozing out of every orifice, like acid, slowly dissolving all that I am in its wake. I flash on your eyes, fixed and empty, your mouth forming the words "I don't like you," and I want to go back and possess my former self so that I might leap at you nails first and tear the very flesh from your face. It doesn't matter if those words were true for you or if you only said them to wound me. Either way, I got wounded. I felt worthless and foolish and wholly unlovable. And you didn't care.

Why didn't you care?

The question alone is incendiary. It causes me to spiral down a mental list I've made of all the times you didn't care, all the moments when the care you claimed to have for me was cancelled out by acts of cruelty or, at best, profound thoughtlessness. I think of all the ways in which you hurt, humiliated, and rejected me, lashed out at me in anger, or put your own gratification ahead of my well-being. How you bulldozed over my boundaries, made promises you couldn't possibly keep, stepped over and around my feelings like toys strewn on a carpet, and I let you. For far too long, I let you.

Another why.

Why did I stay?

Because I had hope. Too much, by all accounts.

I picture old-fashioned weighing scales, with one side laden with all the hope I had for us—a gleaming, glittering heap of the stuff. In the beginning, it seemed like hope was all I had, and nothing could ever shift the balance. But soon enough, the other side began slowly descending as, little by little, evidence piled up—evidence that I shouldn't stay. I wanted to. I really did. So much so that I began adding every scrap of hope I could find—each rare good day or loving gesture—desperately trying to outweigh the bad with the good. For a long time the scales wavered back and forth, but in the end, the stack of evidence grew so heavy that it tipped the scales completely, and no amount of hope could tip them back.

I've got years' worth of proof now. A head full of memories that come at me in quick, sharp snatches, like I'm toggling through radio stations with the volume turned up full. Endless clipped and broken words and phrases full of vitriol and heat. Slammed doors. Angry footsteps. Vicious stares paired with bursts of blaring white-noise silence. It's enough to make me dizzy.

It's enough, in fact, to bring on something akin to relief. If I can just catch myself, switch the sound off, embrace the quiet—the absence of chaos now that you're gone—then a soothing sensation moves through me. Like ice cream sliding down my throat on a hot day.

And yet.

There are still moments when I find myself floored by the ache in my chest, the longing there for you despite it all.

When I get back to our house this evening, for instance, and find a Christmas tree in the living room, along with a box of baubles and a note that reads, *You've never not had a tree.* Once again you're the version of you I'd hoped for, and I can't remember why I'm letting you go.

With this thought comes a different why.

Why couldn't I just be happy?

This why is much more dangerous. This why has me disregarding the evidence entirely and entertaining the theory that you were perfect, everything was great, and I was just incapable of enjoying it. The junkie in me especially likes this theory, because if I *was* the problem, then maybe there's still hope.

Maybe it was all my fault. For wanting too much. For being too much. For not being satisfied with what you had to offer. Maybe all I need is to want less. To be okay with the odd outburst of anger. Maybe I don't need passion and intimacy and connection as much as I think I do. Maybe having someone who can share the mental load is overrated. Maybe I can change myself, round off my edges so that yours can slot more easily into place. And if all that's true, then I can go get you back and be done with all this grief bollocks.

It wasn't all bad, was it?

The answer, of course, is no. Sometimes it was good. Sometimes it was glorious. Sometimes you were kind and supportive and tender and caring and fun. I picture you on Sunday afternoons, presenting me with a tray full of perfectly roasted potatoes, crisp and sizzling from the oven, like a waiter displaying a fine wine. You, walking me to the train station every night before we lived together, waving me off from the platform like some frantic war wife, chasing after my carriage just because you knew it would make me laugh. You in your studio, listening to some piece of music you just wrote. In this scene, you're wearing nothing but a pair of socks and your massive silver headphones. Hips swaying. Eyes closed. Arms waving like a wizard casting spells. You catch me smiling at you from the doorway and next thing I know we're making heated love on the carpet, dripping sweat like a fever has come over us.

You, packing us a picnic to take to my mother's grave, spending hours there chatting to her as if she could hear us. You, kneeling at the end of our bed, rubbing my feet to help me get to sleep. Crawling up to meet me from under the duvet and landing with a kiss. You naked, you in a suit, you silently selecting the next CD. You glancing at me from across the room at parties, checking that I'm still there, still yours.

I stack up the good bits like a precious house of cards, and in the brief time before it comes toppling down again, I would abandon myself entirely to have you back. I would take the chaos, accept it fully, along with any shred of love you have for me.

I call Fran again.

"He got me a Christmas tree," I tell him.

"That prick."

"I think it was sweet."

"Fuck him being sweet!" he shrieks. "Where was this when you were together?"

I don't answer. I'm staring at the tree, thinking about you picking out the perfect one, dragging it all the way home for me, writing me that little note. Fran hears my thoughts.

"Don't fall for this, my babe," he warns. "Don't you dare fall for this third-act-in-a-rom-com bullshit."

"How can I not?" I ask.

"Because sweeping gestures are easy. Sweeping gestures are his fucking forte! It's the boring day-to-day stuff he couldn't seem to grasp. Remember when he whisked you off to Athens after he slept with that ridiculous lingerie model?"

When I don't reply, Fran says, "I'm sorry."

"That was years ago," I say, "and we were broken up."

"Eight days," Fran reminds me, as if I need reminding. "You'd been broken up eight days, Kate. And he'd been messaging her for months!"

"We don't know that for sure," I say, and I can't believe I'm defending you. To Fran of all people. Fran, who was there the night I found out. At a fucking engagement party of all places. Fran, who brought me home, sat by me while I puked up the twelve shots I'd downed in response to hearing the news. Fran, who put me to bed, stayed with me all night, all week in fact. Fran, who sewed me back together, only to watch me rip the stitches out three months later and take you back.

You'd started seeing a therapist, you said, and you knew

now that you were acting out in response to a fear of commitment. I was the best thing that had ever happened to you, you said, and you'd sabotaged it to stop yourself from getting hurt. Classic, you said. Typical. And a lingerie model? How positively trite! How gross. How empty. "A glorified wank," you called it. Just flesh. No feelings. And now, finally, you knew what you wanted: marriage, kids, a home, a dog, family holidays, the works. And you wanted to do it all with me. Couldn't imagine, you said, growing old with anyone else. It was the first time you'd ever seemed sure. Really sure. Certain, in fact. And I believed it. Like a fucking fool, I believed it.

Why did I go back?

I don't realise I've said it out loud until Fran answers.

"Because, my babe, for a while there, he really was his best self. Things were incredible between you two. We all saw it. We all saw the progress he made. The effort he put in. And it's not like he was lying. He really did want those things. He wanted to be better. He just couldn't maintain it for very long. The anger crept back in because it was never gone; he'd just pushed it down, along with the need to conquer every pair of tits in his periphery."

"Jesus," I say.

"Sorry."

"No, it's fair. Just, ouch."

"The problem with Finn," Fran explains, "is that the distance between his best self and his worst self is a fucking chasm."

"That, and I loved him," I add.

"And you loved him," he says.

"And I kept hoping I could get the good bits without the bad."

"Correct," says Fran.

"Sometimes I need reminding."

"Well, I can remind you as many times as you need. Now, why don't you get a pot of mulled wine on the go, stick some Christmas music on, and get decorating? You might enjoy it!"

"Yeah, you're right. Thanks, Fran."

I hang up and go straight to bed.

Hours later, I'm just about to drift off when my foot finds a pair of your crumpled-up socks at the end of the bed and I completely unravel.

It's always something innocuous and unexpected. With my mother it was half a cup of coffee. I found it on the table by the sofa the day after she died. Just a cold half cup of coffee, with a thin skin forming on the surface. Hardly important in the grand scheme. But it was the last cup of coffee she ever made. And I could still see the sticky mark her berry lip balm left on the porcelain rim. Still smell it, very faintly.

I took the cup to my room. Hid it in my wardrobe. Left it there until the liquid congealed and then hardened. I knew, the whole time, I should just get rid of it, but I couldn't bring myself to do it. One day I got home from school and it was gone; Dad must have found it and washed it. The cup went back into circulation and that was that.

With you, it's a pair of worn socks. I feel them there, imagine you kicking them off in your sleep the way you do, and what little progress I've made comes undone. It might as well be the night you left all over, because your side of the bed becomes suddenly daunting again. So much so that this time, I turn my back to it, realising as I do that if I face away, I can imagine you're asleep behind me. And if I listen hard enough, I can even hear you breathing.

My body doesn't care how much you hurt me. My body wants you back regardless. My body actually feels soothed by the thought of you. You. The reason I'm hurting in the first place. Isn't that stupid? I find it stupid. Millions of years of evolution and we'll still run towards a proverbial lion if it shows us some fucking affection.

The trouble is, I've spent so long being somebody's someone that I've forgotten how to be myself. You were here every day when I woke up. And every night when I fell asleep. And even in those weird, murky hours when the whole world powers down and it was just the two of us, lying next to each other in a room. We spent so much time alone in rooms together. On sofas. In beds. Across from each other in restaurants. People spend years sitting beside someone, not even noticing until there's nobody there anymore.

I saw a version of you that no one else saw. Good and bad, I saw it all. The great shit and the weird shit and the shit that drove me absolutely crazy. And when I think about you moving on, when I imagine you with someone else, the first thought I have is, *She doesn't even know you!* She doesn't know you. And I do! And yes, it will be exciting teaching her all about you, but I already know! And what the hell am I supposed to do with all this information, anyway? Does it just go out the window along with my fluent French and ability to write HTML? Are you a language that I'll lose when I stop speaking it?

People tell me we'll still be friends. That at least I still have you. But I don't. Not the way I used to have you. And you don't have me anymore either. Eventually we'll just be two people, bumping into each other outside a cinema somewhere, saying you look great, so do you, and how've you been, yeah, can't complain. After all that, after everything we've been through, we'll be a couple of strangers who used to know each other.

I can't get my head around it.

I keep hoping I'll get a call and some anonymous but authoritative voice will tell me there's been a mistake. "A dreadful mistake." And it'll turn out this was all just one of my nightmares. "Sorry for the inconvenience," the voice will say. But I won't mind, because I'll wake up and realise it's still six years ago. I'll see you there, crouched in front of me with a concerned look in your eyes, and then you'll wrap your arms around me on a sofa underneath a disco ball and we'll have it all to do over again. Only this time will be different. This time we'll have the wisdom of hindsight on our side. This time we'll avoid the pitfalls and stay happy, and together, and in love. And you won't shout or stray or break my heart.

I've been here before, battling the linear nature of time; in the same way I want to go back to the night we fell, I have wished—more times than I can count—to be allowed back to the day she died. I've gone over every inch of that day, scouring it for ways I could have changed the outcome. What if, for instance, I had lingered just a moment longer to hug her good-bye? Long enough, perhaps, to change the course of her day.

Sometimes, I go back further, to the weekend before, when I was tired and decided not to go to a pyjama party at my best friend's house. Every girl who went to Bernadette's that night caught the flu and missed a week of school. And if I'd just pushed through, gone to the sleepover, and got sick too, my mother would have been at home that Wednesday looking after me.

But she might still have made time for her "daily dip," as she called it.

So I travel further and further back, searching for something airtight.

A year prior, my parents considered sizing down and moving to the west coast. There was a cottage for sale in Killadoon, near my mother's childhood home, the house Aunt Kathy lives in now. But I threw a tantrum about leaving Bernadette, and that put the kibosh on their plans. What if I had let them go? And my mam was hundreds of miles from Colligeen Beach that day?

What if, I wonder on my darkest days, I had never been born at all?

If time would allow me to go back, if it would just be amenable enough to bend slightly, curving around on itself instead of moving accursedly forward, then I could put things right. And if I couldn't save her, maybe I'd make better use of the precious time we had. And if I couldn't save us, maybe I'd stop myself from falling for you instead.

Only it's not six years ago. Or twenty-six for that matter.

The tyranny of entropy prevails. You're gone and so is she. And wishing otherwise is like asking a river to flow back up a mountainside.

I'm sure I've had these exact thoughts before. Reached the exact same conclusions.

I'm exhausted by myself.

Not exhausted enough to sleep, though; I spend two more hours circling the drain of my delusions before finally giving up on rest entirely and making myself a mug of hot chocolate. I get settled on the sofa and put on one of Jay's walking-tour videos, hoping it will help me fall asleep.

In the first one, some poor chap is traipsing around Chicago in the middle of a downpour—I catch sight of his reflection briefly in a shop window, lit by red neon light. He's carrying a massive umbrella and there's a camera strapped to his head. It's incredible, I think, how we keep finding new ways to suffer for our art.

People scurry past in search of shelter. One woman holding a newspaper over her head scowls as she passes, and somewhere nearby but out of frame a dog is barking. Muted chatter floats out from the open doorways of bars and restaurants. This, and the sound of the rain, lulls me to sleep, and when I open my eyes, another video has started autoplaying. It looks like some kind of botanical garden in summertime, vivid green and teeming with couples and families out for an afternoon stroll. I watch a while, then drift back down.

It's still dark when I wake again, but I get the sense that hours have passed. The image on-screen is instantly disquieting: still the point of view of someone walking, but no longer through a bustling city or a picturesque park. This is an empty shopping mall at some indeterminable hour of day or night. The whole scene, in fact, seems to have been abandoned by time, untethered and adrift now at a point outside it. I've never seen this place before. But I have.

The walker passes shop fronts, shuttered and dark; a tiled blue fountain strewn with dry copper pennies; a pair of enormous escalators, both unmoving. Well-trodden carpets with geometric patterns stretch endlessly away—lines and circles and squares repeating in blue then pink then blue then pink. Murky yellow light pools like puddles at the centre of vacant corridors, barely able to keep at bay the grainy shadows that encroach from all around. I realise that I can't hear the walker's footsteps; the sound has been replaced by an atmospheric droning, like wind rolling through a warehouse, which has the effect of turning the camera into a disembodied fourth wall. I am no longer a viewer but a voyeur.

We enter a dark hallway and emerge in an abandoned playground late at night, transitioning seamlessly, as in a dream, from one place to the next, with no thought for how we got here. An overhead floodlight casts long, deep umbras under slides and swings and climbing frames. I can hear ghost children squealing, motionless merry-go-rounds squeaking, but the sound remains unchanged—still that low, unending drone.

Without warning the camera whips to a concrete expanse of car park and then to a disused office space where cracked, stained ceiling tiles look down on a windowless department washed in a woozy greenish glow. We pass row upon row of eerily identical workstations: chunky grey computer monitors with matching keyboards and the same high-backed black computer chairs.

A stairwell.

A motel.

A church.

A child's birthday party with no attendees.

Each scene a familiar setting imbued with a sense of quiet unease. I can feel at all times an implied presence that never takes shape.

When the scene shifts again, I sit up, startled. It's Colligeen Beach. That can't be right. And yet it is. I know the stripey yellow-and-red lifeguard hut next to the tarmac path, the specific rise and fall of sand dunes, and the curve of coastline out towards Caille Point. The pale sea soundlessly reflects an overcast sky above, the kind that constantly threatens rain. The air grows redolent with salt air.

And then we're here, in my house, and my heart is in my throat. I'm looking at my television's point of view—my own living room mirrored back at me—and there I am, mug in hand, face aghast, body frozen to the spot. Everything is the same, down to the smallest detail. Even the sound has returned— the gurgle of the radiators, the low room hum, the tapping of branches against our garden fence—all unnaturally amplified, like they've been added after the fact. Behind me, I can see my desk in the corner, and the naked Christmas tree against the window, where a pink-tinged dawn tussles with the last of the night. I raise my arm and the me on TV raises hers; I lower it and so does she. I turn my head this way and that. She follows suit. I start to play with the skin of my face, pushing and pulling at my forehead and cheeks, watching her do the same. She looks tired.

I am so engrossed in her that I don't even notice the figure, which begins as a shadow and then slowly takes form. It approaches her from behind, a tall, winged creature with my mother's head and torso—sleek dark hair framing a featureless face, from the centre of which protrudes a long, serrated beak. Clawed feet click-clack loudly on the wood floor as the beast twitches forwards on fledgling legs, pecking blindly at the air as it goes. The pink glow from the window grows brighter now, melting into a blinding red that envelops the whole room.

It's at this point I know I'm in a nightmare. But that does nothing to assuage my fear; real or not, this is happening.

And I can't move.

I can only look on as the wretched thing gets closer to the version of me on-screen, unable to reach for the remote or glance over my shoulder to see if it's really behind me. I urge my other self to get up, to run, but I know she can't. And so I watch as the creature raises one slick black wing above her head.

It stops, looking right down the lens. Right at me.

"Look!" it cries, like I have any other choice. I'm looking at my doppelgänger as its feathers caress her face. I'm looking as it leans in close, draws back its scrawny neck, and its beak snaps forward, piercing her skull. I feel my own mind shatter, and then—

I'm awake. It's light out. The TV is off. My empty mug has rolled onto the floor and landed on its side.

I spend the day writing, but what comes out is unusable. Non-sense about abandoned malls and playgrounds at night. Futile endeavours to turn time around. And a nightmare in which my mother, in the form of a human-bird hybrid, pecks through my skull with a jagged, knifelike beak. I also jot down my conversation with Fran, noting how pathetic I sound. It's all childish. Amateur. Drivel. I hate it.

I manage to ignore the tree, my unwritten novel, and the out-side world all week. I tell Fran I'm seeing Jenna. I tell Jenna I'm seeing Fran. I tell Alexis that I'm busy with the book.

It's getting silly now. The tree most of all. I leave for Christmas at my father's house in two days and I'm still tiptoe-ing round a bare tree. I haven't even bought a gift for him, or Kathy, who will no doubt be joining us.

Town is unbearable. I have borrowed a pair of your bulkiest headphones and am blasting the heaviest music I can bear, but it's still not enough to drown out the incessant Christmas mu-sic and the raucous swarm of the crowds. I know the tea shop on William Street has the exact brand of oolong my dad likes. The one "you got him" last year—I bought it, wrapped it, and put your name on it. He hasn't stopped raving about it since, so I reckon it's a safe bet. As for Kathy, I picked up a bottle of her favourite perfume, as always, and I'm queuing at the bus stop to go home when someone crashes into me.

"Sorry!" says the stranger, immediately bending down to help me gather up the bags I dropped, and as we both stand up I see her face. She's older up close than I'd imagined, late forties maybe, and her brown hair is actually tinged slightly purple. But it's definitely her.

"You're the painter!" I blurt, realising I don't know this woman's name.

"I am," she says, bewildered. "But I also go by Maeve. Sorry, do I know you?"

"No, sorry, I'm Kate. I'm a friend of Fran's."

"Ah."

"I've seen your show seven times," I say, unable to restrain myself. "It's incredible."

"Wow. Thank you," she says, though I can tell the compliment is hard to absorb.

"I didn't actually pay for my ticket," I admit. "Fran let me sneak in because I'm sad and your show made me feel better."

"*My* show?" asks Maeve, incredulous. "Made you feel . . . *better*?"

"Well, not *better*," I say, and as she watches me trying and failing to find the right words, I note how different this woman in front of me is from her onstage self. She expands there like a river bursting its banks, devouring everything in its path. Here, she's a skinny little rivulet, her slight frame lost in an oversized coat and scarf and a pair of chunky boots.

"To be honest I still haven't figured out how the show

makes me feel," I say finally. "But whatever the feeling is, it's addictive. I'd have kept going, only Fran said I was taking the piss."

"That's fair," says Maeve, scowling at a woman who just smacked her in the legs with a handful of shopping bags. By this point people are swerving around us, bumping our shoulders as they pass.

"Listen, I'm on my way to see a film," she tells me. "I've got a few hours to kill before tonight's show."

"Of course," I say, realising I've taken up too much of her time, but then she adds, "You're welcome to join me. And talk somewhere that's not the middle of a busy street."

"Won't the cinema be packed?" I ask, itchy to be somewhere quiet now.

"It's an IFI screening of *Mirror*"—she smirks—"a semi-autobiographical Andrei Tarkovsky film from 1975 in which a dying man reminisces about his childhood during World War II."

There's a beat before she adds, "In Russian. With subtitles."

"Right," I say. "Well, in that case lead the way."

The screening is part of a wider Tarkovsky exhibition; rows of flimsy white walls have been erected in the mezzanine, all adorned with blown-up versions of the director's film stills and photographs. I find myself lingering in front of his Polaroids, all intimate, unhurried portraits of places—buildings and backyards, fields and streets and ordinary rooms—devoid of life. The few souls who do feature are obscure shapes in the distance, their faces crushed in dimness or ablaze in light. The photos elicit in me a feeling akin to that of Maeve's paintings, or the eerie videos that preceded my most recent nightmare. In them I see no past. No future. Just infinite present. And the threat of something unseen. What that thing is, I can't tell, but there's a lack in each one, a romanticised longing. I feel I could fall into them, that even as I stand here now, I am free-falling. And this, I realise, is the feeling I failed to articulate earlier. The one I feel during her show. I try to explain it to Maeve as she stands next to me, staring at a square image of a kitchen table suspended in two shafts of cold blue sunlight. On the table is a glass vase full of flowers and a place setting for one.

Maeve nods as I talk, never taking her eyes off the photo, and for a short time I wonder if she's been listening at all.

"So this free fall," she asks finally, "is it pleasant or unpleasant?"

"Neither," I say. Then: "Both. I don't know. It's terrifying and exhilarating at the same time. I feel liberated. And also like the ground might smack me in the face at any second. But it never does."

"Huh," says Maeve, her gaze still on the Polaroid. I can't tell if she's responding to me or to it.

"Why are you sad?" she asks, catching me off guard.

"What?"

"Earlier, you said you were sad."

"Oh. Right. Breakup."

Then she turns to me, her eyes bright and wide.

"Congratulations!"

"Thanks?"

Maeve is still smiling as the doors of the auditorium are swung open and the audience moves inside.

She and I stretch out across multiple seats and settle in for the film, which she now tells me has been described as a kind of cinematic Rorschach test. I can't help but be aware of this throughout. Aware of what the film is stirring in me. Exposing, even. I have the solipsistic sense that my own inner world, and not Tarkovsky's, is being projected up there for everyone to see.

I keep having this dream, says the narrator. *I am used to it.*

The dream is of his childhood home, which we see in fractured fragments that walk the line between real and imagined; a nonlinear impressionistic hellscape of memories that, real or not, were real to him, this child who is removed from his own life, confined to a room of mirrors that offer no reflection. And though our stories couldn't be more different on paper, the images of this house—its walls charred and crumbling as water comes crashing through the ceiling—and of his mother, standing hunched in a nightgown or levitating above a bed, and the central premise, a tormented soul beseeching the universe to let him go back, to redo what has been done, all cut a little too close to the quick.

When it's over we sit through the credits in silence, remaining in our seats as long as we can, just like I did at Maeve's shows. I'm grateful for the lack of conversation, the pause between that world and this one as we gather our things and wander instinctively back to the café, and I'm still a bit dazed as she orders two Irish coffees, looking to me for confirmation before nodding at the waiter to go ahead. When we both breathe in together and let out a long exhale, Maeve grins at me.

"Wow," I say, and she nods. "Thanks for letting me tag along."

"Not at all," replies Maeve, with a wave of one bony, paint-splattered hand. "All my friends have kids and *actual* jobs, so it's nice to have company for once."

"I hear you," I say, and she asks what I do. I tell her I'm a writer.

"Oh lovely," she says. "Fiction?"

I nod, and without a moment's hesitation Maeve asks me how that feels. A laugh escapes me.

"What's funny?" she asks.

"Not funny," I say. "Refreshing."

"How so?"

"Nobody ever asks me how it feels."

"What do they ask, then?"

"How much of it is true," I say.

"Really?" She seems genuinely shocked.

"My first novel was the worst," I explain. "Everyone who read it—friends, strangers, each and every radio and podcast host that Alexis, my agent, set up interviews with—wanted to know if it was true. 'It's a novel,' I'd reply. 'Yes,' they'd say, 'but there are so many resemblances to your own life.' My go-to response was, 'It's as true as it needs to be.' Alexis told me to say that. And it usually ended the line of questioning. But one particularly persistent interviewer kept going . . . 'In order to do what?' she asked. 'To achieve the desired outcome,' I replied. She was bemused, to say the least. 'Which is what?' At this point I became what my now ex-boyfriend later referred to as 'snotty.'"

Maeve chuckles at this.

"'You want me to tell you what the desired outcome of art is?' I asked her. And she nodded. The woman actually nodded!"

"And what did you say?" asks Maeve, leaning forward a little.

"I said, 'I'm not sure I'm qualified to answer that question, Pamela. But I do know that I spent years writing horror stories and was never once asked if they were "true." It just so happens that most of the horror I write is lifted directly from my own night terrors, and believe you me, there are few things more honest than the darkest recesses of someone's subconscious. But as soon as I write a love story the whole world wants to know if it's true. As if that matters! As if the heartbreak behind it wasn't satisfying enough. Well, what if I told you it was twelve percent true? Or forty-eight percent? What exact percentage of truth is enough for you, Pamela? How much pain do I need to endure for you to enjoy my art? Give me a number and let's settle this debate once and for all.'"

"Fuck," says Maeve, and I notice our coffees have arrived. The waiter must have dropped them off when I was mid-rant.

"Or something along those lines," I joke, suddenly self-conscious.

"What did Pamela say then?" asks Maeve, blowing on her drink to cool it down.

"That was 'all we had time for,' as it happened."

"Of course," she says with a smirk. "And when did your boyfriend—sorry, ex-boyfriend—call you snotty?"

"In the car on the way home. He said I'd come across as

pretentious in that interview. A lot of people online agreed, actually. Though most of them did misspell the word 'pretentious.'"

"It's a dumb choice of word, anyway," she scoffs. "It implies that you're overstating the importance of something. And you're not. Art *is* important."

"Right? I mean, didn't we all agree on that some time ago? Isn't it sort of . . . widely fucking recognised that art is one of if not *the* most important thing we do?"

I love this sort of conversation, where it sounds like you're arguing but you're vehemently agreeing with each other.

"It is." Maeve nods. "We did. If humans were to disappear tomorrow, the one thing the universe would miss about us is our art. And yet every individual who expresses this opinion gets the word 'pretentious' slung at them like cabbage at a criminal."

"How have we become a race of people who think it's cool to hate and embarrassing to care?" I ask. Maeve just shrugs and shakes her head.

"First novel," she says after a pause. "Is there a second?"

"There is. But I can't seem to get it out of me."

"Ah, that old chestnut."

"It's a lot like a chestnut, actually. Trying to crack the fucker open."

Maeve laughs knowingly.

"I don't know how you do it every night," I tell her with a shake of my head. "Create something so beautiful so quickly, and in front of that many people."

"Oh, but that's my secret," she confides. "I can *only* create quickly and in front of people. The pressure sort of . . . splits me open, and then—whether I like it or not—my insides come pouring out. Half the time it's like I'm not even in the room when it happens. I enter a space between intense focus and complete dissociation. It's hard to describe."

"No need," I say. "I know what you mean." Then I hesitate before adding, "It's a bit like sex."

"It is!" she says, her eyebrows arching in delight.

"After a particularly good writing session," I admit, "I come away with the same feeling I have after great sex; satiated and totally depleted."

"And starving!" adds Maeve.

"Ravenous." I nod. "I'll eat whatever's put in front of me."

"Most nights I grab a pizza and take it home. I'm never happier than I am eating a postshow Margherita alone in bed, knowing I've created something lasting that day."

"Is that why you do it? To create something lasting?"

"No," she replies, deadpan, "I do it for the money," and we both cackle.

"My dad genuinely can't seem to understand why I'm not a millionaire," I joke. "'But you've sold so many books!' he'll say, like that means anything."

But she's avoiding the honest response.

"Why do you really do it?" I ask.

"Fear," she says, without missing a beat. And for a split second I can see it flicker behind her eyes, like a monster she summoned just by saying its name.

"Of?"

"Forgetting."

She punctuates this with a sigh.

"My dad had Alzheimer's," she begins. "By the time I turned forty he was all but lost to us. Then, after he died, we found out his sister had it too. So I got tested a few years ago. And it turns out I inherited a gene mutation called presenilin 1. Which is annoying, really, I'd rather it had a cooler name. Anyway, it basically means that if I live long enough, I will develop Alzheimer's. Unless the extremely experimental medication I'm taking works."

She recites it like a performance. Even the joke in the middle feels scripted.

"What a steaming pile of shit," I say.

"Isn't it?" she responds, draining the end of her drink.

"But I don't understand."

"Which part?" she asks as she wiggles her empty glass at the waiter and holds up two fingers. She doesn't check with me this time. I guess we're having another round.

"You said you paint to remember," I say, "but you destroy everything you paint."

"I didn't say I painted to remember. I said I paint because I'm afraid to forget."

When I say nothing, she goes on.

"I was a dancer my whole life, Kate," she begins, "and when I got the diagnosis I stopped. Stopped dancing. Stopped eating. Stopped sleeping. Just sort of . . . stopped living, really. I figured, what's the point in making memories if I'm just going to forget them all?"

"I imagine that's quite a normal reaction," I offer, and she nods.

"One doctor suggested painting as therapy. So I painted. And I liked it. I even got good at it. But it didn't help. That is until one day I got so angry at something—I can't remember what now, ironically enough—that I took a knife to a painting I'd just finished and tore it apart. Then another. And another. I trashed my entire studio. And it felt incredible! It was the closest I'd come to feeling calm since hearing the news."

I picture Maeve on a rampage through all the scenes I've watched her paint. And then it dawns on me.

"They're memories," I say.

"They are." Maeve smiles. "And this way I get to dress rehearse their destruction. Preemptively grieve their loss. This way I get to do something. Instead of sitting around, waiting to forget."

For a moment while she's speaking I have that free-falling sensation. This time it's clear I'm falling towards something in particular, but the feeling passes before I can grasp what that something is.

"If they're all memories, then that's you kneeling by the edge of the bed praying."

Maeve throws her head back and barks laughter.

"I wasn't praying; I was masturbating."

This line lands just as the waiter is delivering our drinks. He pretends not to hear and hurries away, which only makes us laugh more.

"Well, to be fair," I say, "you're much more likely to see God that way."

And at this, we erupt further.

"Right," says Maeve, catching her breath. "Your turn. Why do you write?"

"Christ. I don't know."

I'm trying to avoid answering, but Maeve gives me a look. *Come on*, it says, *I told you my story.*

"I've been thinking about this a lot, actually. But I'm no closer to figuring out what art is or why any of us do it. I suppose, right now, I feel like if I make something sufficiently beautiful, then maybe I can rest."

"Is that what you want?" she asks. "To rest?"

"More than anything. Lately I—"

"Oh shit!" says Maeve, suddenly noticing the time. "I'm so sorry, Kate, I'd better get to the theatre." And as we're downing our drinks she says, "I haven't lost track of time like that in ages."

"Me either. Thank you."

"Thank *you*," she says, and squeezes my hand.

I walk with her to the Arena, happy to kill more time before going back to our house. On the way I tell Maeve why I'm so hesitant to go home.

"It sounds silly now, saying it out loud; I'm avoiding a Christmas tree."

"You want my advice?" she asks when we get to the stage door, then she dishes it out before I can answer. "Decorate the bloody tree. Who knows how many more Christmases you'll have, or trees you'll get to decorate. So savour this one. Imagine it's your last."

It occurs to me that this is how she must live life, draining every drop from it and leaving nothing for later, dealing only in last times and nevermores. With memory removed from the equation, the present moment becomes all the more sacred.

"I'd ask you to stay for the show," says Maeve impishly, "but you've got work to do."

"Thanks again," I say, and we hug before she slips inside the theatre door into that other world she occupies.

When I get home, I do exactly as Maeve said. Working in complete silence, I detangle the string of lights and drape them around the tree before gently lifting each bauble and trinket from the cardboard box labelled CHRISTMAS and hanging them with care. I pay close attention to each and every ornament, the feel of it in my hand and the way the branch dips softly under its weight. There's the little robin redbreast that belonged to my mam, the gleaming silver angels my grandmother left to me, and the porcelain snowflakes you and I bought at that market in Prague.

I have to use a ladder to place the star on top. I drag it in from the shed, and as I climb up, I have visions of myself toppling into the tree, being found here by you on Sunday evening. But I manage it alone. Then I get down and stand back to admire my work. And here's a new feeling: a warm sense of satisfaction with this moment, and with it a desire, stronger than ever, for you to be here to share it with me. Since the breakup, I've missed you most when I'm at my lowest, but for the first time I'm not lonely, and I don't need you, I just want you all the same. When we moved in here a few months ago,

I'd imagined us hauling a tree home together, you curating a Christmas playlist for us to work to, ambling through markets and buying new decorations. Ones we'd take out years from now. Ones our kids would someday lift lovingly from a cardboard box and think of us, think of home.

Another thing I have to let go of. Another home I'll never know.

I sink to the floor where I sit and bawl so hard that I can't catch my breath. Then I pick up my phone and type out a message to you, trying to think of a good enough reason to get in touch.

"So sorry to bother you," I begin, knowing and not caring one iota how stupid this is. "Just wanted to say thank you for the tree."

You've read it within seconds, and you reply straightaway.

"My pleasure," you say. But I don't want that to be the end of it.

"Don't suppose you know where the ladder is? I need it to put the star on."

A pause. And then.

"Try the shed down the end of the garden."

"I'll have a look," I reply, then I continue to sit with my back against the sofa and knees pulled up to my chest. After an appropriate amount of time has passed, I send another message. "Got it. Thanks so much!"

"No worries," you say, and that's that. The hit is short-lived and doesn't help at all. In fact, being within such close reach of you makes me feel even further away. Then I see you type. And stop. Type. And stop. I realise I'm holding my breath, clutching the phone in two hands, staring at it like something magical is about to happen. Finally another message comes through.

"Just so you know, I'm heading home for Christmas this weekend. I'll be there all week, so if you need to come back at all the place is yours. I know your dad's house can get a bit much."

At this, a fresh wave of tears begins to flow. Because you know me. And I can't imagine teaching all of me to someone new. Learning a new language from scratch. I can't fathom anyone but you joining me for the non-week between Christmas and New Year's to act as a conversational buffer between me and my dad, listening to him bang on about whichever politician's biography he's just read in order to avoid talking about anything real. Last year we got a two-hour monologue on de Valera and you sat patiently through the whole thing, refilling his tea every time he ran out, joking afterwards that you thought he might eventually need a toilet break, but no, he just kept going. I don't want someone else in that situation. I want the devil I know, the devil who knows me.

It's been fifteen minutes since your last message. I'm dragging this out now. Not wanting to close our thin line of communication.

"I'll probably try and stick it out. Haven't seen him much this year. But thanks, Finn. Thanks for knowing."

I delete and retype this last line a few times and then finally hit send.

"Of course," you say. And another ten minutes pass, in which

I wonder where you are right now. What you're doing. Whether you're alone on your brother's sofa or out at a pub with friends. Maybe you're on a date, preoccupied and struggling to keep up with the conversation while you think of what to say to me. Or is this not a big deal to you? Are you barely giving it a second thought? You're hardly sitting on the floor crying over it, are you?

"At the cinema with Scott. About to go in now."

"What are you seeing?" I ask, aware this is the first official deviation from anything strictly logistical.

"*Die Hard*."

"Classic."

"Knew you'd appreciate that."

But before I can reply you say, "Okay, gotta go. I hope you have a nice Christmas."

"You too, Finn."

Again, you type and stop. Type and stop. Then say, "Be careful on that ladder please."

"I will."

I read over and over this brief exchange, wringing it dry for hidden meaning. And for the next few hours I rest easy knowing where you are, who you're with, and that I'm on your mind.

THE KEENING

I wake up at home. And by home, I mean my father's house in Colligeen. It takes me a moment to adjust to my childhood bedroom: the imposing brown wardrobe and dark wood floors, the sky-blue wallpaper dotted all over with little white m's—faraway seagulls in flight.

I hear the swish-swash of the sea below. An arrhythmic thumping. And from there the nightmare takes its usual course.

I'm barefoot on the landing. I'm descending the mahogany stairs. The front door is flung wide open as always. In the living room, stale yellow light. In the kitchen, I burn my hand on a coffeepot. In the basement, the music stops, and I reach to close the high, thin window at the back of the room before turning to see my mother.

A twist.

She is facing away from me—not drowned, not human at all, but moulded from clay: a striking white statue towering on a stone plinth at the centre of the room. Her pristine marble back is rounded forward, unable to bear the weight of the co-lossal wings that protrude from her shoulder blades, breaking through the skin like fractured bones and rising impossibly high. She is the antithesis of the *Winged Victory*, her posture one not of heart-forward triumph but of hunched defeat, and her face carved into a look of resigned agony.

On the walls all around me, displayed in baroque frames, are portraits of my mother, the faces of which have been smeared beyond recognition. Beside each one is a tiny descriptive plaque. I'm trying to read one when suddenly the sculpture's wings start to crack and break. Plumes of thick, velvety black feathers burst through the marble as it falls away in chalky chunks onto the floor. And then the wings begin to beat, labo-riously lifting and lowering, gathering momentum and creat-ing gusts of dusty wind as they go. They flutter and flail up and down, up and down, but she's too heavy; they can't possibly lift her. The wind gathers, growing so forceful that I have to shield my eyes as shards of broken rock are flung my way. As I turn my face, I can just about make out the sound of her scream-ing in the din.

"Look!" she shrieks, and I'm awake in my bed again. Star-ing at the seagulls on the walls. Listening to the sea outside. A strong breeze blows through the house. My bedroom door rattles on its hinges. *Here we go again*, I think, as I pull on a robe and float downstairs to investigate. The front door is flung wide open. A gust of wind rushing in. But this time, I see my father outside. He's walking towards the house with an old leather suitcase in his hand. Then he lifts his head and stares straight at me, his face stern.

"Look!" he shouts.

"What?" I manage.

"Look who's here!" And with that a gloved hand lands on my shoulder. I scream. Aunt Kathy screams back. She's standing behind me in a burgundy duffle coat, face flushed pink from the cold.

"Jesus!" she yelps, placing one hand on her heart.

"Shit," I say. "Sorry."

"What's wrong with the pair of you at all?" asks my father, shaking his head as he plops the suitcase by the bottom of the stairs and closes the front door, stopping the breeze as he does so.

"She started it," jokes Kathy, then she pulls me in for a hug and switches to Gaelic. "Nollaig Shona duit, a stór."

"Happy Christmas, Aunt Kathy," I reply into her shoulder, still readjusting to the waking world.

"I was beginning to think you weren't joining us for the big day," says my dad, and I feign a laugh.

"What time is it?" I groan.

"Never mind him, treasure, it's just gone 10 a.m.," says Kathy, and she squeezes me harder while my dad fusses about.

"You're shaking," she says, drawing back to get a proper look at me. It's exactly the same look my mother gave me as a child, when I'd fallen off my bike or banged my head on something. She'd grip me by the shoulders and stare into my face with a dour expression.

"What's the matter?" Kathy asks.

"Nothing," I say. Because telling her would mean admitting that the nightmares never stopped, and that's a lie I've harboured too long now to let go of.

"Just got a fright," I add, but Kathy can read me just as well as my mam could, and as she screws up her face, I can see her mentally logging this for later.

"C'mere," she says, and hugs me again, more tenderly this time. I'm savouring the feel of her bobbly coat against my cheek as my dad barrels past us towards the kitchen, mumbling something about a ham.

"Ah yes, the ham," says Kathy.

"Imported from Norway," I say.

"Fifteen percent off!" we chime together.

"So, you've heard, then," she says.

"I've been here for five days, Kathy."

"Say no more," she says, and laughs. "You go get ready and I'll hold down the fort." Then she follows my dad into the kitchen, shouting, "Smells delicious, Tony!"

It was Aunt Kathy who stopped the clocks. The day of my mother's wake. Then she covered the mirrors and opened all the windows and doors to help Mam's spirit on its way. Old Irish traditions all, the same ones she'd observed for her mother and father when they died, but I doubt she ever thought she'd be shepherding her little sister's soul into the otherworld. My father was there, and technically the job should have fallen to him, but much like my mother he was present only in the sense that his body was in the room. We may as well have laid him in a shroud on the table next to her and decorated him with wildflowers too.

Kathy had me pick the flowers from the garden, one of the

many tasks she delegated to me that day. At the time I resented being asked to do so much—after all, my mother had just died—but now I understand what she knew then, that idleness is a dear friend of despair. And so, together, we adorned my mother's linen chrysalis in daisies and cowslips, buttercups, brambles, and sea aster, as all the while my aunt cried silently, saving her voice for the keening to come.

It wasn't till the sandwiches were made and the tea was brewed, customs observed and loved ones gathered round, that Kathy allowed herself to keen. As I've said, grief waits. And it waited patiently for her that day.

I had never seen, or heard, a keening; the ancient pagan practice was stamped out by the Church, along with so many of our ways. I was standing next to my father, who was seated by my mother's feet, his right hand resting on her ankle, the other gripping a glass of whisky—the only time I've ever seen him drink. Aunt Kathy was stood at the head of the table, and all around us were the faces of adults I somewhat knew: friends and colleagues who had come and gone over the years, some more often than others. A hush fell. And I remember the wrenching dread that came over me, how my tummy turned and my little limbs grew rigid when my aunt opened her mouth, and instead of the dulcet Connemara brogue I'd come to know, a primaeval roar escaped her lips. It was as though a demon had been caged inside her ribs this whole time and was finally set loose.

Somewhere between a scream, a song, and a convulsion,

the sound she emitted was like grief in motion, rushing through the room fast as wildfire. Occasionally, its flames were dampened as though by a wet cloth, then they rose once again in another wail of unbridled anguish. I can still hear it to this day, that sound. That brutal stream of raw, wordless rites that erupted from her with such force that I felt displaced, rooted in neither this realm nor the next. Aunt Kathy's voice soared, carrying with it the cries of her ancestors—the bean chaointe, the keening women, the thousands of grieving mothers and sisters and daughters who came before—and together, for a brief time, they turned our ordinary dining room into a threshold between worlds. It's the closest I've felt to my mother since she died, the veil between us thinner in that moment than in any other since.

Later, at the graveside, Kathy recited one final prayer in a hoarse and raspy whisper, barely audible to anyone but her.

She stayed with us for a few weeks after that, her presence like a salve on an open wound. Each day she got me up and dressed, out for brisk walks on the beach and lunches at the local GAA club—we'd bring our books with us and get multiple refills of tea—and all the while we'd talk about my mother, her sister, in a way that made missing her okay. Meanwhile, my father was aggressively avoiding grief, moving quickly to deny what had happened.

You hear about widowers keeping their wives' belongings for years. Everything exactly as it was. Oxidising. Gathering dust. But before a month had passed, my father had removed most traces of my mother from our home, like letters tossed into a fire, their scarlet paper hissing and then marrying the air. Kathy made him keep her odd-shaped pottery, all the framed wedding photos, and the oil painting above the stairs. She even helped me pick out photos of my mam to hang in my bedroom—I noted there were none left in his.

Evenings, after I'd been put to bed, I'd sneak back to the top of the stairs and listen to them talking in the living room. One night, I heard him ask my aunt to stay with us, and I remember leaning forward, my hands gripping the bannisters, as I listened for her answer. But Kathy had gone through her first cancer scare just a year prior, and she needed to get back to her beloved west coast—which she still talks about each time she visits like a creature she can't bear to be without. "There's healing there," she told me once, when I asked why she loves her home so much. Besides, she told my dad, her sister had just died. And she needed to grieve too, on her own time, in her own way.

"Right you be," was all he said to that.

Kathy told him I was welcome to visit. She said she'd love to have me. And that was when he asked her to take me with her. Just like that.

"Take her," he said, and I didn't wait to hear the reply. I was back in bed, screaming into my pillow, before she could answer him.

"Will you have another spud there, Katie?" But he's already putting it on my plate before I can tell him I'm full.

"Katherine? One for you?"

"Go on so," she says, and he dishes out another. He's

wearing a pink paper crown and smiling contentedly at the scene before him: empty plates, gravy stains on the tablecloth, Christmas crackers ripped in half. We already read all the shitty jokes aloud. That killed about five minutes.

The dinner itself was delicious—I forget sometimes how good a cook he is. Although he still doesn't seem to derive much joy from it; the man assembles each meal like he's defusing a bomb—tense, meticulous, bristling at every slight disturbance.

"Well, have you any news for me at all, Tony?" asks Kathy, smothering her potato in salt.

"Divil a bit, Kathy," Dad replies, then winces as she pops the oversalted potato in her mouth, just like my mother used to. They are so alike; Kathy has the same dark hair and sea-blue eyes, only hers are wilder on both counts, the yang to my mother's yin. Certain mannerisms are the same—the way they park themselves in front of an open fireplace or lean against a kitchen counter as they talk. The way they absentmindedly carry tea towels from room to room, leaving them all over the house and then wondering aloud where all the towels have got to. Kathy is a much sturdier woman—Mam had a dainty physique—but still, in certain lights the two were often confused for each other. In fact, Kathy borrowed one of my mother's black dresses for the funeral—she had rushed all the way across the country and didn't think to bring one—and several times throughout the day I thought it was her, standing in our hall, leaning in the doorway of the church, crouched by her own graveside. Today I find myself staring at Kathy—the wiry greys in her hair, the delicate lines around her eyes—and wondering if this is how my mother would have looked if she had lived. How time might have changed her, had it been given the chance.

"And yourself?" Kathy asks me. "How's Finn? Will he be joining us tomorrow?"

"Not this year," is all I say, and they exchange a look.

"Right you be," says my dad, at which point I excuse myself to go cry in the bathroom for twenty minutes, making some comment about eating too many Brussels sprouts as I leave the table.

This wasn't how I pictured it. Any of it. But especially today. This was supposed to be our first Christmas together, in a home that we had made. We were supposed to visit our families and then go back to that home to hide in each other till the New Year. We were supposed to be starting something, not ending it.

Sitting on the edge of the bath, I bite on my knuckles to stop my cries from escaping. Everything in me wants to reach out to you for comfort. Everything in me thinks the weight of your arms around me will end the pain I feel.

Because you look and sound so much like him, the man I miss, the man I love. But you're not him. You haven't been for some time. And crawling back to you would be no different from crawling inside my mother's coffin to be with her; she wasn't in there, just something that looked a lot like her.

And suddenly it's not you I want, but her. Her arms around me. Her voice in my ear. Her hand smoothing my hair down my back.

I want my mammy.

I could scream. I could open my mouth and wail like Kathy did all those years ago. I could call forth all the women who've grieved before me and let their voices tear into this world like demons being birthed. Allow my body to be nothing but a conduit for grief. A bridge between worlds. I could fucking howl. But I don't. I wipe my eyes, splash some water on my face, practice smiling in the mirror, and head back downstairs.

Kathy suggests a game of Monopoly. That kills another two hours.

We pass the evening in front of the TV—a monolithic flatscreen that, along with the induction hob and the ice maker on the fridge, has no place in this house, with its mismatched dad decor that hasn't seen an update in well over a decade: the brown floral carpet that bleeds into the wallpaper, the curtains that fall too far below the sill and too high above the floor. I can abide it only by telling myself what I tell myself when it comes to any aspect of my father: he tried.

I absent myself from *It's a Wonderful Life* several times, making my fourth trip to the loo just as George Bailey is about to lose all hope. This time, Aunt Kathy follows me and I step out of the bathroom to find her leaning on the bannister with her arms folded, her face a gentle frown. She doesn't say anything.

"We broke up," I tell her. She nods. She knew.

"Heartbreak is the fucking worst," she concedes, as I slouch against the doorframe.

"How did you cope after Sarah left?" I ask, and a desperate laugh escapes her.

"I didn't!" she says. "I didn't cope at all. Almost flung my-self off the Cliffs of Moher one night."

"Jesus," I say.

Sarah left the moment Kathy recovered from the mastec-tomy. She nursed her back to health, then announced she'd been seeing some twenty-two-year-old diving instructor she met on holiday in Portugal. Classic. She moved out the next day. Left Kathy in an awful state. Worse than I'd realised, ap-parently.

"That's what grief does to you." Kathy shrugs. "But here I am almost a decade later, cancer-free, chaos-free, happy as a pig in shite. There's not a day goes by that I don't count as a blessing. And would you believe, last week I thought about Sarah, and I couldn't remember her last name!?"

I smile my first real smile of the day.

"Almost killed myself over the bitch and now I can't even remember her name!"

We're both laughing when Dad calls up from the bottom of the stairs, "Cheese and crackers, anyone? Mince pies? Pud-ding? I could whip up some cream!"

"I'd love a mince pie, thanks, Tony," shouts Kathy, as she throws me a lopsided smile that says, *He's trying.*

"Same for me, thanks," I add.

"I'll leave the film on pause till ye come down," he says, and plods off to the kitchen. Kathy's smile grows nostalgic then, and her eyes come to rest on something long gone.

"I have him to thank, you know. For saving me."

"Who? Tony?"

"Yes." She laughs. "Tony."

"I can't imagine he offered much sage counsel in your time of need."

"I didn't need counsel," she tells me. "I needed someone to be there. And he was. He came to Connemara. Stayed almost a month. Repaid the favour, I suppose."

"I'd no idea."

"Well, he probably didn't want to worry you."

I can tell she's trying to kindle my sympathy for him, but somehow this only makes me angrier; she got to experience a version of him I never did.

"Make your peace with him, love."

"I don't know how," I snap. "I don't know how to make peace with any of it." Something about this house reduces me to a teenager. I can feel it happening but I'm powerless to stop it. Kathy notices I'm fighting back tears and once again she hugs me, smoothing my hair down my back until I can't hold them in anymore.

"You'll find the answer," she whispers. "You just have to look."

But I'm distracted by the sight of my mother's painting over Kathy's shoulder. My whole life, this oil on canvas—which has always hung here, unchanging—has taken on different meanings depending on my mood. There are days the sky is bluer, the sunrise brighter, the sea a little calmer. There are days the waves threaten to swallow the lone figure at the centre of the scene, standing with her back to us. Days she seems lost, days she seems fierce, days she seems resolute. Tonight, through my tears, the scene ripples and distorts, and for the first time, the woman on the beach is not alone. There are two

women standing side by side. And the sun isn't rising but setting. The silhouettes wobble and waver and I feel myself lurch
in Aunt Kathy's arms. The free fall. The onrushing ground.
Then I blink and the woman is alone once again. Kathy's gripping me by the shoulders, searching my face, then she turns to
follow my gaze.

"Abbie was a very talented painter," she says.

I can't focus on the rest of the film. As George Bailey darts
about his hometown, confronted by memories of a life he
didn't live, I'm thinking about my conversation with Maeve
last week; how I spent a whole day with a painter and didn't
think to tell her that my mother was a painter too. I'm not entirely sure I saw her as one.

She painted. She loved to paint. But was she a painter?

People talk a lot about the things they didn't get to say to
loved ones while they were alive. I've never found that to be
the case—after all, I was nine, and nine-year-olds don't have
a lot of important shit to say. There are things I'd tell her now,
of course. Every day since the day she left there have been
things I've wanted to tell her, about her death, about my life,
about all the breakups and breakdowns and breakthroughs I've
had. A year after she died, I wanted to tell her that I found the
floral notebook I thought I'd lost—it had slipped between
the back seats of dad's car and stayed there till he folded them
one morning to fit some luggage in. She'd spent a whole day
looking for that notebook with me. And it seemed important that
she know it had been found. When I was sixteen, on a school

trip to London, I wanted to tell her that I saw her favourite shade of lipstick in a pharmacy near Soho Square, and bought one for myself. When I was twenty-one, I wanted to tell her I had missed my period and I might be pregnant with the baby of some boy I'd slept with at a party. Turns out I wasn't, but I wanted to tell her that too. I wanted to tell her about Charlie, and you, and writing my first book. Last winter, I wanted to tell her that I made the perfect pot of soup.

Mostly, though, I have questions. I've had a million questions over the years, about thongs and tits and boys and blood and choosing the perfect partner or the right foundation for my skin tone. Lately, I want to ask her about her. I want to know her better. I want to know the woman she was and the woman she wanted to be. And today, I add a new question to the list: Did she consider herself a painter?

She never exhibited her work. But there are plenty of well-known painters who never sold or even showed a painting in their lifetime. Van Gogh is the most obvious example—"Van Gogh never sold a painting" being the phrase we wheel out every time an artist doubts their talent based on a lack of money or fame. The truth is that Van Gogh did sell at least one painting, *The Red Vineyard*, but that's beside the point; he's one of the world's most revered and renowned artists and he had no idea while he was alive.

Then there are those who knew exactly what their work meant and chose to keep it from us all the same. Mam used to tell me the story of Hilma af Klint (only she called her Hilma, like they were on first-name terms). Hilma was a Swedish painter who started out painting landscapes, just like my mother, but her work was drastically altered by her life experiences. When she was eighteen, her ten-year-old sister, Hermina, died from influenza and Hilma's interest in spiritualism was ignited. Every week for ten years, she conducted seances with four other women artists, and they became known as the Five. They believed that other realities existed beyond the observable world and, as well as attempting to commune with these other planes of existence, they would experiment with automatic writing and drawing guided by the unconscious— something the surrealists wouldn't attempt for decades to come. It was during one of these meetings with the Five that Hilma says an entity named Amaliel came to her and "commissioned" her to paint what would become known as the *Paintings for the Temple*, a series of 193 astonishing works spanning almost a decade of Hilma's life and culminating in the *Altarpieces*, my mother's three favourite paintings. Framed prints of the trio have been hanging side by side in our living room since long before I was born—one of the few things my dad would never dare get rid of. I glance over at them now and am struck, as ever, by how powerful yet calming they are; brimming with intense colours and commanding geometric shapes, the paintings take me on a journey while simultaneously grounding me in the present moment. They are more like blueprints for spiritual healing than brushstrokes on a page, and it makes sense, looking at them now, that Hilma claimed to have been merely a medium through which the universe itself brought these works into being.

I know that feeling, or at least I have known it; when the words seem to be coming *through* me, not *from* me. There have been moments in my writing life when it was as though the words already existed, invisible transmissions beaming through the ether that I picked up like a radio receiving sound waves, providing them with shape and form.

I wonder if my mother ever felt that way—if she ever slipped into that fugue-like state and emerged to find her blank page full of beauty. Hilma, apparently, experienced this frequently. She painted prolifically, creating monumental masterpieces in a matter of days and then sinking into a postpartum-like depression before being able to resume her work, which she did in secret and never showed to anyone. She was the true pioneer of abstract art, before Kandinsky, Malevich, or Mondrian, and yet she didn't consider herself an artist and didn't want her work to be seen. She even stipulated in her will that her work should not be exhibited until at least twenty years after her death, asserting that the world "wasn't ready for it."

Vivian Maier, a Chicago-based photographer, went one step further; she never exhibited her work and apparently never planned to either. Maier was a nanny for over forty years, during which time she led an entirely separate and secret life as a street photographer, surreptitiously snapping over 150,000 photographs, most of which remained undeveloped. She stashed away the negatives in storage lockers around the city, and in 2007, a real estate agent bought a box of them at an auction. He developed them and, realising the talent he'd stumbled upon, set out to uncover the rest of the collection, as well as the identity of the artist behind them. The woman he found was intensely private, a quiet, careful observer of tiny human moments, humdrum dramas, and sweetly surreal slices of Americana, a woman who saw the divine in the mundane, captured it, then hid it away for reasons beyond anyone's comprehension. Perhaps in Vivian's case, it wasn't the world who wasn't ready for her, but she who wasn't ready for the world. Perhaps she understood the sad truth, that had she been able to afford the printing and exhibiting required to make a name for herself, her pictures might not have been taken seriously, or worse still, they might have been stolen.

I often wonder if the mystery surrounding her motives and the tantalising nature of this serendipitous discovery were required to propel her into the limelight. Her story is unquestionably appealing. So appealing, in fact, that it tends to get in the way of her photos, like a rogue thumb across the lens— people can't see past it to the beauty beyond. And her work is beautiful—she was clearly an accomplished photographer who knew how good she was. A pioneer, just like Hilma, she is constantly compared to her male contemporaries, like Eggleston and Shore, when, also like Hilma, we should really be comparing those men to her. After all, Maier was doing what they became famous for a decade before they did it. And she never asked for anything in return. Not even to be seen. She died penniless in a retirement home after selling most of her possessions, never knowing what would become of her art. Like Moses's parents entrusting him to the world, only instead of a basket of reeds it was a suitcase, and instead of a river, a storage locker in Chicago.

And what of the art that never made it safely to shore? The

countless artists who found catharsis and nothing more. At what point does art become art? Inception? Execution? Publication? Is the work itself enough? Or does art require a witness?

If I pull a rabbit from a hat and there's nobody around to see it . . .

I miss the end of the movie. Dozing off with a plate of half-eaten crackers on my lap, I'm vaguely aware of the sounds around me; the annual reminder that every time a bell rings an angel gets his wings. Aunt Kathy kisses me good night—she's staying in my room—and my father gently takes my plate and covers me in a blanket. He lingers in the doorway for ages like he's got something to say. Then he leaves.

In the morning I am ripped from sleep by a deafening screech and the hectic flapping of a bird about my head. It's a small, mottled thing, no bigger than my fist, that keeps flitting past my face, darting in and out of corners, and then returning to claw at me again. I cover my head with the blanket and wait, knowing that the dream will soon shift—I'll hear the banging in the basement, go investigate, and find her there in some form or other. I consider beginning my journey now, getting it over with, but this bird really is relentless. Its cries are growing more and more distressed each time it circuits the room.

"Look!" it caws. "Look! Look!"

Now my father is here. He comes running into the room all bleary eyes and bed head, shouting my name again and again. I don't respond. I just peek out from the blanket to watch him chase the bird from one wall to the other and back again. At one point he clambers up onto an armchair and leaps at the bird, but it evades him.

"Out you go," he's saying. "Go on, out you go."

He has opened all the windows now and is trying to direct the bird towards them, but it doesn't want to leave. It keeps clinging to the corners, scurrying between them when it sees my father coming.

"Katie," he yelps, "help please!"

I sit up, staring blankly at the scene unfolding around me, and find myself wondering what the symbolism of this particular nightmare means. Does the bird represent my mother's soul? Do I wish my father had done more to help her on her way? Do I resent the fact that he needs my help? Or is my father just an aspect of my own psyche? I've heard that's common in dreams.

"Katie, for the love of God, will you grab me a brush or something?"

It's the TV that gives it away; the television of my dreams is a bulky old box of a thing, a relic from the nineties, but here is my dad's ridiculous flat-screen, with its slick black surface and sharp edges. And there's the pint of water he left for me last night. And my suitcase on the floor.

"Oh," I say, and I stand up to help the man I now realise is my actual father. He looks at me as if to ask where I've been, as together we wrangle the shaking, squawking bird into an alcove. The commotion comes to an abrupt halt when Dad finally catches the bird in his hands, his sturdy old fingers enveloping its wings and feet in a gentle cocoon.

"Poor thing is terrified," he says, carrying the tiny creature to the window, moving slowly so as not to frighten it further. Once there, he pauses, carefully turning the bird over in his hands, checking for injuries. A look of soft concentration comes over his face, accentuating the deep lines around his mouth and eyes. He looks like a well-weathered rock.

"There, there," he murmurs. "It's alright. You're alright."

Visions of me puking in the back of our old Ford Fiesta, somewhere between Courtown and home. Dad pulling over to let me out. Standing with me by the side of the road. My mother rolling down the car window behind us.

"Is she alright, Tony?"

"She'll be grand, love. Just a little carsick."

I can feel the steady slab of his hand on my back.

"There, there. You're alright."

Once satisfied, my father takes a moment to pet the top of the bird's head, then releases it with gusto into the day.

Over breakfast, Dad and Kathy talk at length about the bird, speculating as to where he came from and how he got into the house; the prevailing theory is that he came down the chimney and through the fireplace—though there was no soot on him, and no marks at all on the wallpaper. The pair even go so far as to assure each other that the bird is fine now, reunited with his family no doubt.

"They're probably all sat over breakfast talking about us!" says Kathy, pleased with her own joke. Dad slaps the table laughing, and when his cousin calls for their annual St. Stephen's Day catch-up, the bird is all he wants to talk about, including the part about me being completely useless, of course.

"I don't know what's got into that one," I overhear him saying.

While he gossips on the phone and Kathy packs up her things, I take myself down to the beach for a walk. The breeze has a bite to it today, and despite wrapping up in two coats— my own and my dad's—I have to brace my body against the cold. I stroll along the water's edge where the sand is hardest, but the wind still whips the odd soft patch of it against the side of my face.

I think it's just me on the beach, until I notice someone further down the shoreline; a woman all in black looking out to sea. She's standing completely still and at first this doesn't bother me, but the closer I get to her the more disquieted I feel; she hasn't moved an inch. Five minutes pass. Ten. She grows larger and larger in my field of vision, but still she doesn't move.

"Hello," I call out, but the wind catches my voice and flings it back at me. I decide to give the woman a wide berth, swerving away from the water in a huge semicircle, but as I pass directly behind her, I glance to my right and am struck when I see her dark silhouette dwarfed against the sea, just like my mother's painting.

Suddenly she calls out. She's screaming at the water. But I can't hear what she's saying. One word. Over and over.

I search the length of the beach but there's nobody here. Just me and her and this one word I can't quite make out. Without realising, I've begun walking towards her, my feet crunching through shells as I go. I'm a few feet away when she yells again.

"Larry!" she calls, and with that a golden retriever comes bounding out of the frothy waves, soaking wet and beaming joy. The woman runs to him, hurriedly attaching his leash as he shakes himself off, drenching her in the process. She notices me then and rolls her eyes good-naturedly.

"He got away from me," she shouts over the wind, and I can just about muster a smile in return as she leads Larry away, leaving me alone by the water's edge. Only I'm not alone. Grief is with me. Grief is always with me. Its presence more potent in this place than anywhere else. I turn towards home, and it follows me, like a terrible shadow that can't be seen. A weightless, formless shimmer that leaves no mark in the real world but carves itself onto my insides all the same.

Back at the house, my father is loading up Aunt Kathy's car, stacking the boot with a dozen Tupperware boxes full of yesterday's leftovers.

"Don't worry!" he says. "There's plenty left for dinner tonight."

I hurry past in search of distraction, which I find in the form of Aunt Kathy kneeling by the bookcase in my father's study with a stack of old paperbacks by her side. She's got one pair of glasses on her head and she's holding another broken pair up to her face as she scans the book spines in front of her. I slump into the desk chair, still a bit breathless.

"I'm taking these ones, Tony," she says. Then, turning around: "Oh, it's yourself. Nice walk?"

"Yeah," I say. "What have you got there?"

"Biographies, mostly. Your dad's not really one for fiction."

As well I know. I'm not sure if he's even read my first book. "Well done," he said when I asked him about it. "Fair play."

"Speaking of," says Kathy, lowering her glasses to look at me, "I know you're not supposed to ask a writer how the writing's going . . ."

"But you're asking anyway?"

"I am."

"Well, Kathy. I started writing this book on the first of November, and so far, I have what could generously be described as sweet fuck all."

"November first?" she asks.

"Yeah?" I say, and she grins.

"Your mammy always started new projects on Samhain too."

My ears prick up at the mention of my mother—the promise of information about her evoking a feeling not unlike the one I get when I see a note from you on the wall of our house. A hit. A fix. A tiny taste. Only this one isn't sour.

"Did she? Why?" I ask.

"It's the Celtic New Year," Kathy answers. "I assumed that's why you picked it."

"No. I'd no idea."

"Well, some things you don't need to be taught," says Kathy. "Some knowing runs deeper."

It's comforting, the notion that parts of my mother lie

dormant in me, weaved into the fabric of my being, waiting to make themselves known. But the thought also sends a shiver through me, and I don't know why.

"Why would they have New Year at the start of November?" I ask, eager to change the subject. Kathy's jaw drops in surprise.

"Deary me, child, did my sister teach you nothing?"

With that she's standing up, holding her glasses to her eyes again as she tilts her head to read the titles of the books along the top shelf.

"There's a book here you should read," says Kathy. "Where has it got to?"

She's mumbling to herself about ancient druidic practices while I stare out the window at my father, who has opened Kathy's car bonnet and appears to be refilling her washer fluid.

"Ah!" she says, tugging at the top corner of a leather-bound book, smiling fondly at it as she dusts it off and hands it to me. On the book's dark green cover there are nine trees in a circle, all embossed in faded gold. I run a finger across their branches as I read the title aloud.

"*Imbas*," I say, looking to Kathy for its meaning. She bites her lip as she turns inwards in search of the English word.

"There isn't a direct translation. Imbas is a sort of knowledge. Or inspiration, I suppose. And those are hazel trees." She points. "The tree of wisdom."

She's telling me about the Salmon of Knowledge, and the nine sacred hazel trees that grew around the well where it swam, when I open the book and am caught off guard by the inscription on the first page: *For Abigail. Mo dheirfúir. Mo sholas. Mo chroí.*

"I'd forgotten," says Kathy with a sad smile. "You don't need a translator for that, surely."

"For Abigail," I say. "My sister. My light. My heart." And Kathy's lips curl inwards as her eyes fill with tears.

"I gave it to her for Christmas one year," she says. "And now I'm giving it to you."

I close the book, pressing one palm into its surface as though it might somehow imbue me with a piece of her.

"Thank you, Kathy," I say, and then a question forms on my lips without my meaning it to. "Where are the rest of my mam's paintings?"

She stops short and looks at me, her face full of something I can't quite place. Kathy's about to speak when my dad does instead.

"What do you mean, Katie?" he asks from the doorway. He seems genuinely perplexed. "Sure they're all over the house."

He's right. It's not just the oil painting on the landing. There's a whole collection of watercolours in the study—meadows and mountains and coastlines from around the country. She used to go for long drives, hike up to spots she'd heard about and make sketches there, then return to the basement to paint. Dozens of those sketches are bound together in thick, heavy books that we keep on the coffee table. And last year Aunt Kathy convinced my dad to hang more of her landscapes in the house.

"I suppose so," is all I say. My mind feels like it's reaching for a high note it can't quite hit.

"There's a few more in the attic," he offers. "I can take them down for you if you'd like."

"Okay, yeah, thanks."

Then he looks to my aunt. "Can I help you with those, Katherine?"

Kathy climbs into her car and gets settled for the long drive ahead.

"Sorry to leave so early," she says. "Don't want to be driving in the dark."

"That's okay," I say. "Thanks for coming all this way. And thanks for the book."

She starts the engine, checks her mirrors, and she's about to reverse out of the driveway when she stops and says, "Come visit me in the West."

"I will."

But she's not satisfied with this.

"There's healing there, a stór," says Kathy, delivering the words like she's pressing a note into the palm of my hand, curling my fingers around it for safekeeping.

Over dinner Dad tells me, not unkindly, that I look exhausted, and suggests I turn in early. He's not wrong. I can't remember the last time I slept through the night.

"Will you be alright if I head up?" I ask, and he chuckles to himself. I feel like I'm missing the joke.

"Katie." He smiles. "I'm well used to being on my own."

He's not saying it for sympathy. He's just stating a fact, that he spends most nights alone. And has done for a very long time. But something about the image of him here, night after night, without her—and without me now for the most part—causes a lump to form in my throat. This is the curse of being an only child with a flawed single parent. To know you are their only family. To be aware at all times that you'll miss them when they're gone but be unable to fully enjoy them while they're here. To want to tell them what they mean to you but be rendered unable as a direct result of how they raised you.

I open my mouth to tell him I love him, but the words stick to my insides like a frightened bird clinging to the corners of a room. This, I realise, is my shrapnel. An old wound that flares up when it rains. Some days, I can't say "I love you."

I hug my dad good night instead—even this seems to surprise him—and when I'm settled in bed, he stops by my room to deliver a hot-water bottle. Once again, he lingers in the doorway on his way out.

"I was sorry to hear about Finn," he says, offering me a thin-lipped smile.

"Thanks, Dad," I say. "Good night."

He pulls my door over, leaving it open a crack just like he used to.

"Night, pet," he says. "Sweet dreams."

≡

I sleep soundly, for the first time in a long time, and in the morning, I find my father shuffling about the kitchen with the radio on—Lyric FM, as always. He's got a copy of the morning paper tucked under his arm as he pours himself a cup of coffee, humming along completely off-key.

"One for yourself?" he asks, waggling the coffeepot at me, and I shake my head. The sun is streaming through the window, tiny white flares of it glaring off the silver sink, and the square of sky I can see outside is a cloudless cornflower blue. I decide to make the most of this rare sunny day in late December, grabbing my coat (I don't need two today) and making my way down to the beach, where everyone else seems to have had the same idea; a shoal of windsurfers are skirting the water's surface, carried along by a much milder breeze than yesterday's, and dozens of people are ambling and jogging all along the shore. As I walk, I pass the lady from yesterday with her golden retriever.

"Keeping Larry on the lead today," she calls over her shoulder, and I laugh easily.

"Good plan!" I tell her.

I stroll the whole length of the beach down to the boulders and back—delicious salt air stinging my lungs all the while—and I'm halfway home when I notice a crowd of people at the shoreline. Larry's owner is there. She's screaming his name like she did before, only these screams sound anguished and urgent, like the bleating of an injured lamb. I rush over to see what's going on, and as I do the crowd parts and there's Larry, the shaggy wet mass of him unmoving on the sand. The lady paces back and forth, hands wringing in front of her. There's a man on his knees next to Larry and she's pleading with him to do something.

"Please," she begs, "please help him!"

The man rhythmically pumps poor Larry's chest, but it's clear the dog is beyond saving; his brown eyes are fixed in a doll-like stare and his tongue is swollen and lolling from one side of his mouth. The other people around him are shaking their heads, mouths agape, glowering in disbelief.

"Oh Jesus," says one woman, when the man, breathless and crying now himself, stops pumping and sits back on his heels. I rush in to comfort his owner, who throws her arms around me and bawls into my hair. All around us, people are mumbling about the freak current and Larry's ruptured lung.

How could they possibly know that?

Larry's owner screams in my ear now.

"Look," she cries, and as I pull back it's not her I see but my own face staring back at me.

"Look," says this other me, gesturing towards Larry, and when I look down it's my mother's bloated body on the sand, her skin grey and her face a blurred mess of wet oil paint. The sky darkens as clouds rapidly gather, then the other me disappears, along with the rest of the crowd.

I throw myself down beside my mother and try to scoop her body up. I want to take her home. Away from the encroaching tide. But I can't carry her; I'm only nine years old and my little arms aren't strong enough. I try again, and as I do, pieces of her break and fall away in my hands. Huge chunks of her are sloughing off now, foul black water gushing out. The stench is unthinkable. And then she disintegrates completely, leaving me face down in the sand, with cold seawater lapping at my feet.

I roll over to see the stars above me, countless stars encasing the night, as all around the wind keens for her, wailing its way mournfully down the beach. I want so badly to keen with it, to open my mouth and scream. But nothing comes. I'm shaking so hard now that my back teeth smash together, and then I'm awake, shivering violently in bed, soaked in my own sweat and tears, still sobbing over half-remembered happenings.

Unable to sleep, and aware the sun will soon be rising, I creep downstairs to make myself some tea, then I take it with me to the front step. Bundling myself up in blankets, I wait in the half-light for dawn to come, as overhead a murder of crows rallies round.

Have you ever seen one? A murder? They swoop in. Chaotic perfection. Orderly nonsense. Flying, gliding, dancing, diving. Quiet. Save for the occasional caw. The odd new note heard on the air. They fade into the distance, quick as they came, twirling around some invisible force like embers round a fire. And in their wake, a silent sincerity, an imperfect cadence. A sign of something unfinished. And the threat of something worse on the way.

I KISSED SOMEONE
(IT WASN'T YOU)

I told my dad I had plans for New Year's so that I could come back to our house and spend it alone. Now I'm here and immediately regretting that decision; this place is like a breeding ground for thoughts of you.

I wonder what your Christmas was like, whether you missed me, whether your family missed me. I wonder if I should have texted Ruth. I consider calling you now. Finding some excuse to talk. But as it stands you might be operating under the assumption that I'm out every night, drinking and flirting so heavily that I've forgotten you exist. And I'd hate to rob you of that fear.

The fear is, of course, my own; I'm convinced you're dragging Scott from bar to bar every night, that you haven't thought about me in days. He'll no doubt throw a New Year's Eve party tomorrow, and you'll no doubt kiss someone at midnight. The only solace I can find is in knowing you well enough to know it won't feel the same; you'll wish you were kissing me instead.

"You kiss with your whole body," you'd tell me, and I'd smile, pushing myself harder against you as though to emphasise your point. There's something almost erotic about imagining you with someone else, knowing you'd rather be with me. Is that weird? Probably. I hardly think you're getting turned on by the thought of me with other men. You're more likely beside yourself with rage. But then, there's something sexy about that too . . .

A shower, I decide. A hot shower. Then fresh pyjamas. And whatever shite is on TV. That'll see me through to bedtime.

Except the shower doesn't help. My want for you has become a physical craving that I can't seem to shake. I lean against the cold tiles and let the water pound against my back, all the while remembering that first time—your fingers lifting my mouth to yours, the way we moved together, the bruises on my belly from our hip bones grinding.

I hate that you still make me feel this way.

Slowly, my right hand strokes my left as though it were you touching me, then it slides down my body and I gasp as the first wave of pleasure hits; I haven't done this since you left.

I'm close to the edge when the unmistakable scent of coffee wafts in through the open door, and without hesitation I turn off the shower and grab my towel, wrapping it around me as I walk onto the landing and drift dutifully down the stairs. I know what I'll find but I'm unsure what form it will take tonight. You. Her. A bird. A dead dog. Or some horrific hybrid. It hardly matters.

Wet footprints lead me up the hallway to the kitchen, where I find you, standing with your back to me just like before. A pot of coffee on the boil beside you. Your dark clothes hanging heavy, clinging to your body, dripping water all over the tiles. Tonight, I realise, it's you who has drowned. And as you begin to turn around, I ready myself for the bloated, faceless version of you I'm about to see.

Surprisingly, your face is intact. Pallid. Tired. But intact. You stare straight at me, unspeaking, still dripping, and right on cue, the Moka pot boils over, spilling thick hot coffee across the hob and down the cupboard doors onto the floor. Eyes still on me, you open your mouth to speak but nothing comes out.

"Finn," I say, as always, and as always, you don't move. Dark brown liquid billows.

"Sorry," you say, but that's not your line. You have no lines in this dream. "I thought you were at your dad's."

"Finn?"

As I step towards you, you finally clock the coffeepot and I see the split-second decision registering on your face; you reach out to pull the pot off the stove and I quickly grab your arm. Understanding, you pick up a towel and move the pot with that instead. Then, wetting another towel, I start to mop up the coffee on the floor.

"How did you know?" you ask, crouching down next to me to help, and I turn my hand over to show you the scar on my palm, the one you've traced in the dark a thousand times.

"I burned it on that coffeepot when I was a kid," I say, but I'm not sure if that's true; my nightmares and memories are becoming one.

You're about to ask another question when the doorbell rings.

"I'll get it." And you leap up, disappearing and then reappearing moments later with a huge pizza box.

"Sorry," you say again. "You said you wouldn't be back, so I assumed the house was—"

"Finn," I say, but you're not listening; you're noticing your footprints.

"And sorry for the mess as well. I'll clean that up. I was going to; I just desperately needed a coffee. But, yeah, sorry, it's your week. I'll take this to Scott's or . . ."

"Finn," I repeat.

"Actually, could I grab some dry clothes first because—"

"Finn!"

"Yes?"

You look at me, and for the first time I feel like you've arrived in the room.

"I'm starving," I say, "and that pizza smells really fucking good."

I become instantly aware that I'm still wearing a towel. As do you, it would seem, because your cheeks flush and you politely avert your gaze. Before you do, though, I catch a flicker of something I've not seen in a very long time: you want me.

"I got a large." You smirk, eyes still on the floor.

"Is that so?"

"Mm-hmm. With extra cheese." You glance up mock-seductively and that crooked smile of yours disarms me.

"I'll go put some clothes on."

"No need."

"Finn!" I warn.

"Right. Yeah. Sorry."

"We're just two people eating pizza, okay?"

"I know," you say, dropping the act, "and I'll head off straight after, I promise."

"Okay."

I maintain my composure till I get to the bedroom, where I close the door behind me and force myself to take deep breaths.

I really should ask you to leave.

But I'm not going to do that, am I?

On the sofa with a pizza between us, it's like we're reliving Halloween all over again. The only real difference is the tension between us now, like static on the air before an earthquake.

"The tree looks great," you say. "You did a lovely job with it."

"Thanks."

A few minutes of chewing in silence. Then I take a quick breath and blurt, "Who did you have over for dinner?"

I can't help myself. It's been running on a low hum in the back of my mind since I came home that day.

"When?" you ask, pulling your chin back slightly.

"I'm not sure. A few weeks ago. I smelled fish. You don't eat fish."

My sentences are coming out in a childlike staccato.

"Quite the little detective." You grin.

"That's not an answer."

"Just some hot older woman," you say, with a casual wave of one hand, but you can tell the joke isn't landing when I scowl.

"It was my mam." You sigh. "She came over to cook me dinner. And I didn't have the heart to remind her I hate fish."

"Oh," I say.

"Oh," you repeat.

"I feel silly now."

"No, don't," you say, taking my hand. "I'm glad you asked. Really. And I'm sorry if that was bothering you."

"That's okay. How is Ruth, anyway?"

"She's good. She misses you."

"I miss her too," I admit, and you give my hand a squeeze before letting go.

I suggest we put a movie on and without missing a beat you say, "*Die Hard*?"

"Didn't you just see that?" I ask, but you throw me a withering glance.

"Yes," I say. "Of course. Stick it on."

We're halfway through the film. The pizza's gone. And neither one of us has mentioned you leaving. Somewhere along the way I get swept up in the moment, stretching my legs out, resting my head on the arm of the sofa, and forgetting what must be done, breaking up, leaving you, leaving this house. For a short while, it's just you and me, watching a movie together.

And, as always, what's weird is how not weird this is. How easily we slip back into being us. It feels like taking a holiday in the past; a brief sojourn to some former version of things. And as I choose to just allow it, I can feel my body soften and my mind start to drift.

When I wake up, my feet are in your lap. You've put a cushion under them, and your hands are resting gently on top. The TV is off. Your eyes are closed, head tilted back. I can tell you're awake, though.

"Hey," I mumble.

"Hey."

Then we're both quiet, listening to the rain thrum against the side of the house.

"Have you big plans for New Year's, then?" you ask. You're trying to sound casual.

"Fran's throwing a party at the theatre."

It's not a lie. Fran is throwing a party. I just don't plan on going.

"Right," you say, but what you don't say is much louder; your frown deepens, your jaw hardens, and your hand tightens ever so slightly around my ankle.

I don't ask where you'll be tomorrow night. I don't want to know. Instead, I ask why you needed a coffee so bad, and you hesitate before you answer.

"Just been having a lot of late nights."

"I see."

"No, not like that," you add quickly.

I decide not to press you, but you offer more anyway.

"I don't sleep as well without you."

I wasn't expecting that. Nor was I expecting the rush that floods me when you slide your hand up my leg a little, or the ache in me when you pull it away.

"I should go," you say.

"No."

"No?" You chuckle.

"No," I say petulantly. "It's pissing rain. And I'm already asleep. What difference will it make if you go now or in the morning?"

"Kate. Let's not complicate things."

"Stay," I insist, and you look at me for a moment, understanding everything I'm not saying.

"Okay. I'll take the couch, though. You go on up to bed."

I do as I'm told. But I lie in bed a long time, resisting the urge to go back downstairs and wondering if you feel the same way. The nearness of you is sickening. The want in me bordering on madness. To be this close. To know you're just a few feet away. That I could have you, if I wanted. I make do with thoughts of you instead, then I fall into a blissfully empty sleep and wake in the morning to find you gone.

Were you here?

Did I dream you?

There are two coffee-stained towels hanging out to dry. And a note on the kitchen table: *Thank you*, is all it says.

New Year's Eve finds me staring at an endless loop of liminal spaces: unfinished construction sites, dreamlike swimming pools with no obvious entrance or exit, mono-yellow hallways in some nondescript hotel. I'm reluctant to call it an addiction, but I can no longer go a day without watching these videos, which get me so close to that feeling of falling, and the sense that at any moment the ground will hit and everything will suddenly make sense. I'm already half a bottle of wine deep— fully engrossed in a bus stop on a barren stretch of road—when the text comes in. It's Fran, reminding me about his party. When I don't respond, he sends another message. Then half an hour later he calls.

"Are you coming or not?" he roars over a deafening pop medley.

"Not," I say.

"Kate!" he wails, and I sit up, brushing biscuit crumbs off my chest.

"What time is it?"

"Just gone half eight," he tells me. "You can still make it."

"I don't have anything to wear," I say, but this is Fran I'm talking to.

"Stick on that little navy dress. With the lacy bit."

"The navy dress with the lacy bit?"

"You wore it to my birthday last year. And as I recall, you wound up outside the pub in it, freezing your tits off while you fought with Finn about God knows what."

I can't tell Fran you stayed over, that I asked you to. I've been ripping out my stitches again, and somehow I don't think my friends will sew me back up this time. If I see Fran, I'll either have to lie to him or tell him the truth, and I'm not sure which is worse.

"I'm not feeling up to it," I say.

"Kate," says Fran, suddenly sincere. "Please come. It's important to me."

Fuck's sake.

I have to rescue the navy dress from the bottom of a bag of clothes I've yet to unpack. It's wrinkled and smells a little stale, so I douse myself in perfume and go, haphazardly applying makeup on the bus.

People are spilling out of the foyer when I arrive, an assortment of angular characters with immaculate eye makeup and the kind of haircut I could never pull off. They're all draped in fur stoles and oversized duster coats, lighting cigarettes for one another and puffing plumes of smoke into the frosty air. One man sporting a sequined bodysuit in Barbie pink holds the door open for me as I arrive and tells me I've got legs for days.

"As do you," I say with a wink.

"Weeks, actually," he shouts after me, and I'm laughing as I make my way through the party, which is positively Gatsbyesque—there's even a band playing swing-style covers of pop anthems. I head straight to the bathroom, where I'm attempting to salvage my back-of-a-bus makeup job when a six-foot-tall stranger in full drag sees me struggling and offers to help. She looks at me like she's appraising wreckage, then gets to work, chatting the whole time in a thick inner-city accent about a love triangle she's got herself involved in. Twins, apparently. One of them is her next-door neighbour. After fifteen minutes of silly gossip, which serves to calm my nerves, she lets me look in the mirror.

"Holy shit!" I shout, and she smirks as she pops her lipstick back in her bag.

"Does needing red lippie to feel okay make me a bad feminist?" I ask, making a pouty face at my own reflection.

"No, darling, it makes you a woman."

At the bar I find Jenna draining a glass of champagne. She squeals when she sees me and stumbles into a hug.

"Two more!" she bellows over my shoulder. God knows how many she's had already. I'm wondering how to ask if she's given up entirely on IVF round four, but she beats me to the punch.

"Just taking some time off from being an incubator you know because honestly fuck that I mean I'll try again eventually I just need a fucking break do ya know what I mean holy shit you look amazing!"

All one sentence. Practically all one word.

"Thanks, Jen," I say, as the barman slides two glasses of bubbly towards us. "And yeah, that's perfectly fair. Let your hair down for once."

"Cheers to that!" shouts Jenna, then she clinks my glass rather violently and knocks her drink back.

"Sláinte," I say, wide-eyed.

"Another!" yells Jenna, and I just about manage to get a glass of water into her before she starts on the next one. I sip on mine. She'll need me to be sober later.

"So how are you?" she asks, with the kind of endearing sincerity only a drunk woman can muster.

"Fine."

"No, you're not."

"No?"

"Nope," she says, one eye half-closed, shaking her head on a diagonal. "You're not fine and you haven't been 'busy writing.'"

She almost drops her champagne flute trying to do the air quotes.

"You're sad," she tells me.

"Am I?"

"Yep. But that's okay, you're allowed to be sad. It's very sad."

"It is."

"Be sad for a bit longer but then you have to start stopping being sad, okay?"

"Okay," I say, stifling a laugh.

"I'm serious!"

"Okay!"

"Okay."

Jenna seems happy with that. She sips her drink and casts a glazed stare across the crowd towards the band, who I've just now noticed are called Vicky and the Vulvas. They're doing a cover of "Fancy" and the crowd is loving it.

"They're actually decent," says Jenna.

"They are." I nod.

"The thing is," she says, and I couldn't even begin to guess what the thing is going to be. "He's not very nice."

I say nothing.

"He's not a very nice person, Kate," she repeats.

"I know."

Jenna takes my hand.

"But he was *your* person."

"He was."

"I get it. I do. You deserve better, though."

"Thank you."

"And you really do look great!" she adds with a twisted smile, nodding a little too fast.

"What can I say? Grief looks good on me."

With that Jenna flings herself at me.

"I love you!" she says, throwing her arms around my neck.

"I love you too, babe."

"I'm here for you," she blubbers. "Okay?"

"Okay," I say.

"Promise?"

"Promise what?" But she looks genuinely perplexed.

"I can't remember."

"Okay," I say. "Shall we go find Fran?"

Jenna nods like a toddler being offered sweets.

Fran is standing under the chandelier, chatting up a small crowd. He's wearing a quilted gold smoking jacket, tied at the waist like a dress, with a pair of thigh-high boots and a pearl necklace. I stand back a moment to marvel at him and I catch the end of a debate about artificial intelligence. Of course this is what Fran is doing at his own party.

"Aren't you worried they'll replace us?" asks a woman

with a sharp blonde bob. "One of them made a sculpture last week!"

"AI didn't *make* a sculpture." Fran sighs. "AI is not creating art. Humans are creating art using AI. It's no different to us using a pen or a paintbrush."

"Put it this way," says another lady. "Would you let AI perform here?"

Fran mulls it over, then smirks.

"Only if they're queer," he jokes, and everybody laughs.

"A politician's answer!" says the blonde.

"Tell you what," he says. "Call me when AI starts *appreciating* art. Then I'll worry."

And with that argument well and truly shut down, he turns and spots me and Jenna hovering at the back of the crowd.

"My babes!" he roars and beckons us towards him.

"Welcome to the jungle." He winks at me.

"It's a far cry from that leaky old flat in Cabra," I say. Fran looks around, grinning.

"It is, isn't it?" And as he tucks his hair behind his ear Jenna screams, actually shrieks. I turn towards her expecting to find something very, very wrong, but she's beaming.

"Fuck off!" says Jenna to Fran.

"No," he says. "Shan't."

"What's going on?" I yell, but then I spot the ring on his finger, an emerald-encrusted silver band.

"Fuck off!" I parrot, grabbing his hand to look more closely. "Did you—?"

"I did!" he says. "We did!"

And with that the three of us are hugging one another, cheeks mashed together in a circular embrace.

"Wait, does this mean you're getting your second surgery?" I ask, and he shakes his head.

"We're holding off until we know for sure whether we want kids or not."

Fran glances at Jenna sheepishly, like the mere mention of children might hurt her feelings.

"I think that's a great idea." She smiles. "Wait and see."

Fran takes Jenna's hand and mouths a thank-you at her.

"Wedding!" she shouts.

"Wedding!" he shouts back, then he leads her onto the dance floor, and she grabs my hand as they go, pulling me along with them.

The vomit comes sooner than expected, most likely brought on by all the bouncing. Jenna's kneeling on the bathroom floor, cradling the toilet bowl like a lover as she hurls yellow bile into it with shocking force. I've got her hair caught back in one hand and I'm passing her wads of tissue with the other. Occasionally she reaches up and clambers for the flush, surfacing long enough to take a breath.

"I think I'm done," she'll say, before another wave hits. It's actually quite impressive how much puke comes out of her.

"Should we move in together?" she asks me at one point.

"We can talk about that when you're sober, Jen."

"I am sober!" she says, then she erupts again.

When she's finally done, I stand Jenna next to the sink, prop-
ping her against the wall like a mannequin. Her arms are hanging limp as I wet some tissue and press it gently into her face,
cleaning off the puke and snot and most of her makeup in the
process. I haven't seen her this drunk since college.

"What time is it?" she mumbles. A man at the sink next to
us answers her.

"Half eleven," says his reflection to hers, and suddenly she
comes to life.

"Fuck!" she says. "I have to fix my face before midnight."

"I think you look lovely," says the man, and Jenna scowls
at him before grabbing her bag and rummaging frantically inside it. The man makes a face like a scolded schoolboy and I
giggle to myself.

"Bollocks," she says. "I didn't bring any makeup."

"C'mere, I'll sort you out," I say.

The man's phone rings just as I'm emptying the contents of
my makeup bag onto the counter. I catch him in the mirror,
taking the phone out of his pocket, sighing when he sees the
name on the screen, hesitating before he answers. He turns
away slightly as he says hello, speaking in hushed tones to
whoever's on the line. Jenna and I try to make conversation to
give him some privacy, but we can't help but overhear.

"Just some party," he says. "Declan's here . . . Yeah, fine so
far . . . I've been okay, yeah . . ." Then a pause before, "Right.
Well, now isn't really a good time, Lisa."

Jenna mouths the word "Lisa" at me like we know who the

fuck Lisa is. A few people come and go, engrossed in their own bathroom drama. The man is getting more and more uncomfortable now, folding his arms across his chest and holding the phone further from his ear as Lisa's tinny little voice gets shriller. He looks over his shoulder at us and we pretend to be busy reapplying Jenna's mascara.

"No, it's just— We said we wouldn't— No, it's fine— Look, I don't mean to— Don't be like— Okay, well—"

Lisa is fully audible now.

"Happy fucking New Year, David!" she screams and then hangs up. The man looks at his phone, bewildered, then at us. A moment passes.

"How's Lisa?" I ask, and he lets out a whimper of a laugh.

"Yeah, good," he says. "She sends her best."

"Messy breakup?" asks Jenna, a beat too fast.

"Something like that."

We all nod in unison.

"She's not a bad person," he hastens to add. "Just . . . alone."

More group nodding.

"Anyway, sorry about that."

"Listen, David," says Jenna. "You just heard me regurgitate two bottles of bubbly and a tuna melt. It's only fair we got to hear you have a deeply vulnerable convo with your ex."

"I suppose," he says. Then to me: "Guess it's your turn next."

"To be vulnerable? I'm all good, thanks." I take Jenna by the arm. "Right, let's get Cinderella here back to the ball."

Jenna takes one step towards the door and stumbles immediately.

"Whoa," says David. "Need a hand there?" and she's giggling as he leads her out of the bathroom and onto the dance floor.

"There you are," calls Declan when he sees David approaching. "It's nearly time!"

"FIVE," we shout, "FOUR, THREE, TWO, ONE, HAPPY NEW YEAR!" and the DJ strikes up a dance remix of "Auld Lang Syne" as everybody cheers, corks are popped, and kisses are shared. Fran and Jay are entangled in a particularly passionate embrace, pulling back every few seconds to smile at each other in either adoration or disbelief. When I turn to my left I see Jenna on her tiptoes, making out ferociously with Declan. David is nowhere in sight. He probably pulled an Irish goodbye, and honestly, I don't blame him; New Year's Eve parties are no place for the recently brokenhearted.

I bum a smoke off someone, grab my coat, then slip out the fire exit and down some metal stairs to a loading bay at the side of the building. It's blessedly quiet out here—the noise of the party reduced to a dull pulse. My plan is to enjoy some champagne and a ciggy alone, but as I descend the steps, I find David standing there.

"Looks like we had the same plan," he says, offering me a cigarette. I get the loose one from my pocket and he laughs and lights it for me.

"Classy," he jokes, then we puff away in silence for a few minutes. I'm the first to break it.

"How long were you with Lisa?" I ask.

"Eight years."

"Ouch."

"Yep."

"Married?" I ask.

"Almost," he says, and I wince.

"Sorry," I say.

"How about yourself? Are you married?"

"No," I say. "I'm also doing that whole breakup thing."

"How long was yours?"

"Six years."

"I win," he says, smiling.

"My friend just got engaged," I say. "Oh?"

"And I'm happy for him. Of course."

"Of course."

"But I'm also sort of sad for myself." David nods. Another silence falls. I break it again.

"There," I chide, "is that vulnerable enough for you?"

He chuckles at this.

"Both can be true," he offers, then he becomes suddenly self-conscious.

"I should probably head back in and find Declan," he says, taking one last drag on his cigarette before flicking it away.

"I doubt Declan's even noticed you're gone."

"Jenna?" he asks, his eyes lighting up, and I nod.

"Best not tell him about all the puke," I say.

"And what about you? Did you get a kiss at midnight?"

"Nope."

"Would you like one?" he asks, and I laugh at his directness.

"Jesus," he says, "is it that funny a proposition?" but I'm already stubbing out my cigarette.

"Go on, then," I say, stepping towards him, and he kisses me. Really kisses me. Walking me slowly back to the wall and planting my body against it. It's a good kiss by any standards. David's technique is flawless—starting slow, building pace and intensity, flicking his tongue softly against mine.

It's been so long since I've kissed anyone but you that I have to adjust slightly to the shape of a new mouth, which only makes me think about your mouth.

Your lips.

Your tongue flicking softly against mine.

My head starts to fill with you.

Our first kiss.

Our first night.

All our firsts.

All our lasts.

"Are you okay?" asks David, suddenly pulling back.

"Yeah, why?"

"You're crying," he says.

"No, I'm not!" I protest, almost laughing at the absurdity, but then my hand flies to my face and comes away wet.

"Oh," I say, staring down at my fingers, shiny with tears. "Shit."

"It's okay," says David, stepping back now, giving me space. "Look, I'm really sorry if I came on too strong."

"No," I say. "It's me— I'm just— Fuck, I'm so sorry."

And then my feet are taking me away. David's trying to

reassure me, but, propelled by blind panic, I apologise and run, not knowing where I'm running to.

I find myself around the back of the theatre, prying open a huge metal door, stepping inside, fumbling for a light switch. There is none. And as the door slams shut behind me, I realise I'm in the basement. It's the odour that gives it away—of drying paint and turpentine-soaked rags. It renders me a child again, lost in a graveyard, lost in a supermarket, descending the staircase of my childhood home, searching for my mother, dead or alive.

I should go back. I want to go back. But somehow, I know I have to move forward.

So I begin to make my way across the room, remembering the door on the other side, and beyond that, the skinny corridor leading to an elevator that will take me out of here. I can't see or hear the party above me—not even the thud of music makes its way through the ceiling—but I trust that it's all still up there waiting for me, if I can just take this first step.

With my arms outstretched, I inch forward. Just like that night in Dublin Bay, I'm shrouded in a darkness so dense that I might as well be blindfolded—I can't even see my own hands, which occasionally brush against some unidentified object. Each time I touch something, a blade of fear cuts through me as I quickly adjust course, my high heels digging deeper into the backs of my ankles as I go. If I could look down, I'm sure I would see frilly white socks with bright red stains at the back. I kick the heels off and keep going.

I lost my shoes.

Never mind about that.

Ten steps in, and I'm trembling all over, surer still with every step that somewhere in this room, my mother waits for me. I'm terrified my fingers will find the rotting flesh of her un-breathing belly, the sea-soaked nightgown that clings to her grey skin night after night. She's down here with me. I know it. And by twenty steps, I would almost welcome her—the devil I know. So afflicted am I by visions of things I can't see, things I have yet to see, that I would bury my face in the hem of her skirt and cry us both an ocean to drown in. I would sink gladly and never surface.

When something moves against my hip, I scream and pull away, but then it moves again, buzzing violently until I realise it's my phone vibrating in my bag. I rush to answer it, but as I do the signal disappears and the call cuts off. It was you. Your name I saw on the screen. Why were you calling me? I need to get upstairs. I need to call you back. And with that I re-member my phone is also a torch! For a moment I'm filled with a newfound sense of resolve as my shaky fingers find the light and shine it on the path ahead. I take one brave stride across the room, then another. I'm halfway there now. But as I lift my gaze, I see what my hands were brushing against.

Filling the room from side to side and end to end, Maeve's paintings, or what's left of them, are propped up on wooden easels. Row after row of tattered pictures—the remnants of every show she's performed—gutted, preserved, and presented here, like carcasses strung up by their hind legs. As I walk among them, some canvases fall into shadow as others are caught in the grim white glare. It illuminates scenes without centres, memories with no middle, fragments of a life, lived and forgotten. It's like moving through the bowels of a demented mind; shrivelled and porous as a lump of sandstone, riddled with holes, and leaking moments quick as they come.

I turn to run.

But I fall and all my thoughts come tumbling with me. A jumble of fractal split-second memories all spliced together into one long reel that rushes through a projector at lightning speed like some cosmic supercut of her. I see my whole life happening right now. And as I plummet headlong towards the ground, reality breaks down, like an image unrendering before my eyes. The walls on all sides seem to crack and come away until there are none left, and life is just one seamless circle inside which everything is visible and clear.

I see my mother. Really see her. Maybe for the first time.

And I feel it more vividly than ever now: that full-body lurch, that weightless descent, that grisly unending onrush of air as I wait for an impact that never comes. Then my knees smack the concrete, and the palms of my hands fly out but barely break my fall. This time, finally, the ground hits and I land, face down, sprawled across the floor, listening to the contents of my bag spilling all around me. The light goes out. And the next few seconds are filled with the sound of loose coins spinning to a stop.

Nothing but the jagged sound of my breath.

And then.

Click-clack. Click-clack.

I lift my head towards the sound. It's coming from the corridor.

Click-clack. Click-clack.

Then the door swings open and I see it, its gangly, feath-ered outline looming black inside a sickly green rectangle, like a portal between worlds. There it is. The creature from my dreams made flesh. And fresh tears fall now as it steps towards me and I hold my breath, remembering its eyeless face and the feel of its serrated beak against my neck.

Please.

No.

The portal slides shut. A grating metallic clang. My shak-ing hands attempt to lift me up, but I collapse back down, depleted. In the darkness I can't see it; I can only listen as the creature's clawed feet step into the room.

Click-clack. Click-clack.

A blinding light. I cover my eyes.

Click-clack. Click-clack. Click-clack.

Suddenly it's on me. I can feel its feathers, prickly and soft, as it jostles me this way and that. I keep my arms crossed tight over my head, shouting at it now to go away, begging it to please, please leave me alone.

"Kate," says the creature, in a woman's voice—not my mother's but a voice I know.

"Kate," it says again, but I'm screaming over and over, "LEAVE ME ALONE!"

I push it off me, hear it land with a thump nearby. The creature doesn't move. Nor do I.

"Kate?" it says, quiet now, and I peek out through the cracks in my fingers at one of its feet.

No claws. Just a scarlet-red stiletto.

I let my gaze move up the creature's legs (both human) to its torso (human too) and then its face. Maeve is looking back at me, her features fearful but soft. She's sat amidst a bundle of silk skirts. Her corset is made entirely of feathers, which creep up like vines around her neck and face.

"Put me in a cab," I say. "I want to go home."

REPRISE

A saline breeze hits me as I step out of the taxi, and with my high heels hooked over two fingers, I pass a row of sleepy houses, their windows dark and shuttered against a gathering coastal storm. The sky above me is a charcoal void. The only sound a rising wind and the swish-swash of a squally sea.

I make it inside just as the rain hits. Dumping my stuff by the front door—a lifelong habit that used to drive my mother mad—I am about to head upstairs when I notice the kitchen light still on. Through the mottled glass door at the end of the hall I can see my dad's distorted outline standing by the sink.

"Katie?" he calls out. "Is that you?"

"Yes, Dad. Only me."

I used to turn up here after the odd night out. Lulled by the thought of my childhood bed and the promise of a proper fry-up the next morning, I'd climb into a cab and recite this address instead of whatever flat or college dorm I was living in at the time. Muscle memory kicked in as I drunkenly directed drivers down the intricate tangle of streets it takes to get here, avoiding train crossings and cul-de-sacs on the way, making small talk about the weather or the traffic or whichever government was in power at the time. More often than not, my dad was asleep when I got in, so I'd leave a note on the bathroom door to tell him I was home, and what time I wanted breakfast. It got to be a joke—me putting in my order—to the point that he once stole a room service menu from a hotel he was staying at and left it on my bedside table for my next visit. The thought softens my resolve somewhat, my hand hesitating on the door handle. Then I remember what I came here for.

In the kitchen, Dad's got his back to me, forearms plunged in soapy water.

"You're up late," I say, heading straight to the fridge, opening it, and staring vacantly at the food inside. I'm ravenous. All I've had today is a packet of biscuits.

"Can I make you something?" he asks over his shoulder.

"No, thanks. I'm not hungry."

"Well, will you close the fridge in that case? You're letting all the cold out."

Another habit of mine that bothered my mam. Dad never used to mind, but when she died, he took up caring about all the things she'd cared about—the doors I left open, the lights I left on, the piles of my stuff all over the house. I close the fridge door and lean against the counter, restless. I can feel my fists clenching, my jaw tensing, my toes tapping on the tiled floor.

"I caught the New Year's Eve concert on RTÉ," he says, filling the silence as he stacks his dishes on the drying rack. "Load of shite, but sure it's something to watch."

"Was Mam sick?" I ask, and for a split second my father freezes—shoulders stiffening, hand pausing in midair—before resuming what he was doing. He drains the sink, takes a few deliberate breaths, and turns around. I notice him drying his hands on his dressing gown, and without thinking, I grab a tea towel from the second drawer down and hang it on the oven door. Then I return to leaning, arms folded, against the counter. My father sits down at the table. He still hasn't looked at me.

"Yes, love," he says finally. "She was."

"What was it?" My voice sounds empty and far away, like the radio's been left on in the next room.

"Early-onset Alzheimer's. Which became dementia. Will you sit down with me please?"

He gestures to the seat opposite him. The seat I've been sitting in my whole life. I shake my head.

"You want to know why I never told you." He's sitting back, regarding me now.

I just keep glaring at the floor with my teeth clamped together.

"She didn't want you to know," he says.

"And *you*?" I snap.

"That didn't matter."

"Why not?"

"Because I made a promise, pet."

Everything he says makes me angrier. His calm detachment, which I'm sure is intended to be soothing, riles me up instead. Even now he can't manage to summon just a scrap of emotion for me.

"I don't understand," I say to my feet.

"I don't expect you to."

"Fuck's sake, will you quit it with the Zen shit?"

He doesn't answer.

"How long did she know?" I demand. I'm lobbing questions at him like rocks, but they land like flowers at his feet.

"We started to suspect just after her fortieth. She got the diagnosis at forty-one. You came along soon after that."

"Then why the hell did she have me? If she knew?" I watch tears drip down my nose and onto the tiles.

"She didn't plan to have a baby. You know that. You were her—"

"Don't say it," I say, flinging a palm up in protest.

Noisy little miracle.

"We were told it wasn't possible," he goes on. "We'd long since given up on ever having kids. She was four months in before she even realised. Thought it was the menopause. All those hot flushes and hormones and what have you."

He's looking straight ahead now, his gaze reaching beyond this kitchen and into the past. A weary smile creeps across his face.

"She was so happy when she found out. And sad too. She knew she wouldn't be around for all of it."

"*It* being my life," I scoff, walking to the back door. "I need a smoke."

"Wait," says my father, his joints creaking as he lifts himself up out of his seat and walks to the dresser. "It's lashing out there."

He takes Mam's old ashtray down from a high shelf, blows the dust off it, and places it on the table. It's a ridiculous-looking thing. A huge hunk of angular glass. You could do real damage with it. I tap a cigarette out of the packet and light it up. Then I offer one to my dad, and to my surprise he takes it, lights up, and inhales deeply with his eyes closed. When he pulls it away from his lips, he regards it for a moment, nodding satisfaction.

"That's lovely."

"Menthol," I say, showing him the pack.

"They didn't have those in my day."

"Probably for the best," I say, and he pretends not to notice as I sit down across from him.

"I used to keep a pack in the shed," he confesses. "After Abbie made me quit, I'd sneak out there at night to have one."

"I know," I say, half rolling my eyes. "We all knew, Dad."

My father and I inhale and exhale together for a while, pausing at the top, pausing at the bottom. Sometimes it's not the caffeine you need, but the tea ceremony itself. I'm not sure who said that.

"How did you find out?" asks my father.

"You weren't particularly quiet," I say, but he's shaking his head, amused.

"I mean about your mam, being sick."

"Oh," I say. "I don't know. Some things just suddenly got clearer."

He nods. We both tap ash into Mam's glass monstrosity. And I think of her hands doing just this. I must have seen it a thousand times—the delicate flick of her long fingers, the modest emerald on her left hand, her nails kept short and always flecked with paint. She never did quit smoking, but she insisted that Dad should. Now I understand why.

"I got lost in the supermarket once," I tell him. "I'd stopped to read the back of a cereal box, and when I looked up, she was gone. It felt like hours went by before I found her. It was probably only a minute or two. I heard her laughing and followed the sound."

He smiles at this. I wonder if he gets the same hit I do at being offered new information about her.

"When I found her, she was talking to a friend. Not looking for me. Not panicking. She didn't even seem to notice I was gone. And when she saw me, I could have sworn she didn't know who I was. There wasn't so much as a drop of recognition in her eyes. It lasted less than a second. Then suddenly she was my mam again."

He's nodding now. He's seen the look I'm talking about.

"She was always forgetting things," I say. "Losing things. Running late. She left me at the school gates more than once. She would constantly make coffee, put it down somewhere, and go pour a fresh cup. They'd be all over the house. One time she left her wallet on top of the car, did I ever tell you that? And drove off. Mrs. O'Kelly found it and brought it back. Then there was the night she accidentally cooked dinner twice. Remember?"

Of course he remembers. It was a symptom of an ever-worsening illness, and he was forced to play it off as a joke.

"All this time, I thought she was just quirky. Scatterbrained," I tell him through gritted teeth. "I told myself stories to make it make sense. But it never did. Stories weren't enough. I needed the truth, Dad. You should have told me the truth." I glare over at him now and he stares into my face like he's trying to read some foreign language etched across it.

"Should I have?" he's genuinely asking. "Would that have made things easier?"

"I don't know. Maybe. I'm not—" But I don't know how to tell him, whether to tell him.

"Not what, pet?"

"I'm not okay, Dad! I still have nightmares, you know. They never went away."

A hint of something in his eyes. Though I can't tell what. Anger? Or guilt.

"You never did tell me what they were about," he says, and that's when I snap.

"You didn't want to know!" I yell. "You pawned me off on some child psychologist. Some woman I'd never even met. I had to talk to her instead of my own father!"

It's like watching a mask slide off his face now. His brow knits together in a tight knot. His lips form a pale line. The lump at the front of his throat undulates as he swallows down emotions. But this only spurs me on.

"You stopped talking about Mam. You tried to get rid of her. And me! I heard you ask Aunt Kathy to take me, by the way. I heard you!"

I sound like a child. But I'm not. I'm a grown woman and I'm slinging everything I have at him now; decades' worth of rage—some of which belongs to him, some of which doesn't—and he just sits there, steadfast, taking it. I think of the day I found my cat run over in the street. How I stood by her broken little body and screamed at my father to fix it, pounding at his legs with tiny balled-up fists, kicking at his shins. And how he remained, unflinching, and utterly helpless. Some things were bigger even than him. But I wasn't ready to see that.

He reaches across the table now for my hand, but I don't give it to him.

"You disappeared when I needed you the most, Dad. You just . . . fucking . . . receded. I lost you both the day she died. One parent would have been enough, I could have got by with one, but I had none. And what's worse is you were right there. The whole time!"

"I'm so sorry," he says, and it's almost the worst thing he could say. At least if he defended himself, I could keep fighting. Keep shouting. Keep pounding my little fists against his legs. Instead he collects himself and says, "You must be starving. Can I make you a sandwich?"

I swear to God, he actually offers me a sandwich.

"Jesus Christ!" I screech.

"Well, I don't know what to say, Katie! When I was sad, my mammy would make me a sandwich."

And there it is. When he was sad, his mammy would make him a sandwich.

It isn't enough to forgive him. But it is enough to understand him. And I suppose understanding is the first step towards forgiveness.

"Alright," I say, and his knees creak again as he gets up. I watch him shuffle about the kitchen, moving much slower now than I remember.

When did that happen?

He returns with a plate full of sandwiches, which he places on the table between us, and I continue to cry as I eat them.

"Thanks," I say when I'm done, wiping away tears and crumbs.

"What are your nightmares about?" he asks, and I eye him cautiously. He nods for me to go on, then sits back to listen.

"Her," I say, closing my eyes. "They're about her.

"I wake up here. Alone. There's a noise I can't make out. A banging. I come downstairs. The front door is open. The wind is rushing through. I walk to the kitchen. There's coffee on the floor. I burn my hand on the pot. Then I go down to the basement. And she's there. But . . ."

I open my eyes to look at him.

"But she's drowned. She's already drowned. Her nightdress is wet. And her face is all . . . smudged."

I mime the action across my own face, like I'm smearing my features with my hand.

"And sometimes there's more than one of her. There are dozens of her, all faceless. She sees me. And she screams. It's—"

But I don't have the words for what it is.

"Then I wake up."

My father drops his chin to his chest and draws a long ragged breath.

"That was real," he says, and my stomach tenses as he continues, talking in slow, deliberate sentences that wash over me like huge waves.

"Not long before your mammy died," he begins, "I woke

up one Sunday morning to find her gone. It was early. Six or seven o'clock. The front door was open and, you're right, it was blustery outside. She was on the high street, outside the chemist where she used to work. Still in her nightdress. Soaked through from the rain. She kept saying she was late. Insisting that she get inside. She didn't know who I was."

"I'm sorry," I say, but he bats it away.

"It wasn't the first time; she'd already started to slip. That's what she called it—slipping. She said it was like being on a boat in a storm. Watching things slide across the floor in front of her. Reaching out for them and being unable to grab on. She was better with words than she thought, you know. You didn't lick that off the ground."

He gives me a smile, and I offer one back.

"Anyway, the chemist was closed, thank God. So I brought her home. Cleaned up the mess in the kitchen. And went upstairs to check on you. But you weren't in your bed. Or anywhere else in the house. Jaysis, I was like a madman looking for you. I thought you'd wandered off down the beach or something."

"Where was I?"

"In your playhouse, at the end of the garden, nursing a burned hand. So I dressed the wound and put you back to bed. Then I found Abbie in the basement. Just standing there."

His demeanour shifts suddenly. He twists in his chair.

"She always kept it locked, pet, I didn't know you'd been down there. That you'd seen . . ."

"Seen what?"

He hesitates.

"Her paintings."

"But I've seen all Mam's paintings," I protest weakly. "You said so yourself."

Dad's shaking his head, tears and guilt filling his eyes.

"She'd been painting portraits of herself. Since the diagnosis. She said it helped."

He's talking with that faraway stare again.

"There were so many. A hundred. Maybe more. And they'd started . . . changing."

"Changing how?" I ask, but I already know; I see them almost every night.

"Well, as she deteriorated they got more and more . . . distorted," he says. "By the end they were awful-looking things. Just awful. The hair and clothes were all clear, but the faces . . . Abbie said she didn't recognise herself anymore.

"She said those pictures were how it felt in her head. It broke my heart just to look at them."

This time it's me who reaches out and he takes my hand, squeezing it between both of his.

"She kept it locked," he mumbles. "She always kept it locked."

"Where are they now?" I ask him.

"Gone."

"Gone where?" But again, I know the answer already.

"We got rid of them. Kathy and I. We didn't want you to see. We didn't know you had."

I'm not sure how much more I can absorb. I'm already at saturation point. But still, I persist.

"You said this happened a week before she died?" I know he knows where I'm going with this.

"Let's not," he says, pulling away from me. "I can't."

"I need to know, Dad."

"Please, don't," he begs.

"Was it an accident?"

He stares straight at me then and I see the decision being made; he's going to tell me the truth.

"I don't think so, no."

I stand up. I don't mean to but my body's up and moving, pacing the room.

"After that day, things changed," he says. "But not how I expected. She bounced back! She was clearer than she'd been in years. Asked me to take the week off. And I did. We drove down to Courtown, remember? You puked by the side of the road. All that ice cream . . ."

It's alright. You're alright.

"I didn't see what she was doing," he continues in an almost pleading tone. "I was so blindsided. So keen to believe she was better. That it had just been a blip. Truth be told, I don't think she could bear it. That you got hurt. That we were slipping from her."

He can barely get the next sentence out.

"She didn't recognise her own face, Katie."

"What are you saying, Dad?" I've found myself propped against the wall, gripping my arms across my chest.

"She didn't leave a note," he offers. "Or anything like that. But she was smart, your mother. And there was a warning for the currents that day. She knew better."

He drops his head again.

"I don't know," he mutters. "I'll never know."

I imagine him turning these thoughts over, night after night for twenty-six years, like pieces of sea glass, blunted by time but still heavy in his hands. I glance over at the dishes drying by the sink: one plate, one knife and fork, one champagne flute. And for the first time I feel the weight of his loss on top of my own. I see grief slipping under his door and taking his wife from him piecemeal, while all he could do was look on. I see it lying in bed next to him in place of her, occupying the armchair across from his own, standing beside him in family photos, grinning in the empty space where she should be.

I go to him now and wrap my arms around his neck, and he clutches on to them with both hands as he sobs, his whole body convulsing beneath me.

"It's alright," I tell him. "You're alright."

We stay this way until he's caught his breath, me rocking him like a child, and I think of him holding me when I'd woken from bad dreams. How he always seemed to be right there, without my even needing to call out. It never occurred to me that he was up already, grappling with his own waking nightmare. No wonder he asked Aunt Kathy to take me; how can you be a father when you're barely a human? I can't imagine caring for a child these past few months; I'm hardly able to care for myself.

I make us both a cup of tea and we sit sipping for a long while, listening to each other's thoughts as they go roaring through the kitchen, silent as freight trains.

"Should I get tested?" I ask, and he deflates. He was expecting this.

"*She* didn't want that for you, that's all I know."

When the wind picks up, a draft causes the basement door to rattle on its hinges and a shiver runs through me. I think of her paintings. Another piece of her lost forever. Another thing I need to grieve. And I know he hid them from me, just like he hid the truth, in an effort to protect me. But his good intentions do little to assuage the anguish rising in me now.

"I need to go," I announce. "I need to sleep, and I need to think."

My father loans me a pair of boots and insists on driving me himself. I sit in the passenger seat staring at the rain that's pummelling the windscreen, barely held off by the wipers. The ghost of my bedraggled face swims up to meet me, lit by traffic lights and yellow streetlamps. Rivulets of rain pour down my limp hair and mascara-streaked cheeks. Echoes of her everywhere.

Dawn is creeping when he pulls up outside our house.

"Still leaving lights on, I see."

He's right. The living room light is on.

"That wasn't me," I say. "Finn must be here."

He can sense my hesitation, I'm sure.

"I'll drive you back home if you like."

"It's okay, thanks. I'd like to see him."

"Alright," he says. Then: "Something struck me about your nightmare."

He looks to me for permission to go on and I nod.

"It's just, you said the front door is always open, but you keep going down to the basement, even though you know what's waiting for you there."

"It's a dream," I say, a little confused. "I don't get to choose."

"I know, pet. Just something to think about."

My dad waits until I've let myself in before driving away. I'm still waving him off when I hear your voice coming from the kitchen.

"Hold on," I hear you say to someone, before appearing in the doorway at the end of the hall. By the looks of it, you're still wearing the suit you went out in last night, only it's wrinkled in places, your hair is a mess, and your eyes are red raw. You're holding a phone to your ear.

"She's just walked in the door, Jenna. Will you let Fran know? Thanks." And you hang up as you rush towards me, enveloping me in your arms, kissing the top of my head over and over.

"I was so worried," you say.

"Hello," I mumble into your chest, and relief escapes you in the form of a weak laugh.

"Hello, honey."

"What are you doing here, Finn?"

You're crying when you pull back to look at me, taking me in like an apparition.

"I called you last night," you say, and I remember now, seeing your name lit up on my phone. That feels like a different lifetime.

"When you didn't answer, I tried again but it didn't even ring. None of my messages were going through. I called Fran to make sure you were okay, and he told me you'd gone home in a taxi. He said you were upset, but you wouldn't say why. So I came over to check on you, but you never came home, and it got later and later, and I tried not to panic but—"

You can't seem to finish the sentence. You just stare into my face like it's the only thing you've ever seen. I'd be lying if I said I hadn't pictured some version of this moment a thousand times.

"What happened?" you ask me. "Are you okay?"

But that's too big a question, and I don't have an answer for you.

"Could you just kiss me please?" I ask.

Without hesitation you take my face in your hands, running one thumb back and forth across my lips as my eyes close and my head tilts slowly back, like a baby bird eager to be fed. Then I feel your lips, lingering just a hair's breadth from my own, and as you hover there agonisingly close, the air escaping your mouth flows into mine and I breathe you in, gasping as your hands find my hips, thumbs pressing hard into the tender hollows there.

"Ask me again," you mumble into my mouth.

"Kiss me," I say. And you do. And it's everything I imagined. Everything I remembered. And before I know it, you're lifting my dress over my head and I'm unbuckling your belt and we can't seem to get naked enough or close enough as we fall to the floor, pressing our bodies greedily together like we're trying to crawl inside each other's skin. Like nothing short of that will do. We lick and bite and grab at every morsel of flesh available to us, making love over and over, till I'm screaming your name to the bare white walls of this house we never quite made a home, moving with an almost religious fervour; like a pair of penitent sinners desperately seeking absolution. It's as though we've been told that this is how to repent, that somehow, if we can just fuck each other hard enough and loud enough and long enough we can exorcise what plagues us—all the pain we've accumulated over time, all the history we've scrawled, all the reasons why we simply do not work—and be granted deliverance. A new life. A fresh start. A blessed blank page on which to write a new story with a happy ending.

We've made our way to the bedroom now, and morning light comes creeping through the curtains as I lie in your arms, head on your shoulder like the first night, like the last night, like you never even left.

"I've been writing to you," I say.

"Oh? I didn't get anything . . ."

I smile into your skin.

"Not like that. It's just that every time I try to write, I find myself writing to you."

"I see. And what do you tell me?" you ask, your fingertips lazily tracing my spine.

"All sorts. Things you know already. Things you don't. Things you never will."

"Maybe I'll read them someday," you say.

"Maybe."

I sit up on the edge of the bed, rummaging in the top drawer for some cigarettes.

"I told myself I'd quit in the New Year," I say, taking one out. "Do you mind?"

You shake your head. I open a window and lean next to it, still naked, watching you watching me. There's a look of sleepy satisfaction on your face.

"Where were you, anyway?" you ask.

"At my dad's house."

"Is everything okay?" But I don't want to talk about that.

"Why did you call me last night, Finn?"

"I needed to see you," you say, matter-of-fact.

"Why?"

"I missed you."

"That's it?" I ask, and you nod.

"You just . . . missed me, and needed to see me?"

"Isn't that enough?"

"I suppose," I say. "But I don't believe you." And you throw back your head and roll your eyes like a teenager.

"Fine. I was at a shit party in Scott's flat."

Then you stop, like that's the end of the story.

"And?"

"And I was talking to some girl."

"Okay . . . ?"

"And she was pretty, but . . ."

"But what?"

"It's so stupid," you say, hiding your face in a pillow now. I have no idea what you're about to say. I realise I'm holding my breath waiting for an answer.

"But what, Finn?"

"Her mascara was all clumpy."

Except you mumble it into the pillow so I can barely understand. I sit next to you and pull the pillow away.

"What?"

"Her mascara was all clumpy!" you repeat, and I can't help but laugh, exhaling a cloud of smoke as I do.

"It's true!" you insist. "The whole time she was talking to me, all I could focus on was her clumpy fucking mascara."

"So?"

"So, your mascara's never clumpy. And it made me realise, no matter how pretty, or funny, or lovely someone else is, she won't be you. There'll always be some dumb thing that'll remind me how much better I had it."

I stub out the cigarette, buying myself time.

"Did you kiss her at midnight?" I ask, hoping you don't notice me skirting around what you just said. You shake your head and then I watch as realisation blooms on your face.

"Did you kiss anyone?" But before I can answer you say, "No, don't tell me, I don't want to know."

I think you can tell that I did. Or at least you're imagining it happening. Because you sit up next to me now and kiss me like you're trying to prove a point. That no one will ever kiss me like this again.

We spend the next few days drifting from the bed to the sofa and back again. Occasionally nipping out for bread or eggs or more cigarettes. By the third day, I wake from a nap to hear you in your studio, your fingers fumbling across the frets, and the clumsy beginnings of some new song. But it's not new, not entirely. It reminds me of that score you wrote the first year we were together—the one that sounded like me. The melody is similar. Almost a reprise.

I'm still lying in bed when your phone rings, and I pick up without thinking. It's your mother.

"Katie! Hi!"

I can tell I've caught her off guard.

"Sorry," she says, "I just . . . didn't expect to hear your voice. Finn said you two were having a bit of a break is all."

"We were," I say. "We are."

Are we?

"I just came over for a chat," I tell her.

"Oh good," she says, her relief palpable. "That's good. I knew you two would work it out."

"Did you want to talk to Finn?" I ask.

"No, you're grand. I was just in the area, and I thought I might swing by and see the house. But I'll leave you two to have your chat."

"Okay, Ruth. I'll get him to call you later."

Then it hits me.

"Wait," I say. "See the house?"

"Yes, love."

"But you've seen it already."

"No, love," she says. "Sure when would I have seen it?"

I'm sitting on the edge of the bed when you emerge from your studio, complaining about a broken guitar string, saying you need to pop out for a new one. You're putting on your coat,

wrapping my burgundy scarf around your neck. You tell me
you're borrowing it. I say that's fine.

"Are you alright?" you ask, and I nod unconvincingly. I'm
staring at my navy dress, still crumpled on the floor, and your
suit jacket draped over a pile of unpacked boxes.

"Where are you going?" I ask.

"Into town, to buy strings, like I said."

"Oh yeah."

"Are you sure you're okay?"

"Yes, fine."

"Okay, well, I won't be long." And although the conversation is over, you're still looking at me like you've got something to
say. Then you're walking over to me, kneeling down, placing
your hands in mine and staring up into my eyes.

"I'll do whatever it takes to make this work, Kate. I'll go
to couples' counselling. My own therapy. Whatever you want.
I'll do anything. If it means I get to keep you."

You're smiling at me and I'm fairly sure I'm smiling back.

"You'll see," you're saying. "This time it'll be different."

Now you're standing up, kissing me on the forehead, and
your lips land like a gavel coming down.

When you leave, I pack a suitcase, then I go to the living
room and write you one last note.

GOODBYE

This is the last time I'll write to you, Finn.

I'm sorry I didn't say goodbye. I think by now we both know how that goes.

The house is yours, till February.

Kate

THE SPACE
BETWEEN BREATH

It was a Wednesday morning in mid-September, and the light was turning from silver to gold as you pulled my bedroom curtains open on a rough grey sea. At breakfast, you held Dad's hand across the table and sipped your coffee. Then you packed my lunch—a ham sandwich, two biscuits, a banana—and saw us to the door. You stood waving as we backed out of the driveway, blowing kisses from the tips of your paint-speckled fingers. Now your sister stands in the doorway of her bungalow, raising one hand to greet me as I drag my suitcase up the narrow path. And although I know you're gone—and although it's been over twenty-six years between that moment and this—for the slimmest sliver of time, brief as the beat of a moth's silk wing, it's as though the clocks did stop, after all, and here you are, welcoming me home.

"Fáilte, a stór," says Kathy, cupping my face in her hands. "Welcome back."

She sees me to a room at the front of the house and tells me that it used to be yours.

"I remember," I say, setting my bag on the bed as I take in the view of the Atlantic Ocean through a small bay window. My memories of this place are those of a toddler: oddly selected sights, sounds, and smells, messily collected in scrapbook fashion. I've seen that window before. Slept next to you in this bed. And over there I played with a box of your old toys on a fluffy sheepskin rug. The rug is gone now, as are the toys, but the walls and shelves still teem with your belongings: sketches, paintings, souvenirs, precious tokens of your many walks on Killadoon Bay Beach—stones and shells, driftwood and razors—carefully collected and curated. This was just a room then. Now it's a shrine. A thin place, where at any moment I might hear your voice in the next room, catch the scent of your perfume in the hallway, or the shape of you crouched by the hearth, building us a fire for the evening ahead.

"Have you slept?" asks Kathy, and I blink back from wherever I just was.

"A little, on the train," I say. She's got that furrowed concern about her again.

"Why don't you put your head down for an hour, treasure?"

"Alright, yeah."

"I'll call you for dinner," she says, then she turns to go and stops at the door, looking back with lucent eyes. "Happy New Year, I suppose."

"Happy New Year, Kathy," I say, and a tired laugh escapes me.

Laughter comes easily in this place. I remember that, as well. The pair of you, howling in the kitchen late at night, sharing a bottle of Baileys and ancient jokes that only sisters know. Screeching as you ran along the shoreline or leapt hand in hand with me over huge west-coast waves. I remember us, sitting at the sea's foam edge. You, feeding me crisps and sandy sandwiches. Bundling me up in a coarse beach towel and holding me against your chest.

But quick as memories come, they are rewritten, altered by the knowledge that you knew then how little time we had. And soon this knowing starts to seep through my whole mind, like ink in water, tainting every memory I have of you, darkening the tone of my whole childhood. I thought that I had mourned you fully. That there would be no more mourning left to do. But this is a fresh, graveside grief, raw and untamed, that doesn't so much slip under the door as burst through it, demanding my attention.

I look away from my thoughts and out across the water, where a plump saffron sun hangs heavy as an orange, ripe and dipping from its bough. Briefly soothed, I watch it sink below the world, leaving in its wake a scene straight from one of your landscapes: gauzy clouds and one thick rose-coloured streak, sweeping straight across a lilac sky. It's like heaven itself just came into bloom. And then I think of you. Sitting here. Watching sunsets. Wondering how many more you'd see.

When Kathy comes to wake me, I haven't slept. She finds me curled up on the bed, babbling and struggling to breathe.

"She could have gone anywhere," I sputter angrily as she sits down next to me. "She could have seen the world. She could have seen the whole world. And painted it! But she stayed in one tiny place. She was trapped. Because of me."

Kathy's back is straight. Her chin lifted.

"You're right," she says. "She could have gone anywhere. So why didn't she?"

I shake my head, wiping my nose. "I don't know."

I think of you, tucking me in every night, waving me off every morning. The same routine. The same four walls. The same beige stretch of sand. And it's more than I can bear.

"Oh, darling, isn't it obvious? She stayed because she wanted to stay. She chose this life. She chose you. To her very last breath, she chose you."

"But she lost herself," I wail. "She lost herself."

"To a disease, love. Not to you. You didn't rob her of this world. *You* are how she remains in it. You, and me, and your dad, and her art. All the pieces of herself she left behind."

I gaze up now through bleary eyes at your sketches on the wall. Of beaches and craggy bridges, seagulls and curlews, snails and spiders. I can all but feel them crawling on my skin.

"She could have been a great artist."

"She *was* a great artist," says Kathy, taking me by the hand and pulling me to my feet. "Come with me, Kate."

In the failing light, Kathy leads me through the kitchen, out the back door, and down a mossy path to a windowless red-brick shed at the end of her garden, its flat roof overgrown with wildflowers. Clusters of long grass graze against my legs as we go. Bees throng, unseen, in the hedges. And all around us, birds flit dancingly from branch to branch, calling out their twilight chorus—less a warning now than a welcome. Overhead, the crescent moon is perched in its zenith like a silver chalice waiting to be filled. It's as though this place has lain in wait for me and is now making ready for my return.

Kathy unlocks the door—on which has been painted, in yellow cursive, *Abigail*. It reminds me of the box of photographs I found in the attic, and makes me wonder if we store the dead in sheds and shrines and boxes, encase them inside concrete and cardboard, in order to create new containers for them in lieu of bodies, ones with edges we can comprehend.

Kathy moves aside, gesturing for me to come forward, and as I step through the doorway and into the shed, I can just about make out the shapes of canvases, sheathed in clear plastic wrapping. There's a row of them on a wooden shelf encircling the room, another at ground level, and upright stacks of them spread across the floor. Kathy reaches over my left shoulder and pulls a light switch dangling there. An exposed bulb at the centre of the room blinks on and I close my eyes instinctively against the glare. When I open them, I see Kathy's face, which for a moment could just as easily be yours.

"Look," she says.

And here you are, captured in a hundred or so portraits in a thousand different shades. Here is your interpretation of existence, your frenzied dig for meaning, your dive within for the parts of yourself you couldn't fully know until you put them on the page.

Here is the act of art. That lightning-in-a-bottle-blink-and-you'll-miss-it moment our science has no answer for. Here is the alchemic instant when creation meets consumption and becomes communion; a fleeting fellowship of souls across space and time, life and death, this world and the next, sharing in something that can't ever be explained, described, or recreated.

Your paintings are beautiful. This experience divine.

Soundlessly, I drop to the floor, my legs unable to carry the weight of revelation. Kathy quickly lands beside me, pulling my torso up onto her lap as she drapes her body over mine. One of my hands moves to my heart, the other to my head, palms pressing hard into my chest and forehead as though trying to contain the swell of emotion that rises in me now. When Kathy rests her hands on top of mine, buttressing my efforts, I flash on the keening, how she held this exact same pose as she rocked back and forth above your body, one hand on her heart, the other on her head, the very picture of grief. And with that I can hear the sound that came from her that day, the one I prayed I'd never hear again. Only this time it's my own voice, my own pain, my own demons being loosed into the world. Loss splits me at the seams and gushes from me, filling this whole space and spilling out into the deepening night. I lost you. I lost the father I could have known, the family I could have had, the life I could have lived—had that not all died with you. I lost love, lost time, lost sleep, lost home after home, dream after dream. I lost my words. I lost myself. I've been losing myself, Mam. Slipping from myself just like we slipped from you, unable to recognise my own face in the mirror some days, unsure of who I am and terrified of what that means. I've been so afraid to see beyond the nightmare, to peel it back and look at reality, that I chose to live inside it instead.

Kathy doesn't flinch. She doesn't try to stop me or soothe me. She lets me roar until my throat burns and my voice fails me, till my arms go limp and I lie sobbing in her lap, wracked by the worst loss of all, the loss of the veil that separated me from a truth more terrifying than any nightmare—evidence, bare and undeniable, of the thing I feared most and so refused to see: that you and I are the same, and that this is both my greatest blessing and perhaps my greatest curse.

The skies stay clear all month. And I watch the passing phases of the moon through what used to be your window. Ice lies thick on the hardened ground, and it seems for the longest time like nothing will grow here again. Like nothing could. But on my walk down to the beach this evening I spot the first sprouting of crocuses, their green shoots bravely bursting through the frost, and I feel winter ebbing from the shores of Killadoon.

I still open my door sometimes to find grief waiting there for me. But now, instead of fighting or running away, I welcome her home. Like a loyal pet returning from her travels, I look, unflinching, at the gift in grief's jaw, grotesque as it may be, grateful for whatever she has brought. I set a place at the table and invite her to sit with me. I share my meals and books and thoughts. I take her on long walks and into hot baths at the end of each day. Because I know now who she is—her mask can't fool me anymore. Standing on my doorstep, disguised as a monster, is love, begging to be let in.

This is why the cloak of grief hangs so heavy; it's not one cloak, but two. And on days when I can hardly move under the weight of it, I remind myself that grief and love are intricately woven together, and healing isn't about shedding one or the other, it's about becoming strong enough to bear them both. This pain is a productive pain, a fortifying pain, no different to the itchy ache of bones that knit together after breaking. And just like broken bones need rest, so too do hearts.

Like days when the words won't come, I see these pauses now as part of the process. With life, as with art, there's the in breath, the out breath, and the space in between. And this is where I feel you most, in the space between breath.

≣

Making my way across the beach today, I hear your voice in my head as I battle a gale that's brewing off the coast.

"That'll blow the cobwebs away," you say.

At the water's edge, the ocean is hungrily sucking at the shoreline, sending swarms of pebbles scraping over and under one another as they're dragged up and down, up and down. I close my eyes to listen to the sound.

Suaitiú

Suaitiú

Then the ocean becomes your voice. Only this time I don't hear it in my head; you're standing right next to me, teaching me a new word.

"Suaitiú," you say, then you repeat it phonetically, "Suet-choo."

You smile down at me like the sun on a warm spring day.

"That's the sound the sea makes when it pulls at the shore."

"There's a word for that?" I ask, and your eyes crease in laughter.

"The Irish have a word for everything."

"Suaitiú," I say, wrapping my mouth around the sound.

"Good girl." You wink. "Maith an cailín."

I have no idea when we are. Only that you are here. And as the wind sweeps my hair across my neck, feeling just like the palm of your hand, it's easy to imagine that if someone were to paint this scene, from somewhere up in the dunes perhaps, there'd be a sweep of sand, the shoreline, the sunset and sky, and two women standing side by side.

February fast approaches, the beginning of spring and the feast of Imbolc—which Kathy tells me comes from the Gaelic "im-bolg"—in the belly. It's a time of rebirth, new life, and lengthening light, a celebration of Brigit, goddess of poetry and healing, midwifery and craft.

"If you could make it with your hands," says Kathy, "it was Brigit's domain."

She tells me of Brigit, of the old gods and the old ways. She picks up where you left off, speaking about spirits and folktales as though they were real; not myth or legend, but part of a long-forgotten past. She tells me of the Tuatha Dé Danann—a supernatural race who walked this island before us—and Tír na nÓg—the land of the young—an otherworld found far out at sea. Sometimes, she pictures you there, in a realm of eternal beauty, joy, and youth. An absurd concept, I'll admit, but no more so than death itself.

Kathy has enough stories to see us through winter, of the people and the place that I came from, and the woman I came from too. We stay up late at night, cackling in the kitchen just like you did, over tales of your adventures. Like the time you both skipped school and went to Dublin, determined to catch a glimpse of the Rolling Stones at the airport, only you got lost on the way and your dad had to come collect you.

"We didn't even make it past Westport," she says, and I'm giggling as I pour us both another Baileys.

Or the time you tried to sneak out your bedroom window, fell a few feet, and broke your ankle, as well as your mother's precious rosebush.

"Your granny was more concerned with the roses than she was with the ankle," Kathy jokes, wiping a tear from the corner of one eye with the back of her finger.

And then there were the college years, full of music and men and all manner of drugs, as Kathy tells it. I struggle to imagine you in this role—untamed and unabashed, hungry for the world and eager to eat it raw. I imagine us both in our twenties, meeting in a dorm room, waxing lyrical all night about life, the universe, and everything, and I feel a strange new grief in realising that had you lived to see me grow up, we might have become more than mother and daughter; we might well have been friends.

Kathy says that the day you found out you were pregnant,

there was no doubt, not even for a second, that you would keep me.

"Did you worry?" I ask her.

"Of course I worried! We were told a pregnancy might accelerate her condition. And I won't lie, I asked her to consider her options, but she wouldn't hear it. Stubborn to the end, your mam."

"Do you think she made the right choice?" I ask her, and she frowns at me.

"There was only ever one choice, treasure. Abbie wanted you from the day she was born. *She* was the one pushing prams around while I was in the garden building forts out of bits of bricks and planks of wood I'd found. I made them sturdy and rainproof, and when I was done, your mammy made them beautiful. She made everything more beautiful."

"You've done that here," I offer, and she smiles fondly, looking around at the home she's built before growing sombre once more.

"She knew what she wanted, Kate. And she took the leap with her eyes wide open."

I know we're talking about both my birth and your death. We've talked a lot about it. Openly and honestly. We've talked about your diagnosis and decline, though in that regard there isn't much Aunt Kathy can tell me that your paintings haven't already said.

Kathy says her decision to keep them was not unlike your decision to keep me; that really, there was no other choice. She had been your protector in life, and that job didn't end when you died. Since then, she's been protecting all the pieces of you she could—me, my dad, this home, and your paintings. Like the huntsman in "Snow White," Kathy couldn't bring herself to do what was asked of her; to destroy what you'd made would be akin to cutting out your heart, she says. And so she kept them. And waited. Not knowing exactly what she was waiting for.

When I arrived on her doorstep, she knew that was part of the reason, but not all of it.

"I want you to exhibit her work," she tells me over breakfast one morning. Another decision that isn't a decision at all. The answer feels already writ. The request merely a formality.

"Of course I will," I say, and she's smiling while she butters her toast.

Fran volunteered the Arena as a venue, and Jenna says she'll help with the logistics. I'm moving in with her when I get back—turns out her drunken proclamation was a genuine offer after all. She said she's not done trying for a baby yet, but in the meantime, she can't bear to look at those yellow splotches in that empty room.

"You can paint it any colour you want," she tells me over the phone.

"I don't care," I say, "as long as it's not eggshell white."

Jenna laughs and then sighs.

"Who'd have thought you'd end up raising a child with me?" she jokes. "Hardly the life you expected."

"No," I say. "But I release that life now, to make way for a better one."

The longer I'm away from that life, that house, that relationship, the clearer it is to me. Just another nightmare I'm slowly waking up from. The woman I was with Finn feels like an old acquaintance—someone I still think about from time to time, still care about and wish the best for, but no longer want to see. The longing in me to leave this world has been replaced by a fierce ache to live in it, to know it deeply and capture it the best I can. As the words begin to flow again, transmuting trauma into art, their very passage helps me understand that I write for the same reason you painted. I write to press myself between the pages, firmly but tenderly, like a handful of flowers, in the hopes of preserving some dried, flattened simulacrum of life.

Tomorrow morning I leave for Dublin, and I'm spending my last night here curled up with your book, the one Kathy gave me. I've been reading it sparingly, trying to make it last—not because of the stories themselves, charming as they are, but because its pages are full of you, the margins and blank spaces filled with your sketches and notes. Several times, I've reached to underline a passage, only to notice you already have, and I was moved to tears to see that one of these passages concerned imbas. The word literally means "light that illuminates," and according to this book it's more than just inspiration:

> *Imbas, short for imbas forosnai, is the channelling of mystic energies into poetic practice, the difference between art created by the limits of human ability, and that which is gifted from the gods. It is a divine knowing, a sacred foresight, that is often sought in the threshold between worlds.*

Under these words there's a faint pencil line, and beside it, in your handwriting, *Not all of my paintings come from me.*

It was like you'd heard the question I asked myself—whether you ever felt what I feel when I write—and found a way to answer me from wherever you are.

The last chapter, the one I'm reading tonight, is about Samhain, and it explains why the Celtic New Year happens in November: the Celts didn't fear the dark, they celebrated it, believing that each day started at sunset, that darkness brought forth magic and rebirth, and that only in a space of complete nothingness were all things possible. Samhain is the end of the summer, the end of the harvest, the end of the light, and therefore the beginning of something new. Like the universe, which was forged in cosmic night, or the dreams we conjure in the gloom of sleep, our filí, poet-seers, and our draoithe, druid magic makers, understood that in order to receive the light that illuminates one must first embrace the dark. One must surrender to imbas just as the riverbed crumbles, giving up no less than itself to make way for the water's flow.

As we say good night, Kathy asks me if I want to know whether I carry your fate and I tell her I don't plan to seek an answer.

We spend our whole lives waiting. Waiting for spring. Waiting for summer. Waiting to fall in love. Waiting to fall out of it again. Waiting to get pregnant. Waiting for permission. Waiting for remission. Waiting for the surgery that may or may not help. We wait for those results. That piece of news. That text, that call, that knock at the door. We wait for our kids to be born, go to school, go away, have kids of their own. Then we wait for them to come back. We wait for inspiration. Wait for that promotion. Wait and wait for something to happen that we think will make it all better. *I'll be happy when*, we say. *When this, when that.* Never *now*, never *here*. Meanwhile, life happens in the waiting. It takes place in the in-between. When you've let go of the last rung and before you've caught hold of the next. Life happens in the reach, the release, the free fall. While you sit, remembering then and imagining when, life unfurls, blooms, and withers without your even noticing.

I think of you, wilfully entering the ultimate liminal space, that yawning chasm between this world and the next, as vast as forever and no wider than a breath. I think of you, taking an inhale, knowing it would be your last, and devastating as that thought is, I know why you did it. You died before you lost us and yourself completely. You died before the choice to die was taken from you. But mostly, you died for the sake of the story, my story. You wrote your own tragic ending so that I might have a happy one. You died so that I could live a life unburdened by fate, and I refuse to spend it waiting to forget.

CODA

I get home from the exhibition, exhausted but elated, having spent another evening watching people walk the length of your illness from death to diagnosis—I chose to arrange your portraits from most to least recent so that I and everyone else could see the disease slip from you, and not the other way around.

Dropping my things by the front door, I catch myself, then take them through to the kitchen, where I find Jenna stirring a pot of soup.

"Honey, I'm home," I say, hugging her around her waist. She feeds me a spoonful over her shoulder, and I nod with closed eyes.

"That's incredible," I tell her as she turns around to give me a proper hug.

"Emotional. Exhausting. I'll be sad when it's over."

Then I sneak another spoonful of soup behind her back. "How'd the scan go?"

"Good," she says. "Really good." And her face is scrunched up with joy when she pulls away. She's radiant.

"Oh! There's a package for you," says Jenna. "I think it's from Maeve."

I turn and spot a huge rectangular parcel leaning against the wall. Above it, there are two blank spaces where your first and last portraits usually hang, but they're on loan this week to the Arena, bookending the exhibition.

Ripping back the parcel's brown paper, I see a glint of silver frame, and I begin to wonder if this is one of Maeve's new works. Jenna helps me pull the paper further from one corner, revealing blank borders behind glass.

"It's empty," she says.

But then I see it: in the middle of the frame is a circular picture with tattered edges, of a young woman kneeling by a bed. The colours—fuchsia, violet, and electric blue—all blur as my eyes fill with tears, not of pain but of awe.

All this time I wondered how Maeve could destroy what she made, but amidst the destruction was more creation. I hadn't considered the centres. The middles. The magnificent gaps. These pieces of her that seemed lost weren't lost at all, just dried out, flattened, and preserved.

Attached to the frame is part of a Christina Rossetti poem, in Maeve's handwriting, which I catch myself noticing has already started to deteriorate. I sit down, and Jenna takes my shaking hand in hers as I read the words aloud:

Yet if you should forget me for a while
And afterwards remember, do not grieve:
For if the darkness and corruption leave
A vestige of the thoughts that once I had,
Better by far you should forget and smile
Than that you should remember and be sad.

ACKNOWLEDGEMENTS

I'd like to thank the universe for this book, strange as that may sound. For the imbas that flowed from the first page to the last, for the words that came through me, not from me, and for all the people, places, and circumstances that converged in order to get them on the page. In particular, I'm thankful for the heartbreaks I've endured—they taught me the language of loss. I'm thankful for the island I come from—its thin places and deep lore. And I'm thankful for the women who shepherded me through my most liminal year—a time of moving, mending, and magic-making all over the world.

To my darling Dodie for being my home, and to Anna and Rosie for providing me with one when I needed it most. To Amelia, for the drives. To Cayleigh, for the frogs. To Reb, Louise, Tessa, Ellen, Sadhbh, Naomi, Imelda, Helen, Becca, Pema, Lucy, Lan, and countless others, for giving me the space and support, sofas and songs, words and wisdom I needed to see this through. To Laura for the cúpla focail. To Kathy and

Anne for the bit of draíocht towards the end. To Anna G., my white witch back home. And to Sabrina and Cassidy and the whole team at Dutton for putting your trust in me again.

Finally, I'm thankful for you, dear reader, without whom I would be a grown woman, alone in a room, cursing at a box full of rabbits.

ABOUT THE AUTHOR

HAZEL HAYES is an Irish-born London-based writer and director who for many years wrote primarily for the screen. After graduating from Dublin City University with a degree in journalism, she went on to study creative writing at the Irish Writers Centre before honing her craft as a screenwriter through numerous short films and sketches. Her eight-part horror, *PrankMe*, won the award for excellence in storytelling at Buffer Festival in Toronto. *Out of Love* was her first novel.